Adventures in Criticism

Arthur Quiller-Couch

Alpha Editions

This edition published in 2024

ISBN : 9789362928931

Design and Setting By
Alpha Editions
www.alphaedis.com
Email - info@alphaedis.com

As per information held with us this book is in Public Domain.
This book is a reproduction of an important historical work. Alpha Editions uses the best technology to reproduce historical work in the same manner it was first published to preserve its original nature. Any marks or number seen are left intentionally to preserve its true form.

Contents

CHAUCER	- 1 -
"THE PASSIONATE PILGRIM."	- 14 -
SHAKESPEARE'S LYRICS	- 18 -
SAMUEL DANIEL	- 23 -
WILLIAM BROWNE	- 28 -
THOMAS CAREW	- 32 -
"ROBINSON CRUSOE"	- 36 -
LAWRENCE STERNE	- 43 -
SCOTT AND BURNS	- 49 -
CHARLES READE	- 59 -
HENRY KINGSLEY	- 62 -
ALEXANDER WILLIAM KINGLAKE	- 66 -
C.S.C. and J.K.S.	- 69 -
ROBERT LOUIS STEVENSON	- 73 -
M. ZOLA	- 88 -
SELECTION	- 91 -
EXTERNALS	- 94 -
CLUB TALK	- 102 -
EXCURSIONISTS IN POETRY	- 105 -
THE POPULAR CONCEPTION OF A POET	- 108 -
POETS ON THEIR OWN ART	- 113 -
THE ATTITUDE OF THE PUBLIC TOWARDS LETTERS	- 117 -
A CASE OF BOOKSTALL CENSORSHIP	- 124 -
THE POOR LITTLE PENNY DREADFUL	- 128 -
IBSEN'S "PEER GYNT"	- 131 -

MR. SWINBURNE'S LATER MANNER .... - 138 -
A MORNING WITH A BOOK .... - 142 -
MR. JOHN DAVIDSON .... - 146 -
BJÖRNSTERNE BJÖRNSON .... - 155 -
MR. GEORGE MOORE .... - 159 -
MRS. MARGARET L. WOODS... - 163 -
MR. HALL CAINE .... - 171 -
MR. ANTHONY HOPE .... - 175 -
"TRILBY"... - 178 -
MR. STOCKTON .... - 181 -
BOW-WOW .... - 184 -
OF SEASONABLE NUMBERS: .... - 186 -

CHAUCER

March 17, 1894. Professor Skeat's Chaucer.

After twenty-five years of close toil, Professor Skeat has completed his great edition of Chaucer.[A] It is obviously easier to be dithyrambic than critical in chronicling this event; to which indeed dithyrambs are more appropriate than criticism. For when a man writes *Opus vitæ meæ* at the conclusion of such a task as this, and so lays down his pen, he must be a churl (even if he be also a competent critic) who will allow no pause for admiration. And where, churl or no churl, is the competent critic to be found? The Professor has here compiled an entirely new text of Chaucer, founded solely on the manuscripts and the earliest printed editions that are accessible. Where Chaucer has translated, the originals have been carefully studied: "the requirements of metre and grammar have been carefully considered throughout": and "the phonology and spelling of every word have received particular attention." We may add that all the materials for a Life of Chaucer have been sought out, examined, and pieced together with exemplary care.

All this has taken Professor Skeat twenty-five years, and in order to pass competent judgment on his conclusions the critic must follow him step by step through his researches—which will take the critic (even if we are charitable enough to suppose his mental equipment equal to Professor Skeat's) another ten years at least. For our time, then, and probably for many generations after, this edition of Chaucer will be accepted as final.

And the Clarendon Press.

And I seem to see in this edition of Chaucer the beginning of the realization of a dream which I have cherished since first I stood within the quadrangle of the Clarendon Press—that fine combination of the factory and the palace. The aspect of the Press itself repeats, as it were, the characteristics of its government, which is conducted by an elected body as an honorable trust. Its delegates are not intent only on money-getting. And yet the Clarendon Press makes money, and the University can depend upon it for handsome subsidies. It may well depend upon it for much more. As the Bank of England—to which in its system of government it may be likened—is the focus of all the other banks, private or joint-stock, in the kingdom, and the treasure-house, not only of the nation's gold, but of its commercial honor, so the Clarendon Press—traditionally careful in its selections and munificent in its rewards—might become the academy or central temple of English literature. If it would but follow up Professor Skeat's Chaucer with a resolution to publish, at a pace suitable to so large an undertaking, *all the great*

English classics, edited with all the scholarship its wealth can command, I believe that before long the Clarendon Press would be found to be exercising an influence on English letters which is at present lacking, and the lack of which drives many to call, from time to time, for the institution in this country of something corresponding to the French Academy. I need only cite the examples of the Royal Society and the Marylebone Cricket Club to show that to create an authority in this manner is consonant with our national practice. We should have that centre of correct information, correct judgment, correct taste—that intellectual metropolis, in short—which is the surest check upon provinciality in literature; we should have a standard of English scholarship and an authoritative dictionary of the English language; and at the same time we should escape all that business of the green coat and palm branches which has at times exposed the French Academy to much vulgar intrigue.

Also, I may add, we should have the books. Where now is the great edition of Bunyan, of Defoe, of Gibbon? The Oxford Press did once publish an edition of Gibbon, worthy enough as far as type and paper could make it worthy. But this is only to be found in second-hand book-shops. Why are two rival London houses now publishing editions of Scott, the better illustrated with silly pictures "out of the artists' heads"? Where is the final edition of Ben Jonson?

These and the rest are to come, perhaps. Of late we have had from Oxford a great Boswell and a great Chaucer, and the magnificent Dictionary is under weigh. So that it may be the dream is in process of being realized, though none of us shall live to see its full realization. Meanwhile such a work as Professor Skeat's Chaucer is not only an answer to much chatter that goes up from time to time about nine-tenths of the work on English literature being done out of England. This and similar works are the best of all possible answers to those gentlemen who so often interrupt their own chrematistic pursuits to point out in the monthly magazines the short-comings of our two great Universities as nurseries of chrematistic youth. In this case it is Oxford that publishes, while Cambridge supplies the learning: and from a natural affection I had rather it were always Oxford that published, attracting to her service the learning, scholarship, intelligence of all parts of the kingdom, or, for that matter, of the world. So might she securely found new Schools of English Literature—were she so minded, a dozen every year. They would do no particular harm; and meanwhile, in Walton Street, out of earshot of the New Schools, the Clarendon Press would go on serenely performing its great work.

March 23, 1895. Essentials and Accidents of Poetry.

A work such as Professor Skeat's Chaucer puts the critic into a frame of mind that lies about midway between modesty and cowardice. One asks—"What right have I, who have given but a very few hours of my life to the enjoying of Chaucer; who have never collated his MSS.; who have taken the events of his life on trust from his biographers; who am no authority on his spelling, his rhythms, his inflections, or the spelling, rhythms, inflections of his age; who have read him only as I have read other great poets, for the pleasure of reading—what right have I to express any opinion on a work of this character, with its imposing commentary, its patient research, its enormous accumulation of special information?"

Nevertheless, this diffidence, I am sure, may be carried too far. After all is said and done, we, with our average life of three-score years and ten, are the heirs of all the poetry of all the ages. We must do our best in our allotted time, and Chaucer is but one of the poets. He did not write for specialists in his own age, and his main value for succeeding ages resides, not in his vocabulary, nor in his inflections, nor in his indebtedness to foreign originals, nor in the metrical uniformities or anomalies that may be discovered in his poems; but in his *poetry*. Other things are accidental; his poetry is essential. Other interests—historical, philological, antiquarian—must be recognized; but the poetical, or (let us say) the spiritual, interest stands first and far ahead of all others. By virtue of it Chaucer, now as always, makes his chief and his convincing appeal to that which is spiritual in men. He appeals by the poetical quality of such lines as these, from Emilia's prayer to Diana:

"Chaste goddesse, wel wostow that I
Desire to been a mayden al my lyf,
Ne never wol I be no love ne wyf.

I am, thou woost, yet of thy companye,
A mayde, and love hunting and venerye,
And for to walken in the wodes wilde,
And noght to been a wyf, and be with childe..."

Or of these two from the Prioresses' Prologue:

"O moder mayde! O mayde moder free!
O bush unbrent, brenninge in Moyses sighte..."

Or of these from the general Prologue—also thoroughly poetical, though the quality differs:

"Ther was also a Nonne, a Prioresse,
That of hir smyling was ful simple and coy;
Hir gretteste ooth was but by sëynt Loy;

And she was cleped madame Eglentyne.
Ful wel she song the service divyne,
Entuned in hir nose ful semely;
And Frensh she spak ful faire and fetisly,
After the scole of Stratford atte Bowe,
For Frensh of Paris was to hir unknowe..."

Now the essential quality of this and of all very great poetry is also what we may call a *universal* quality; it appeals to those sympathies which, unequally distributed and often distorted or suppressed, are yet the common possessions of our species. This quality is the real antiseptic of poetry: this it is that keeps a line of Homer perennially fresh and in bloom:—

" Ὣς φάτο τοὺς δ' ἤδη κατέχεν φυσίζοος αἶα
ἐν Λακεδαίμονι αὖθι, φίλῃ ἐν πατρίδι γαιῃ."

These lines live because they contain something which is also permanent in man: they depend confidently on us, and will as confidently depend on our great-grandchildren. I was glad to see this point very courageously put the other day by Professor Hiram Corson, of Cornell University, in an address on "The Aims of Literary Study"—an address which Messrs. Macmillan have printed and published here and in America. "All works of genius," says Mr. Corson, "render the best service, in literary education, when they are first assimilated in their absolute character. It is, of course, important to know their relations to the several times and places in which they were produced; but such knowledge is not for the tyro in literary study. He must first know literature, if he is constituted so to know it, in its absolute character. He can go into the philosophy of its relationships later, if he like, when he has a true literary education, and when the 'years that bring the philosophic mind' have been reached. Every great production of genius is, in fact, in its essential character, no more related to one age than to another. It is only in its phenomenal character (its outward manifestations) that it has a *special* relationship." And Mr. Corson very appositely quotes Mr. Ruskin on Shakespeare's historical plays—

"If it be said that Shakespeare wrote perfect historical plays on subjects belonging to the preceding centuries, I answer that they *are* perfect plays just because there is no care about centuries in them, but a life which all men recognize for the human life of all time; and this it is, not because Shakespeare sought to give universal truth, but because, painting honestly and completely from the men about him, he painted that human nature which is, indeed, constant enough—a rogue in the fifteenth century being *at heart* what a rogue is in the nineteenth century and was in the twelfth; and an honest or knightly man being, in like manner, very similar to other such at any other time. And the work of these great idealists is, therefore, always universal: not because it is *not portrait*, but because it is *complete* portrait down to the heart, which is the same in all ages; and the work of the mean idealists is *not* universal, not because it is portrait, but because it is *half* portrait—of the outside, the manners and the dress, not of the heart. Thus Tintoret and Shakespeare paint, both of them, simply Venetian and English nature as they saw it in their time, down to the root; and it does for *all* time; but as for any care to cast themselves into the particular ways of thought, or custom, of past time in their historical work, you will find it in neither of them, nor in any other perfectly great man that I know of."—*Modern Painters*.

It will be observed that Mr. Corson, whose address deals primarily with literary training, speaks of these absolute qualities of the great masterpieces as the *first* object of study. But his words, and Ruskin's words, fairly support my further contention that they remain the *most important* object of study, no matter how far one's literary training may have proceeded. To the most erudite student of Chaucer in the wide world Chaucer's poetry should be the dominant object of interest in connection with Chaucer.

But when the elaborate specialist confronts us, we are apt to forget that poetry is meant for mankind, and that its appeal is, or should be, universal. We pay tribute to the unusual: and so far as this implies respect for protracted industry and indefatigable learning, we do right. But in so far as it implies even a momentary confusion of the essentials with the accidentals of poetry, we do wrong. And the specialist himself continues admirable only so long as he keeps them distinct.

I hasten to add that Professor Skeat *does* keep them distinct very successfully. In a single sentence of admirable brevity he tells us that of Chaucer's poetical excellence "it is superfluous to speak; Lowell's essay on Chaucer in 'My Study Windows' gives a just estimate of his powers." And with this, taking the poetical excellence for granted, he proceeds upon his really invaluable work of preparing a standard text of Chaucer and illustrating it out of the stores of his apparently inexhaustible learning. The result is a monument to Chaucer's memory such as never yet was reared to English poet. Douglas Jerrold assured Mrs. Cowden Clarke that, when her time came to enter Heaven, Shakespeare would advance and greet her with the first kiss of welcome, "*even* should her husband happen to be present." One can hardly with decorum imagine Professor Skeat being kissed; but Chaucer assuredly will greet him with a transcendent smile.

The Professor's genuine admiration, however, for the poetical excellence of his poet needs to be insisted upon, not only because the nature of his task keeps him reticent, but because his extraordinary learning seems now and then to stand between him and the natural appreciation of a passage. It was not quite at haphazard that I chose just now the famous description of the Prioresse as an illustration of Chaucer's poetical quality. The Professor has a long note upon the French of Stratford atte Bowe. Most of us have hitherto believed the passage to be an example, and a very pretty one, of Chaucer's playfulness. The Professor almost loses his temper over this: he speaks of it as a view "commonly adopted by newspaper-writers who know only this one line of Chaucer, and cannot forbear to use it in jest." "Even Tyrwhitt and Wright," he adds more in sorrow than in anger, "have thoughtlessly given currency to this idea." "Chaucer," the Professor explains, "merely states a *fact*" (the italics are his own), "viz., that the Prioress spoke the usual Anglo-French of the English Court, of the English law-courts, and of the English ecclesiastics of higher ranks. The poet, however, had been himself in France, and knew precisely the difference between the two dialects; but he had no special reason for thinking *more highly*" (the Professor's italics again) "of the Parisian than of the Anglo-French.... Warton's note on the line is quite sane. He shows that Queen Philippa wrote business letters in French (doubtless Anglo-French) with 'great propriety'" ... and so on. You see, there was a Benedictine nunnery at Stratford-le-Bow; and as "Mr. Cutts says, very justly, 'She spoke French correctly, though with an accent which savored of the Benedictine Convent at Stratford-le-Bow, where she had been educated, rather than of Paris.'" So there you have a fact.

And, now you have it, doesn't it look rather like Bitzer's horse?

"Bitzer," said Thomas Gradgrind. "Your definition of a horse?"

"Quadruped. Graminivorous. Forty teeth, namely twenty-four grinders, four eye-teeth, and twelve incisive. Sheds coat in the spring; in marshy countries sheds hoofs too. Hoofs hard, but requiring to be shod with iron. Age known by marks in mouth." Thus (and much more) Bitzer.

March 30, 1895. The Texts of the "Canterbury Tales."

It follows, I hope, from what I said last week, that by far the most important service an editor can render to Chaucer and to us is to give us a pure text, through which the native beauty of the poetry may best shine. Such a text Professor Skeat has been able to prepare, in part by his own great industry, in part because he has entered into the fruit of other men's labors. The epoch-making event in the history of the Canterbury Tales (with which alone we are concerned here) was Dr. Furnivall's publication for the Chaucer Society of the famous "Six-Text Edition." Dr. Furnivall set to work upon this in 1868.

The Six Texts were these:—

1. The great "Ellesmere" MS. (so called after its owner, the Earl of Ellesmere). "The finest and best of all the MSS. now extant."

2. The "Hengwrt" MS., belonging to Mr. William W.E. Wynne, of Peniarth; very closely agreeing with the "Ellesmere."

3. The "Cambridge" MS. Gg 4.27, in the University Library. The best copy in any public library. This also follows the "Ellesmere" closely.

4. The "Corpus" MS., in the library of Corpus Christi College, Oxford.

5. The "Petworth" MS., belonging to Lord Leconfield.

6. The "Lansdowne" MS. in the British Museum. "Not a good MS., being certainly the worst of the six; but worth reprinting owing to the frequent use that has been made of it by editors."

In his Introduction, Professor Skeat enumerates no fewer than fifty-nine MSS. of the Tales: but of these the above six (and a seventh to be mentioned presently) are the most important. The most important of all is the "Ellesmere"—the great "find" of the Six-Text Edition. "The best in nearly every respect," says Professor Skeat. "It not only gives good lines and good sense, but is also (usually) grammatically accurate and thoroughly well spelt. The publication of it has been a great boon to all Chaucer students, for which Dr. Furnivall will be ever gratefully remembered.... This splendid MS. has also the great merit of being complete, requiring no supplement from any other source, except in a few cases when a line or two has been missed."

Professor Skeat has therefore chiefly employed the Six-Text Edition, supplemented by a seventh famous MS., the "Harleian 7334"—printed in full for the Chaucer Society in 1885—a MS. of great importance, differing considerably from the "Ellesmere." But the Professor judges it "a most dangerous MS. to trust to, unless constantly corrected by others, and not at all fitted to be taken as the basis of a text." For the basis of his text, then, he takes the Ellesmere MS., correcting it freely by the other seven MSS. mentioned.

Now, as fate would have it, in the year 1888 Dr. Furnivall invited Mr. Alfred W. Pollard to collaborate with him in an edition of Chaucer which he had for many years promised to bring out for Messrs. Macmillan. The basis of their text of the Tales was almost precisely that chosen by Professor Skeat, *i.e.* a careful collation of the Six Texts and the Harleian 7334, due preponderance being given to the Ellesmere MS., and all variations from it stated in the notes. "A beginning was made," says Mr. Pollard, "but the giant in the partnership had been used for a quarter of a century to doing, for nothing, all the hard work for other people, and could not spare from his pioneering the time necessary to enter into the fruit of his own Chaucer labors. Thus the partner who was not a giant was left to go on pretty much by himself. When I had made some progress, Professor Skeat informed us that the notes which he had been for years accumulating encouraged him to undertake an edition on a large scale, and I gladly abandoned, in favor of an editor of so much greater width of reading, the Library Edition which had been arranged for in the original agreement of Dr. Furnivall and myself with Messrs. Macmillan. I thought, however, that the work which I had done might fairly be used for an edition on a less extensive plan and intended for a less stalwart class of readers, and of this the present issue of the Canterbury Tales is an instalment."[B]

So it comes about that we have two texts before us, each based on a collation of the Six-Text edition and the Harleian MS. 7334—the chief difference being that Mr. Pollard adheres closely to the Ellesmere MS., while Professor Skeat allows himself more freedom. This is how they start—

"Whán that Apríllë with híse shourës soote
The droghte of March hath percëd to the roote,
And bathed every veyne in swich licóur
Of which vertú engendred is the flour;
Whan Zephirus eck with his swetë breeth   5
Inspirëd hath in every holt and heeth
The tendrë croppës, and the yongë sonne
Hath in the Ram his halfë cours y-ronne,
And smalë fowelës maken melodye
That slepen al the nvght with open eye,—   10
So priketh hem Natúre in hir coráges,—
Thanne longen folk to goon on pilgrimages ..."
(*Pollard.*)

"Whan that Aprille with his shoures sote
The droghte of Marche hath perced to the rote,
And bathed every veyne in swich licour
Of which vertu engendred is the flour;
Whan Zephirus eek with his swete breeth   5
Inspired hath in every holt and heeth
The tendre croppes, and the yong sonne
Hath in the Ram his halfe cours y ronne,
And smale fowles maken melodye,
That slepen al the night with open yë,   10
(So priketh hem nature in hir corages:)

Than longen folk to goon on pilgrimages..."
(*Skeat.*)

On these two extracts it must be observed (1) that the accents and the dotted e's in the first are Mr. Pollard's own contrivances for helping the scansion; (2) in the second, l. 10, "yë" is a special contrivance of Professor Skeat. "The scribes," he says (Introd. Vol. IV. p. xix.), "usually write *eye* in the middle of a line, but when they come to it at the end of one, they are fairly puzzled. In l. 10, the scribe of Hn ('Hengwrt') writes *lye*, and that of Ln ('Lansdowne') writes *yhe*; and the variations on this theme are curious. The spelling *ye* (= yë) is, however, common.... I print it 'yë' to distinguish it from *ye*, the pl. pronoun." The other differences are accounted for by the varying degrees in which the two editors depend on the Ellesmere MS. Mr. Pollard sticks to the Ellesmere. Professor Skeat corrects it by the others. Obviously the editor who allows himself the wider range lays himself open to more criticism, point by point. He has to justify himself in each particular case, while the other's excuse is set down once for all in his preface. But after comparing the two texts in over a dozen passages, I have had to vote in almost every case for Professor Skeat.

The Alleged Difficulty of Reading Chaucer.

The differences, however, are always trifling. The reader will allow that in each case we have a clear, intelligible text: a text that allows Chaucer to be read and enjoyed without toil or vexation. For my part, I hope there is no presumption in saying that I could very well do without Mr. Pollard's accents and dotted e's. Remove them, and I contend that any Englishman with an ear for poetry can read either of the two texts without difficulty. A great deal too much fuss is made over the pronunciation and scansion of Chaucer. After all, we are Englishmen, with an instinct for understanding the language we inherit; in the evolution of our language we move on the same lines as our fathers; and Chaucer's English is at least no further removed from us than the Lowland dialect of Scott's novels. Moreover, we have in reading Chaucer what we lack in reading Scott—the assistance of rhythm; and the rhythm of Chaucer is as clearly marked as that of Tennyson. Professor Skeat might very well have allowed his admirable text to stand alone. For his rules of pronunciation, with their elaborate system of signs and symbols, seem to me (to put it coarsely) phonetics gone mad. This, for instance, is how he would have us read the Tales:—

"Whán-dhat Áprílla/wídh iz-shúurez sóotə
dhə-drúuht' ov-Márchə/hath pérsed tóo dhə róotə,
ənd-báadhed év'ri véinə/in-swích likúur,
ov-whích vertýy/enjéndred iz dhə flúur...."

—and so on? I think it may safely be said that if a man need this sort of assistance in reading or pronouncing Chaucer, he had better let Chaucer alone altogether, or read him in a German prose translation.

April 6, 1895.

Why is Chaucer so easy to read? At a first glance a page of the "Canterbury Tales" appears more formidable than a page of the "Faërie Queene." As a matter of fact, it is less formidable; or, if this be denied, everyone will admit that twenty pages of the "Canterbury Tales" are less formidable than twenty pages of the "Faërie Queene." I might bring several recent editors and critics to testify that, after the first shock of the archaic spelling and the final "e," an intelligent public will soon come to terms with Chaucer; but the unconscious testimony of the intelligent public itself is more convincing. Chaucer is read year after year by a large number of men and women. Spenser, in many respects a greater poet, is also read; but by far fewer. Nobody, I imagine, will deny this. But what is the reason of it?

The first and chief reason is this—Forms of language change, but the great art of narrative appeals eternally to men, and its rules rest on principles older than Homer. And whatever else may be said of Chaucer, he is a superb narrator. To borrow a phrase from another venerable art, he is always "on the ball." He pursues the story—the story, and again the story. Mr. Ward once put this admirably—

"The vivacity of joyousness of Chaucer's poetic temperament ... make him amusingly impatient of epical lengths, abrupt in his transitions, and anxious, with an anxiety usually manifested by readers rather than by writers, to come to the point, 'to the great effect,' as he is wont to call it. 'Men,' he says, 'may overlade a ship or barge, and therefore I will skip at once to the effect, and let all the rest slip.' And he unconsciously suggests a striking difference between himself and the great Elizabethan epic poet who owes so much to him, when he declines to make as long a tale of the chaff or of the straw as of the corn, and to describe all the details of a marriage-feast *seriatim*:

'The fruit of every tale is for to say:
They eat and drink, and dance and sing and play.'

This may be the fruit; but epic poets, from Homer downward, have been generally in the habit of not neglecting the foliage. Spenser in particular has that impartial copiousness which we think it our duty to admire in the Ionic epos, but which, if truth were told, has prevented generations of Englishmen from acquiring an intimate personal acquaintance with the 'Fairy Queen.' With Chaucer the danger certainly rather lay in the opposite direction."

Now, if we are once interested in a story, small difficulties of speech or spelling will not readily daunt us in the time-honored pursuit of "what happens next"—certainly not if we know enough of our author to feel sure he will come to the point and tell us what happens next with the least possible palaver. We have a definite want and a certainty of being satisfied promptly. But with Spenser this satisfaction may, and almost certainly will, be delayed over many pages: and though in the meanwhile a thousand casual beauties may appeal to us, the main thread of our attention is sensibly relaxed. Chaucer is the minister and Spenser the master: and the difference between pursuing what we want and pursuing we-know-not-what must affect the ardor of the chase. Even if we take the future on trust, and follow Spenser to the end, we cannot look back on a book of the "Faërie Queene" as on part of a good story: for it is admittedly an unsatisfying and ill-constructed story. But my point is that an ordinary reader resents being asked to take the future on trust while the author luxuriates in casual beauties of speech upon every mortal subject but the one in hand. The first principle of good narrative is to stick to the subject; the second, to carry the audience along in a series of small surprises—satisfying expectation and going just a little beyond. If it were necessary to read fifty pages before enjoying Chaucer, though the sum of eventual enjoyment were as great as it now is, Chaucer would never be read. We master small difficulties line by line because our recompense comes line by line.

Moreover, it is as certain as can be that we read Chaucer to-day more easily than our fathers read him one hundred, two hundred, three hundred years ago. And I make haste to add that the credit of this does not belong to the philologists.

The Elizabethans, from Spenser onward, found Chaucer distressingly archaic. When Sir Francis Kynaston, *temp.* Charles I., translated "Troilus and Criseyde," Cartwright congratulated him that he had at length made it possible to read Chaucer without a dictionary. And from Dryden's time to Wordsworth's he was an "uncouthe unkiste" barbarian, full of wit, but only tolerable in polite paraphrase. Chaucer himself seems to have foreboded this, towards the close of his "Troilus and Criseyde," when he addresses his "litel book"—

"And for there is so great diversitee
In English, and in wryting of our tonge,
So preye I God that noon miswryte thee,
Ne thee mismetre for defaute of tonge.
And red wher-so thou be, or elles songe,
That thou be understoude I God besechel!..."

And therewith, as though on purpose to defeat his fears, he proceeded to turn three stanzas of Boccaccio into English that tastes almost as freshly after five hundred years as on the day it was written. He is speaking of Hector's death:—

"And whan that he was slayn in this manere,
His lighte goost ful blisfully it went
Up to the holownesse of the seventh spere
In convers leting every element;
And ther he saugh, with ful avysement,
The erratik starres, herkening armonye
With sownes ful of hevenish melodye.

"And down from thennes faste he gan avyse
This litel spot of erthe, that with the see
Embraced is, and fully gan despyse
This wrecched world, and held al vanitee
To respect of the pleyn felicitee
That is in hevene above; and at the laste,
Ther he was slayn, his loking down he caste;

"And in himself he lough right at the wo
Of hem that wepten for his death so faste;
And dampned al our werk that folweth so
The blinde lust, the which that may not laste,
And sholden al our harte on hevene caste.
And forth he wente, shortly for to telle,
Ther as Mercurie sorted him to dwelle...."

Who have prepared our ears to admit this passage, and many as fine? Not the editors, who point out very properly that it is a close translation from Boccaccio's "Teseide," xi. 1-3. The information is valuable, as far as it goes; but what it fails to explain is just the marvel of the passage—viz., the abiding "Englishness" of it, the native ring of it in our ears after five centuries of linguistic and metrical development. To whom, besides Chaucer himself, do we owe this? For while Chaucer has remained substantially the same, apparently we have an aptitude that our grandfathers and great-grandfathers had not. The answer surely is: We owe it to our nineteenth century poets, and particularly to Tennyson, Swinburne, and William Morris. Years ago Mr. R.H. Horne said most acutely that the principle of Chaucer's rhythm is "inseparable from a full and fair exercise of the genius of our language in versification." This "full and fair exercise" became a despised, almost a lost, tradition after Chaucer's death. The rhythms of Skelton, of Surrey, and Wyatt, were produced on alien and narrower lines. Revived by Shakespeare and the later Elizabethans, it fell into contempt again until Cowper once more began to claim freedom for English rhythm, and after him Coleridge, and the despised Leigh Hunt. But never has its full liberty been so triumphantly asserted as by the three poets I have named above. If we are at home as we read Chaucer, it is because they have instructed us in the liberty which Chaucer divined as the only true way.

FOOTNOTES:

[A] The Complete Works of Geoffrey Chaucer. Edited, from numerous manuscripts, by the Rev. Walter W. Skeat, Litt. D., LL.D., M.A. In six volumes. Oxford: At the Clarendon Press. 1894.

[B] Chaucer's Canterbury Tales. Edited, with Notes and Introduction, by Alfred W. Pollard. London: Macmillan & Co.

"THE PASSIONATE PILGRIM."

January 5, 1805. "The Passionate Pilgrim."

The Passionate Pilgrim (1599). *Reprinted with a Note about the Book, by Arthur L. Humphreys. London: Privately Printed by Arthur L. Humphreys, of* 187, *Piccadilly. MDCCCXCIV.*

I was about to congratulate Mr. Humphreys on his printing when, upon turning to the end of this dainty little volume, I discovered the well-known colophon of the Chiswick Press—"Charles Whittingham & Co., Took's Court, Chancery Lane, London." So I congratulate Messrs. Charles Whittingham & Co. instead, and suggest that the imprint should have run "Privately Printed *for* Arthur L. Humphreys."

This famous (or, if you like it, infamous) little anthology of thirty leaves has been singularly unfortunate in its title-pages. It was first published in 1599 as *The Passionate Pilgrims. By W. Shakespeare. At London. Printed for W. Jaggard, and are to be sold by W. Leake, at the Greyhound in Paules Churchyard.* This, of course, was disingenuous. Some of the numbers were by Shakespeare: but the authorship of some remains doubtful to this day, and others the enterprising Jaggard had boldly conveyed from Marlowe, Richard Barnefield, and Bartholomew Griffin. In short, to adapt a famous line upon a famous lexicon, "the best part was Shakespeare, the rest was not." For this, Jaggard has been execrated from time to time with sufficient heartiness. Mr. Swinburne, in his latest volume of Essays, calls him an "infamous pirate, liar, and thief." Mr. Humphreys remarks, less vivaciously, that "He was not careful and prudent, or he would not have attached the name of Shakespeare to a volume which was only partly by the bard—that was his crime. Had Jaggard foreseen the tantrums and contradictions he caused some commentators—Mr. Payne Collier, for instance—he would doubtless have substituted 'By William Shakespeare *and others*' for 'By William Shakespeare.' Thus he might have saved his reputation, and this hornets' nest which now and then rouses itself afresh around his aged ghost of three centuries ago."

That a ghost can suffer no inconvenience from hornets I take to be indisputable: but as a defence of Jaggard the above hardly seems convincing. One might as plausibly justify a forger on the ground that, had he foreseen the indignation of the prosecuting counsel, he would doubtless have saved his reputation by forbearing to forge. But before constructing a better defence, let us hear the whole tale of the alleged misdeeds. Of the second edition of *The Passionate Pilgrim* no copy exists. Nothing whatever is known of it, and the whole edition may have been but an ideal construction of

Jaggard's sportive fancy. But in 1612 appeared *The Passionate Pilgrime, or certaine amorous Sonnets between Venus and Adonis, newly corrected and augmented. By W. Shakespeare. The third edition. Whereunto is newly added two Love Epistles, the first from Paris to Hellen, and Hellen's answere back again to Paris. Printed by W. Jaggard.* (These "two Love Epistles" were really by Thomas Heywood.) This title-page was very quickly cancelled, and Shakespeare's name omitted.

Mr. Humphrey's Hypothesis.

These are the bare facts. Now observe how they appear when set forth by Mr. Humphreys:—

"Shakespeare, who, when the first edition was issued, was aged thirty-five, acted his part as a great man very well, for he with dignity took no notice of the error on the title-page of the first edition, attributing to him poems which he had never written. But when Jaggard went on sinning, and the third edition appeared under Shakespeare's name *solely*, though it had poems by Thomas Heywood, and others as well, Jaggard was promptly pulled up by both Shakespeare and Heywood. Upon this the publisher appears very properly to have printed a new title-page, omitting the name of Shakespeare."

Upon this I beg leave to observe—(1) That although it may very likely have been at Shakespeare's own request that his name was removed from the title-page of the third edition, Mr. Humphreys has no right to state this as an ascertained fact. (2) That I fail to understand, if Shakespeare acted properly in case of the third edition, why we should talk nonsense about his "acting the part of a great man very well" and "with dignity taking no notice of the error" in the first edition. In the first edition he was wrongly credited with pieces that belonged to Marlowe, Barnefield, Griffin, and some authors unknown. In the third he was credited with these and some pieces by Heywood as well. In the name of common logic I ask why, if it were "dignified" to say nothing in the case of Marlowe and Barnefield, it suddenly became right and proper to protest in the case of Heywood? But (3) what right have we to assume that Shakespeare "took no notice of the error on the title-page of the first edition"? We know this only—that if he protested, he did not prevail as far as the first edition was concerned. That edition may have been already exhausted. It is even possible that he *did* prevail in the matter of the second edition, and that Jaggard reverted to his old courses in the third. I don't for a moment suppose this was the case. I merely suggest that where so many hypotheses will fit the scanty data known, it is best to lay down no particular hypothesis as fact.

Another.

For I imagine that anyone can, in five minutes, fit up an hypothesis quite as valuable as Mr. Humphreys'. Here is one which at least has the merit of not making Shakespeare look a fool:—W. Jaggard, publisher, comes to William Shakespeare, poet, with the information that he intends to bring out a small miscellany of verse. If the poet has an unconsidered trifle or so to spare, Jaggard will not mind giving a few shillings for them. "You may have, if you like," says Shakespeare, "the rough copies of some songs in my *Love's Labour's Lost*, published last year"; and, being further encouraged, searches among his rough MSS., and tosses Jaggard a lyric or two and a couple of sonnets. Jaggard pays his money, and departs with the verses. When the miscellany appears, Shakespeare finds his name alone upon the title-page, and remonstrates. But, of the defrauded ones, Marlowe is dead; Barnefield has retired to live the life of a country gentleman in Shropshire; Griffin dwells in Coventry (where he died, three years later). These are the men injured; and if they cannot, or will not, move in the business, Shakespeare (whose case at law would be more difficult) can hardly be expected to. So he contents himself with strong expressions at The Mermaid. But in 1612 Jaggard repeats his offence, and is indiscreet enough to add Heywood to the list of the spoiled. Heywood lives in London, on the spot; and Shakespeare, now retired to Stratford, is of more importance than he was in 1599. Armed with Shakespeare's authority Heywood goes to Jaggard and threatens; and the publisher gives way.

Whatever our hypothesis, we cannot maintain that Jaggard behaved well. On the other hand, it were foolish to judge his offence as if the man had committed it the day before yesterday. Conscience in matters of literary copyright has been a plant of slow growth. But a year or two ago respectable citizens of the United States were publishing our books "free of authorial expenses," and even corrected our imperfect works without consulting us. We must admit that Jaggard acted up to Luther's maxim, "*Pecca fortiter.*" He went so far as to include a piece so well known as Marlowe's *Live with me and be my love*—which proves at any rate his indifference to the chances of detection. But to speak of him as one would speak of a similar offender in this New Year of Grace is simply to forfeit one's claim to an historical sense.

The Book.

What further palliation can we find? Mr. Swinburne calls the book "a worthless little volume of stolen and mutilated poetry, patched up and padded out with dirty and dreary doggrel, under the senseless and preposterous title of *The Passionate Pilgrim*." On the other hand, Mr. Humphreys maintains that "Jaggard, at any rate, had very good taste. This is partly seen in the choice of a title. Few books have so charming a name as

The Passionate Pilgrim. It is a perfect title. Jaggard also set up a good precedent, for this collection was published a year before *England's Helicon,* and, of course, very many years before any authorized collection of Shakespeare's 'Poems' was issued. We see in *The Passionate Pilgrim* a forerunner of *The Golden Treasury* and other anthologies."

Now, as for the title, if the value of a title lie in its application, Mr. Swinburne is right. It has little relevance to the verses in the volume. On the other hand, as a portly and attractive mouthful of syllables *The Passionate Pilgrim* can hardly be surpassed. If not "a perfect title," it is surely "a charming name." But Mr. Humphreys' contention that Jaggard "set up a good precedent" and produced a "forerunner" of English anthologies becomes absurd when we remember that *Tottel's Miscellany* was published in June, 1557 (just forty-two years before *The Passionate Pilgrim*), and had reached an eighth edition by 1587; that *The Paradise of Dainty Devices* appeared in 1576; *A Gorgeous Gallery of Gallant Inventions* in 1578; *A Handfull of Pleasant Delights* in 1584; and *The Phoenix' Nest* in 1593.

Almost as wide of the mark is Mr. Swinburne's description of the volume as "worthless." It contains twenty-one numbers, besides that lofty dirge, so unapproachably solemn, *The Phoenix and the Turtle.* Of these, five are undoubtedly by Shakespeare. A sixth (*Crabbed age and youth*), if not by Shakespeare, is one of the loveliest lyrics in the language, and I for my part could give it to no other man. Note also that but for Jaggard's enterprise this jewel had been irrevocably lost to us, since it is known only through *The Passionate Pilgrim.* Marlowe's *Live with me and be my love,* and Barnefield's *As it fell upon a day,* make numbers seven and eight. And I imagine that even Mr. Swinburne cannot afford to scorn *Sweet rose, fair flower, untimely pluck'd, soon vaded*—which again only occurs in *The Passionate Pilgrim.* These nine numbers, with *The Phoenix and the Turtle,* make up more than half the book. Among the rest we have the pretty and respectable lyrics, *If music and sweet poetry agree; Good night, good rest; Lord, how mine eyes throw gazes to the east. When as thine eye hath chose the dame,* and the gay little song, *It was a Lording's daughter.* There remain the *Venus and Adonis* sonnets and *My flocks feed not.* Mr. Swinburne may call these "dirty and dreary doggrel," an he list, with no more risk than of being held a somewhat over-anxious moralist. But to call the whole book worthless is mere abuse of words.

It is true, nevertheless, that one of the only two copies existing of the first edition was bought for three halfpence.

SHAKESPEARE'S LYRICS

August 25, 1894. Shakespeare's Lyrics.

In their re-issue of *The Aldine Poets*, Messrs. George Bell & Sons have made a number of concessions to public taste. The new binding is far more pleasing than the old; and in some cases, where the notes and introductory memoirs had fallen out of date, new editors have been set to work, with satisfactory results. It is therefore no small disappointment to find that the latest volume, "The Poems of Shakespeare," is but a reprint from stereotyped plates of the Rev. Alexander Dyce's text, notes and memoir.

The Rev. A. Dyce.

Now, of the Rev. Alexander Dyce it may be fearlessly asserted that his criticism is not for all time. Even had he been less prone to accept the word of John Payne Collier for gospel; even had Shakespearian criticism made no perceptible advance during the last quarter of a century, yet there is that in the Rev. Alexander Dyce's treatment of his poet which would warn us to pause before accepting his word as final. As a test of his æsthetic judgment we may turn to the "Songs from the Plays of Shakespeare" with which this volume concludes. It had been as well, in a work of this sort, to include all the songs; but he gives us a selection only, and an uncommonly bad selection. I have tried in vain to discover a single principle of taste underlying it. On what principle, for instance, can a man include the song "Come away, come away, death" from *Twelfth Night*, and omit "O mistress mine, where are you roaming?"; or include Amiens' two songs from *As you Like It*, and omit the incomparable "It was a lover and his lass"? Or what but stark insensibility can explain the omission of "Take, O take those lips away," and the bridal song "Roses, their sharp spines being gone," that opens *The Two Noble Kinsmen*? But stay: the Rev. Alexander Dyce may attribute this last pair to Fletcher. "Take, O take those lips away" certainly occurs (with a second and inferior stanza) in Fletcher's *The Bloody Brother*, first published in 1639; but Dyce gives no hint of his belief that Fletcher wrote it. We are, therefore, left to conclude that Dyce thought it unworthy of a place in his collection. On *The Two Noble Kinsmen* (first published in 1634) Dyce is more explicit. In a footnote to the Memoir he says: "The title-page of the first edition of Fletcher's *Two Noble Kinsmen* attributes the play partly to Shakespeare; I do not think our poet had any share in its composition; but I must add that Mr. C. Lamb (a great authority in such matters) inclines to a different opinion." When "Mr. C. Lamb" and the Rev. Alexander Dyce hold opposite opinions, it need not be difficult to choose. And surely, if internal evidence count for anything at all, the lines

"Maiden pinks, of odour faint,
Daisies smell-less, yet most quaint,
And sweet thyme true."

or—

"Oxlips in their cradles growing"

or—

"Not an angel of the air,
Bird melodious, or bird fair,
Be absent hence."

—were written by Shakespeare and not by Fletcher. Nor is it any detraction from Fletcher to take this view. Shakespeare himself has left songs hardly finer than Fletcher wrote at his best—hardly finer, for instance, than that magnificent pair from *Valentinian*. Only the note of Shakespeare happens to be different from the note of Fletcher: and it is Shakespeare's note—the note of

"The cowslips tall her pensioners be"

(also omitted by the inscrutable Dyce) and of

"When daisies pied, and violets blue,
And lady-smocks all silver-white,
And cuckoo buds of yellow hue
Do paint the meadows with delight ..."

—that we hear repeated in this Bridal Song.[A] And if this be so, it is but another proof for us that Dyce was not a critic for all time.

Nor is the accent of finality conspicuous in such passages as this from the Memoir:—

"Wright had heard that Shakespeare 'was a much better poet than player'; and Rowe tells us that soon after his admission into the company, he became distinguished, 'if not as an extraordinary actor, yet as an excellent writer.' Perhaps his execution did not equal his conception of a character, but we may rest assured that he who wrote the incomparable instructions to the player in *Hamlet* would never offend his audience by an injudicious performance."

I have no more to urge against writing of this order than that it has passed out of fashion, and that something different might reasonably have been looked for in a volume that bears the date 1894 on its title-page. The public owes Messrs. Bell & Sons a heavy debt; but at the same time the public has a peculiar interest in such a series as that of *The Aldine Poets*. A purchaser who finds several of these books to his mind, and is thereby induced to embark upon the purchase of the entire series, must feel a natural resentment if succeeding volumes drop below the implied standard. He cannot go back: and to omit the offending volumes is to spoil his set. And I contend that the action taken by Messrs. Bell & Sons in improving several of their more or less obsolete editions will only be entirely praiseworthy if we may take it as an earnest of their desire to place the whole series on a level with contemporary knowledge and criticism.

Nor can anyone who knows how much the industry and enthusiasm of Dyce did, in his day, for the study of Shakespeare, do more than urge that while, viewed historically, Dyce's criticism is entirely respectable, it happens to be a trifle belated in the year 1894. The points of difference between him and Charles Lamb are perhaps too obvious to need indication; but we may sum them up by saying that whereas Lamb, being a genius, belongs to all time, Dyce, being but an industrious person, belongs to a period. It was a period of rapid development, no doubt—how rapid we may learn for ourselves by the easy process of taking down Volume V. of Chalmers's "English Poets," and turning to that immortal passage on Shakespeare's poems which Chalmers put forth in the year 1810:—

"The peremptory decision of Mr. Steevens on the merits of these poems must not be omitted. 'We have not reprinted the Sonnets, etc., of Shakespeare, because the strongest Act of Parliament that could be framed would fail to compel readers into their service. Had Shakespeare produced no other works than these, his name would have reached us with as little celebrity as time has conferred upon that of Thomas Watson, an older and much more elegant sonnetteer.' Severe as this may appear, it only amounts to the general conclusion which modern critics have formed. Still, it cannot be denied that there are many scattered beauties among his Sonnets, and in the Rape of Lucrece; enough, it is hoped, to justify their admission into the present collection, especially as the Songs, etc., from his plays have been added, and a few smaller pieces selected by Mr. Ellis...."

No comment can add to, or take from, the stupendousness of this. And yet it was the criticism proper to its time. "I have only to hope," writes Chalmers in his preface, "that my criticisms will not be found destitute of candour, or improperly interfering with the general and acknowledged principles of taste." Indeed they are not. They were the right opinions for Chalmers; as Dyce's were the right opinions for Dyce: and if, as we hope, ours is a larger appreciation of Shakespeare, we probably hold it by no merit of our own, but as the common possession of our generation, derived through the chastening experiences of our grandfathers. That, however, is no reason why we should not insist on having such editions of Shakespeare as fulfil our requirements, and refuse to study Dyce except as an historical figure.

It is an unwise generation that declines to take all its inheritance. I have heard once or twice of late that English poets in the future will set themselves to express emotions more complex and subtle than have ever yet been treated in poetry. I shall be extremely glad, of course, if this happen in my time. But at present I incline to rejoice rather in an assured inheritance, and, when I hear talk of this kind, to say over to myself one particular sonnet which for mere subtlety of thought seems to me unbeaten by anything that I can select from the poetry of this century:—

Thy bosom is endeared of all hearts
Which I by lacking have supposed dead;
And there reigns Love and all Love's loving parts,
And all those friends which I thought buried.
How many a holy and obsequious Tear
Hath dear religious love stol'n from mine eye,
As interest of the dead, which now appear
But things remov'd that hidden in thee lie!

Thou art the grave where buried love doth live,
Hung with the trophies of my lovers gone,
Who all their parts of me to thee did give;
That due of many now is thine alone!
Their images I lov'd I view in thee,
And thou, all they, hast all the all of me.

FOOTNOTES:

[A] The opening lines of the second stanza of this poem have generally been printed thus:

"Primrose, firstborn child of Ver,
Merry springtime's harbinger,
With her bells dim...."

And many have wondered how Shakespeare or Fletcher came to write of the "bells" of a primrose. Mr. W.J. Linton proposed "With harebell slim": although if we must read "harebell" or "harebells," "dim" would be a pretty and proper word for the color of that flower. The conjecture takes some little plausibility from Shakespeare's elsewhere linking primrose and harebell together:

"Thou shalt not lack

The flower that's like thy face, pale primrose, nor
The azured harebell, like thy veins...."
Cymbeline, iv. 2.

I have always suspected, however, that there should be a semicolon after "Ver," and that "Merry springtime's harbinger, with her bells dim," refers to a totally different flower—the snowdrop, to wit. And I have lately learnt from Dr. Grosart, who has carefully examined the 1634 edition (the only early one), that the text actually gives a semicolon. The snowdrop may very well come after the primrose in this song, which altogether ignores the process of the seasons.

SAMUEL DANIEL

February 24, 1894. Samuel Daniel.

The writings of Samuel Daniel and the circumstances of his life are of course well enough known to all serious students of English poetry. And, though I cannot speak on this point with any certainty, I imagine that our younger singers hold to the tradition of all their fathers, and that Daniel still

renidet in angulo

of their affections, as one who in his day did very much, though quietly, to train the growth of English verse; and proved himself, in everything he wrote, an artist to the bottom of his conscience. As certainly as Spenser, he was a "poet's poet" while he lived. A couple of pages might be filled almost offhand with the genuine compliments of his contemporaries, and he will probably remain a "poet's poet" as long as poets write in English. But the average reader of culture—the person who is honestly moved by good poetry and goes from time to time to his bookshelves for an antidote to the common cares and trivialities of this life—seems to neglect Daniel almost utterly. I judge from the wretched insufficiency of his editions. It is very hard to obtain anything beyond the two small volumes published in 1718 (an imperfect collection), and a volume of selections edited by Mr. John Morris and published by a Bath bookseller in 1855; and even these are only to be picked up here and there. I find it significant, too, that in Mr. Palgrave's *Golden Treasury* Daniel is represented by one sonnet only, and that by no means his best. This neglect will appear the more singular to anyone who has observed how apt is the person whom I have called the "average reader of culture" to be drawn to the perusal of an author's works by some attractive idiosyncrasy in the author's private life or character. Lamb is a staring instance of this attraction. How we all love Lamb, to be sure! Though he rejected it and called out upon it, "gentle" remains Lamb's constant epithet. And, curiously enough, in the gentleness and dignified melancholy of his life, Daniel stands nearer to Lamb than any other English writer, with the possible exception of Scott. His circumstances were less gloomily picturesque. But I defy any feeling man to read the scanty narrative of Daniel's life and think of him thereafter without sympathy and respect.

Life.

He was born in 1562—Fuller says in Somersetshire, not far from Taunton; others say at Beckington, near Philip's Norton, or at Wilmington in Wiltshire. Anthony Wood tells us that he came "of a wealthy family;" Fuller that "his father was a master of music." Of his earlier years next to nothing is known; but in 1579 he was entered as a commoner at Magdalen Hall, Oxford, and left the university three years afterwards without taking a degree. His first book—a translation of Paola Giovio's treatise on Emblems—appeared in 1585, when he was about twenty-two. In 1590 or 1591 he was travelling in Italy, probably with a pupil, and no doubt busy with those studies that finally made him the first Italian scholar of his time. In 1592 he published his "Sonnets to Delia," which at once made his reputation; in 1594 his "Complaint of Rosamond" and "Tragedy of Cleopatra;" and in 1595 four books of his "Civil Wars." On Spenser's death, in 1599, Daniel is said to have succeeded to the office of poet-laureate.

"That wreath which, in Eliza's golden days,
My master dear, divinist Spenser, wore;
That which rewarded Drayton's learned lays,
Which thoughtful Ben and gentle Daniel wore...."

But history traces the Laureateship, as an office, no further back than Jonson, and we need not follow Southey into the mists. It is certain, however, that Daniel was a favorite at Elizabeth's Court, and in some way partook of her bounty. In 1600 he was appointed tutor to the Lady Anne Clifford, a little girl of about eleven, daughter of Margaret, Countess of Cumberland; and his services were gratefully remembered by mother and daughter during his life and after. But Daniel seems to have tired of living in great houses as private tutor to the young. The next year, when presenting his works to Sir Thomas Egerton, he writes:—"Such hath been my misery that whilst I should have written the actions of men, I have been constrained to bide with children, and, contrary to mine own spirit, put out of that sense which nature had made my part."

Self-distrust.

Now there is but one answer to this—that a man of really strong spirit does not suffer himself to be "put out of that sense which nature had made my part." Daniel's words indicate the weakness that in the end made futile all his powers: they indicate a certain "donnish" timidity (if I may use the epithet), a certain distrust of his own genius. Such a timidity and such a distrust often accompany very exquisite faculties: indeed, they may be said to imply a certain exquisiteness of feeling. But they explain why, of the two contemporaries, the robust Ben Jonson is to-day a living figure in most men's conception of those times, while Samuel Daniel is rather a fleeting ghost. And his self-distrust was even then recognized as well as his exquisiteness. He is indeed "well-languaged Daniel," "sweet honey-dropping Daniel," "Rosamund's trumpeter, sweet as the nightingale," revered and admired by all his compeers. But the note of apprehension was also sounded, not only by an unknown contributor to that rare collection of epigrams, *Skialetheia, or the Shadow of Truth*.

"Daniel (as some hold) might mount, *if he list*;
But others say he is a Lucanist"

—but by no meaner a judge than Spenser himself, who wrote in his "Colin Clout's Come Home Again":

"And there is a new shepherd late upsprung
The which doth all afore him far surpass:
Appearing well in that well-tunéd song
Which late he sung unto a scornful lass.
Yet doth his trembling Muse but lowly fly,
As daring not too rashly mount on height;
And doth her tender plumes as yet but try
In love's soft lays, and looser thoughts delight.
Then rouse thy feathers quickly, DANIEL,
And to what course thou please thyself advance;
But most, meseems, thy accent will excel
In tragic plaints and passionate mischance."

Moreover, there is a significant passage in the famous "Return from Parnassus," first acted at Cambridge during the Christmas of 1601:

"Sweet honey-dropping Daniel doth wage
War with the proudest big Italian
That melts his heart in sugar'd sonneting,
Only let him more sparingly make use
Of others' wit and use his own the more."

The 'mauvais pas' of Parnassus.

Now it has been often pointed out that considerable writers fall into two classes—(1) those who begin, having something to say, and are from the first rather occupied with their matter than with the manner of expressing it; and (2) those who begin with the love of expression and intent to be artists in words, *and come through expression to profound thought*. It is fashionable just now, for some reason or another, to account Class 1 as the more respectable; a judgment to which, considering that Shakespeare and Milton belonged undeniably to Class 2, I refuse to assent. The question, however, is not to be argued here. I have only to point out in this place that the early work of all poets in Class 2 is largely imitative. Virgil was imitative, Keats was imitative—to name but a couple of sufficiently striking examples. And Daniel, who belongs to this class, was also imitative. But for a poet of this class to reach the heights of song, there must come a time when out of imitation he forms a genuine style of his own, *and loses no mental fertility in the transformation.* This, if I may use the metaphor, is the *mauvais pas* in the ascent of Parnassus: and here Daniel broke down. He did indeed acquire a style of his own; but the effort exhausted him. He was no longer prolific; his ardor had gone: and his innate self-distrustfulness made him quick to recognize his sterility.

Soon after the accession of James I., Daniel, at the recommendation of his brother-in-law, John Florio, possibly furthered by the interest of the Earl of Pembroke, was given a post as gentleman extraordinary and groom of the privy chamber to Anne of Denmark; and a few months after was appointed to take the oversight of the plays and shows that were performed by the children of the Queen's revels, or children of the Chapel, as they were called under Elizabeth. He had thus a snug position at Court, and might have been happy, had it been another Court. But in nothing was the accession of James more apparent than in the almost instantaneous blasting of the taste, manners, and serious grace that had marked the Court of Elizabeth. The Court of James was a Court of bad taste, bad manners, and no grace whatever: and Daniel—"the remnant of another time," as he calls himself—looked wistfully back upon the days of Elizabeth.

"But whereas he came planted in the spring,
And had the sun before him of respect;
We, set in th' autumn, in the withering
And sullen season of a cold defect,
Must taste those sour distastes the times do bring
Upon the fulness of a cloy'd neglect.
Although the stronger constitutions shall
Wear out th' infection of distemper'd days ... "

And so he stood dejected, while the young men of "stronger constitutions" passed him by.

In this way it happened that Daniel, whom at the outset his contemporaries had praised with wide consent, and who never wrote a loose or unscholarly line, came to pen, in the dedicatory epistle prefixed to his tragedy of "Philotas," these words—perhaps the most pathetic ever uttered by an artist upon his work:

"And therefore since I have outlived the date
Of former grace, acceptance and delight.
I would my lines, late born beyond the fate
Of her[A] spent line, had never come to light;
So had I not been tax'd for wishing well,
Nor now mistaken by the censuring Stage,
Nor in my fame and reputation fell,

Which I esteem more than what all the age
Or the earth can give. *But years hath done this wrong,
To make me write too much, and live too long.*"

Ease of his verse.

I said just now that Daniel had done much, though quietly, to train the growth of English verse. He not only stood up successfully for its natural development at a time when the clever but less largely informed Campion and others threatened it with fantastic changes. He probably did as much as Waller to introduce polish of line into our poetry. Turn to the famous "Ulysses and the Siren," and read. Can anyone tell me of English verses that run more smoothly off the tongue, or with a more temperate grace?

"Well, well, Ulysses, then I see
I shall not have thee here:
And, therefore, I will come to thee,
And take my fortune there.
I must be won that cannot win,
Yet lost were I not won;
For beauty hath created been
T'undo or be undone."

To speak familiarly, this is as easy as an old shoe. To speak yet more familiarly, it looks as if any fool could turn off lines like these. Let the fool try.

And yet to how many anthologies do we not turn in vain for "Ulysses and the Siren"; or for the exquisite spring song, beginning—

"Now each creature joys the other,
Passing happy days and hours;
One bird reports unto another
In the fall of silver showers ..."

—or for that lofty thing, the "Epistle to the Countess of Cumberland"?—which Wordsworth, who quoted it in his "Excursion," declares to be "an admirable picture of the state of a wise man's mind in a time of public commotion." Certainly if ever a critic shall arise to deny poetry the virtue we so commonly claim for her, of fortifying men's souls against calamity, this noble Epistle will be all but the last post from which he will extrude her defenders.

FOOTNOTES:

[A] Sc. Elizabeth's.

WILLIAM BROWNE

April 21, 1894. William Browne of Tavistock.

It has been objected to the author of *Britannia's Pastorals* that their perusal sends you to sleep. It had been subtler criticism, as well as more amiable, to observe that you can wake up again and, starting anew at the precise point where you dropped off, continue the perusal with as much pleasure as ever, neither ashamed of your somnolence nor imputing it as a fault to the poet. For William Browne is perhaps the easiest figure in our literature. He lived easily, he wrote easily, and no doubt he died easily. He no more expected to be read through at a sitting than he tried to write all the story of Marina at a sitting. He took up his pen and composed: when he felt tired he went off to bed, like a sensible man: and when you are tired of reading he expects you to be sensible and do the same.

A placid life.

He was born at Tavistock, in Devon, about the year 1590; and after the manner of mild and sensible men cherished a particular love for his birth-place to the end of his days. From Tavistock Grammar School he passed to Exeter College, Oxford—the old west-country college—and thence to Clifford's Inn and the Inner Temple. His first wife died when he was twenty-three or twenty-four. He took his second courtship quietly and leisurely, marrying the lady at length in 1628, after a wooing of thirteen years. "He seems," says Mr. A.H. Bullen, his latest biographer, "to have acquired in some way a modest competence, which secured him immunity from the troubles that weighed so heavily on men of letters." His second wife also brought him a portion. More than four years before this marriage he had returned to Exeter College, as tutor to the young Robert Dormer, who in due time became Earl of Carnarvon and was killed in Newbury fight. By his fellow-collegians—as by everybody with whom he came into contact—he was highly beloved and esteemed, and in the public Register of the University is styled, "vir omni humana literarum et bonarum artium cognitione instructus." He gained the especial favor of William Herbert, Earl of Pembroke, whom Aubrey calls "the greatest Mæcenas to learned men of any peer of his time or since," and of whom Clarendon says, "He was a great lover of his country, and of the religion and justice, which he believed could only support it; and his friendships were only with men of those principles,"—another tribute to the poet's character. He was familiarly received at Wilton, the home of the Herberts. After his second marriage he moved to Dorking and there settled. He died in or before the year 1645. In the letters of administration granted to his widow (November, 1645) he is described as "late of Dorking, in the county of Surrey, Esquire." But there is no entry of his death in the registers at Dorking or Horsham: so perhaps he went back to lay his bones in his beloved Devon. A William Browne was buried at Tavistock on March 27th, 1643. This may or may not have been our author. "Tavistock,—Wilton,—Dorking," says Mr. Bullen,—"Surely few poets have had a more tranquil journey to the Elysian Fields."

An amiable poet.

As with his life, so with his poetry—he went about it quietly, contentedly. He learned his art, as he confesses, from Spenser and Sidney; and he took it over ready-made, with all the conventions and pastoral stock-in-trade—swains languishing for hard-hearted nymphs, nymphs languishing for hard-hearted swains; sheep-cotes, rustic dances, junketings, anadems, and true-love knots; monsters invented for the perpetual menace of chastity; chastity undergoing the most surprising perils, but always saved in the nick of time, if not by an opportune shepherd, then by an equally opportune river-god or earthquake; episodes innumerable, branching off from the main stem of the narrative at the most critical point, and luxuriating in endless ramifications. Beauty, eluding unwelcome embraces, is never too hotly pressed to dally with an engaging simile or choose the most agreeable words for depicting her tribulation. Why indeed should she hurry? It is all a polite and pleasant make-believe; and when Marina and Doridon are tired, they stand aside and watch the side couples, Fida and Remond, and get their breath again for the next figure. As for the finish of the tale, there is no finish. The narrator will stop when he is tired; just then and no sooner. What became of Marina after Triton rolled away the stone and released her from the Cave of Famine? I am sure I don't know. I have followed her adventures up to that point (though I should be very sorry to attempt a *précis* of them without the book) through some 370 pages of verse. Does this mean that I am greatly interested in her? Not in the least. I am quite content to hear no more about her. Let us have the lamentations of Celadyne for a change—though "for a change" is much too strong an expression. The author is quite able to invent more adventures for Marina, if he chooses to, by the hour together. If he does not choose to, well and good.

Was the composition of *Britannia's Pastorals* then, a useless or inconsiderable feat? Not at all: since to read them is to taste a mild but continuous pleasure. In the first place, it is always pleasant to see a good man thoroughly enjoying himself: and that Browne thoroughly "relisht versing"—to use George Herbert's pretty phrase—would be patent enough, even had he not left us an express assurance:—

"What now I sing is but to pass away
A tedious hour, as some musicians play;
Or make another my own griefs bemoan—"

—rather affected, that, one suspects:

"Or to be least alone when most alone,
In this can I, as oft as I will choose,
Hug sweet content by my retirèd Muse,
And in a study find as much to please
As others in the greatest palaces.
Each man that lives, according to his power,
On what he loves bestows an idle hour.
Instead of hounds that make the wooded hills
Talk in a hundred voices to the rills,
I like the pleasing cadence of a line
Struck by the consort of the sacred Nine.
In lieu of hawks ..."

—and so on. Indeed, unless it be Wither, there is no poet of the time who practised his art with such entire cheerfulness: though Wither's satisfaction had a deeper note, as when he says of his Muse—

"Her true beauty leaves behind
Apprehensions in the mind,
Of more sweetness than all art
Or inventions can impart;
Thoughts too deep to be express'd,
And too strong to be suppressed."

Yet Charles Lamb's nice observation—

"Fame, and that too after death, was all which hitherto the poets had promised themselves from their art. It seems to have been left to Wither to discover that poetry was a present possession as well as a rich reversion, and that the muse had promise of both lives—of this, and of that which was to come."

—must be extended by us, after reading his lines quoted above, to include William Browne. He, at least, had no doubt of the Muse as an earthly companion.

As for posthumous fame, Browne confides to us his aspirations in that matter also:—

"And Time may be so kind to these weak lines
To keep my name enroll'd past his that shines
In gilded marble, or in brazen leaves:
Since verse preserves, when stone and brass deceives.
Or if (as worthless) Time not lets it live

To those full days which others' Muses give,
Yet I am sure I shall be heard and sung
Of most severest eld and kinder young
Beyond my days; and maugre Envy's strife,
Add to my name some hours beyond my life."

This is the amiable hope of one who lived an entirely amiable life in

"homely towns,
Sweetly environ'd with the daisied downs:"

and who is not the less to be beloved because at times his amiability prevents him from attacking even our somnolence too fiercely. If the casual reader but remember Browne as a poet who had the honor to supply Keats with inspiration,[A] there will always be others, and enough of them, to prize his ambling Muse for her own qualities.

FOOTNOTES:

[A] *Cf.* his lament for William Ferrar (brother of Nicholas Ferrar, of Little Gidding), drowned at sea—

"Glide soft, ye silver floods,
And every spring:
Within the shady woods
Let no bird sing...."

THOMAS CAREW

July 28, 1894. A Note on his Name.

Even as there is an M alike in Macedon and Monmouth, so Thomas Carew and I have a common grievance—that our names are constantly mispronounced. It is their own fault, of course; on the face of it they ought to rhyme with "few" and "vouch." And if it be urged (impolitely but with a fair amount of plausibility) that what my name may or may not rhyme with is of no concern to anybody, I have only to reply that, until a month or so back, I cheerfully shared this opinion and acquiesced in the general error. Had I dreamed then of becoming a subject for poetry, I had pointed out—as I do now—for the benefit of all intending bards, that I do not legitimately rhyme with "vouch" (so liable is human judgment to err, even in trifles), unless they pronounce it "vooch," which is awkward. I believe, indeed (speaking as one who has never had occasion to own a Rhyming Dictionary), that the number of English words consonant with my name is exceedingly small; but leave the difficulty to the ingenious Dr. Alexander H. Japp, LL.D., F.R.S.E., who has lately been at the pains to compose and put into private circulation a sprightly lampoon upon me. As it is not my intention to reply with a set of verses upon Dr. Japp, it seems superfluous to inquire if *his* name should be pronounced as it is spelt.

But Carew's case is rather important; and it is really odd that his latest and most learned editor, the Rev. J.F. Ebsworth, should fall into the old error. In a "dedicatory prelude" to his edition of "The Poems and Masque of Thomas Carew" (London: Reeves & Turner), Mr. Ebsworth writes as follows:—

"Hearken strains from one who knew
How to praise and how to sue:
Celia's lover, TOM CAREW."

Thomas Carew (born April 3d, 1590, at Wickham, in Kent) was the son of Sir Matthew Carew, Master in Chancery, and the grandson of Sir Wymond Carew, of East Antony, or Antony St. Jacob, between the Lynher and Tamar rivers in Cornwall, where the family of Pole-Carew lives to this day. Now, the Cornish Carews have always pronounced their name as "Carey," though, as soon as you cross the Tamar and find yourself (let us say) as far east as Haccombe in South Devon, the name becomes "Carew"—pronounced as it is written. The two forms are both of great age, as the old rhyme bears witness—

"Carew, Carey and Courtenay,
When the Conqueror came, were here at play"—

and the name was often written "Carey" or "Cary," as in the case of the famous Lucius Carey, Lord Falkland, and his descendants. In Cornwall, however, where spelling is often an untrustworthy guide to pronunciation (I have known people to write their name "Hix" and pronounce it as "Hic"—when sober, too), it was written "Carew" and pronounced as "Carey"; and there is not the slightest doubt that this was the case with our poet's name. If anyone deny it, let him consider the verse in which Carew is mentioned by his contemporaries: and attempt, for instance, to scan the lines in Robert Baron's "Pocula Castalia," 1650—

"Sweet *Suckling* then, the glory of the Bower
Wherein I've wanton'd many a genial hour,
Fair Plant! whom I have seen *Minerva* wear
An ornament to her well-plaited hair,
On highest days; remove a little from
Thy excellent *Carew*! and thou, dearest *Tom*,
Love's Oracle! lay thee a little off
Thy flourishing *Suckling*, that between you both
I may find room...."

Or this by Suckling—

"*Tom Carew* was next, but he had a fault,
That would not well stand with a Laureat;
His Muse was hard-bound, and th' issue of 's brain
Was seldom brought forth but with trouble and pain."

Or this, by Lord Falkland himself (who surely may be supposed to have known how the name was pronounced), in his "Eclogue on the Death of Ben Jonson"—

"*Let Digby, Carew, Killigrew* and *Maine,
Godolphin, Waller*, that inspired train—
*Or whose rare pen beside deserves the grace
Or of an equal, or a neighbouring place—
Answer thy wish, for none so fit appears
To raise his Tomb, as who are left his heirs.*"

In each case "Carey" scans admirably, while "Carew" gives the line an intolerable limp.

Mr. Ebsworth's championship.

This mistake of Mr. Ebsworth's is the less easy to understand inasmuch as he has been very careful to clear up the popular confusion of our poet Thomas Carew, "gentleman of the Privy Chamber to King Charles I., and cup-bearer to His Majesty," with another Thomas Gary (also a poet), son of the Earl of Monmouth and groom of His Majesty's bed-chamber. But it is one thing to prove that this second Thomas Gary is the original of the "medallion portrait" commonly supposed to be Carew's: it is quite another thing to saddle him, merely upon guess-work, with Carew's reputed indiscretions. Indeed, Mr. Ebsworth lets his enthusiasm for his author run clean away with his sense of fairness. He heads his Introductory Memoir with the words of Pallas in Tennyson's "Œnone"—

"Again she said—'I woo thee not with gifts:
Sequel of guerdon could not alter me
To fairer. Judge thou me by what I am,
So shalt thou find me fairest.'"—

from which I take it that Mr. Ebsworth claims his attitude towards Carew to be much the same as Thackeray's towards Pendennis. But in fact he proves himself a thorough-going partisan, and anyone less enthusiastic may think himself lucky if dismissed by Mr. Ebsworth with nothing worse than a smile of pity mingled with contempt. Now, so long as an editor confines this belligerent enthusiasm to the defence of his author's writings, it is at worst but an amiable weakness; and every word he says in their praise tends indirectly to justify his own labor in editing these meritorious compositions. But when he extends this championship over the author's private life, he not unfrequently becomes something of a nuisance. We may easily forgive such talk as "There must assuredly have been a singular frankness and affectionate simplicity in the disposition of Carew:" talk which is harmless, though hardly more valuable than the reflection beloved of local historians—"If these grey old walls could speak, what a tale might they not unfold!" It is less easy to forgive such a note as this:—

"Sir John Suckling was incapable of understanding Carew in his final days of sickness and depression, as he had been (and this is conceding much) in their earlier days of reckless gallantry. His vile address 'to T—— C——,' etc., 'Troth, *Tom*, I must confess I much admire ...' is nothing more than coarse badinage without foundation; in any case not necessarily addressed to Carew, although they were of close acquaintance; but many other Toms were open to a similar expression, since 'T.C.' might apply to Thomas Carey, to Thomas Crosse, and other T.C. poets."

It is not pleasant to rake up any man's faults; but when an editor begins to suggest some new man against whom nothing is known (except that he wrote indifferent verse)—who is not even known to have been on speaking terms with Suckling—as the proper target of Suckling's coarse raillery, we have a right not only to protest, but to point out that even Clarendon, who liked Carew, wrote of him that, "after fifty years of his life spent with less severity and exactness than it ought to have been, he died with great remorse for that license, and with the greatest manifestation of Christianity that his best friends could desire." If Carew thought fit to feel remorse for that license, it scarcely becomes Mr. Ebsworth to deny its existence, much less to hint that the sinfulness was another's.

A correction.

As a minor criticism, I may point out that the song, "Come, my Celia, let us prove ..." (included by Mr. Ebsworth, with the remark that "there is no external evidence to confirm the attribution of this song to Carew") was written by Ben Jonson, and is to be found in *Volpone*, Act III., sc. 7, 1607.

But, with some imperfections, this is a sound edition—sadly needed—of one of the most brilliant lyrical writers of his time. It contains a charming portrait; and the editor's enthusiasm, when it does not lead him too far, is also charming.

"ROBINSON CRUSOE"

April 13, 1895. Robinson Crusoe.

Many a book has produced a wide and beneficent effect and won a great reputation, and yet this effect and this reputation have been altogether wide of its author's aim. Swift's *Gulliver* is one example. As Mr. Birrell put it the other day, "Swift's gospel of hatred, his testament of woe—his *Gulliver*, upon which he expended the treasures of his wit, and into which he instilled the concentrated essence of his rage—has become a child's book, and has been read with wonder and delight by generations of innocents."

How far is the tale a parable?

Generations of innocents in like manner have accepted *Robinson Crusoe* as a delightful tale about a castaway mariner, a story of adventure pure and simple, without sub-intention of any kind. But we know very well that Defoe in writing it intended a parable—a parable of his own life. In the first place, he distinctly affirms this in his preface to the *Serious Reflections* which form Part iii. of his great story:—

"As the design of everything is said to be first in the intention, and last in the execution, so I come now to acknowledge to my reader that the present work is not merely a product of the two first volumes, but the two first volumes may rather be called the product of this. The fable is always made for the moral, not the moral for the fable...."

He goes on to say that whereas "the envious and ill-disposed part of the world" have accused the story of being feigned, and "all a romance, formed and embellished by invention to impose upon the world," he declares this objection to be an invention scandalous in design, and false in fact, and affirms that the story, "though allegorical, is also historical"; that it is

"the beautiful representation of a life of unexampled misfortunes, and of a variety not to be met with in the world, sincerely adapted to and intended for the common good of mankind, and *designed at first*, as it is now further applied, to the most serious use possible. Farther, that there is a man alive, and well known too, the actions of whose life are the just subject of these volumes, *and to whom all or most part of the story most directly alludes*; this may be depended upon, for truth, and to this I set my name."

He proceeds to assert this in detail of several important passages in the book, and obviously intends us to infer that the adventures of Robinson Crusoe of York, Mariner, were throughout and from the beginning designed as a story in parable of the life and adventures of Daniel Defoe, Gentleman. "But

Defoe may have been lying?" This was never quite flatly asserted. Even his enemy Gildon admitted an analogy between the tale of Crusoe and the stormy life of Defoe with its frequent shipwrecks "more by land than by sea." Gildon admitted this implicitly in the title of his pamphlet, *The Life and Strange Surprising Adventures of Mr. D—— De F——, of London, Hosier, who has lived above Fifty Years by himself in the Kingdoms of North and South Britain.* But the question has always been, To what extent are we to accept Defoe's statement that the story is an allegory? Does it agree step by step and in detail with the circumstances of Defoe's life? Or has it but a general allegorical resemblance?

Hitherto, critics have been content with the general resemblance, and have agreed that it would be a mistake to accept Defoe's statement too literally, to hunt for minute allusions in *Robinson Crusoe*, and search for exact resemblances between incidents in the tale and events in the author's life. But this at any rate may be safely affirmed, that recent discoveries have proved the resemblance to be a great deal closer than anyone suspected a few years ago.

Mr. Wright's hypothesis.

Mr. Aitken supplied the key when he announced in the *Athenæum* for August 23rd, 1890, his discovery that Daniel Defoe was born, not in 1661 (as had hitherto been supposed), but earlier, and probably in the latter part of the year 1659. The story dates Crusoe's birth September 30th, 1632, or just twenty-seven years earlier. Now Mr. Wright, Defoe's latest biographer,[A] maintains that if we add these twenty-seven years to the date of any event in Crusoe's life we shall have the date of the corresponding event in Defoe's life. By this simple calculation he finds that Crusoe's running away to sea corresponds in time with Defoe's departure from the academy at Newington Green; Crusoe's early period on the island (south side) with the years Defoe lived at Tooting; Crusoe's visit to the other side of the island with a journey of Defoe's into Scotland; the footprint and the arrival of the savages with the threatening letters received by Defoe, and the physical assaults made on him after the Sacheverell trial; while Friday stands for a collaborator who helped Defoe with his work.

Defoe expressly states in his *Serious Reflections* that the story of Friday is historical and true in fact—

"It is most real that I had ... such a servant, a savage, and afterwards a Christian, and that his name was called Friday, and that he was ravished from me by force, and died in the hands that took him, which I represent by being killed; this is all literally true, and should I enter into discoveries many alive can testify them. His other conduct and assistance to me also have just references in all their parts to the helps I had from that faithful savage in my real solitudes and disasters."

It may be added that there are strong grounds for believing Defoe to have had about this time assistance in his literary work.

All this is very neatly worked out; but of course the really important event in Crusoe's life is his great shipwreck and his long solitude on the island. Now of what events in Defoe's life are these symbolical?

The 'Silence.'

Well, in the very forefront of his *Serious Reflections*, and in connection with his long confinement in the island, Defoe makes Crusoe tell the following story:—

"I have heard of a man that, upon some extraordinary disgust which he took at the unsuitable conversation of some of his nearest relations, whose society he could not avoid, suddenly resolved never to speak any more. He kept his resolution most rigorously many years; not all the tears or entreaties of his friends—no, not of his wife and children—could prevail with him to break his silence. It seems it was their ill-behaviour to him, at first, that was the occasion of it; for they treated him with provoking language, which frequently put him into undecent passions, and urged him to rash replies; and he took this severe way to punish himself for being provoked, and to punish them for provoking him. But the severity was unjustifiable; it ruined his family and broke up his house. His wife could not bear it, and after endeavouring, by all the ways possible, to alter his rigid silence, went first away from him, and afterwards from herself, turning melancholy and distracted. His children separated, some one way and some another way; and only one daughter, who loved her father above all the rest, kept with him, tended him, talked to him by signs, and lived almost dumb like her father *near twenty-nine years with him; till being very sick, and in a high fever, delirious as we call it, or light-headed, he broke his silence*, not knowing when he did it, and spoke, though wildly at first. He recovered of his illness afterwards, and frequently talked with his daughter, but not much, and very seldom to anybody else."

I italicise some very important words in the above story. Crusoe was wrecked on his island on September 30th, 1659, his twenty-seventh birthday. We are told that he remained on the island twenty-eight years, two months and nineteen days. (Compare with duration of the man's silence in the story.) This puts the date of his departure at December 19th, 1687.

Now add twenty-seven years. We find that Defoe left *his* solitude—whatever that may have been—on December 19th, 1714. Just at that date, as all his biographers record, Defoe was struck down by a fit of apoplexy and lay ill for six weeks. Compare this again with the story.

You divine what is coming. Astounding as it may be, Mr. Wright contends that Defoe himself was the original of the story: that Defoe, provoked by his wife's irritating tongue, made a kind of vow to live a life of silence—and kept it for more than twenty-eight years!

So far back as 1859 the egregious Chadwick nibbled at this theory in his *Life and Times of Daniel Defoe, with Remarks Digressive and Discursive*. The story, he says, "would be very applicable" to Defoe himself, and again, "is very likely to have been taken from his own life"; but at this point Chadwick maunders off with the remark that "perhaps the domestic fireside of the poet or book-writer is not the place we should go to in search of domestic happiness." Perhaps not; but Chadwick, tallyhoing after domestic happiness, misses the scent. Mr. Wright sticks to the scent and rides boldly; but is he after the real fox?

April 20, 1895.

Can we believe it? Can we believe that on the 30th of September, 1686, Defoe, provoked by his wife's nagging tongue, made a vow to live a life of complete silence; that for twenty-eight years and a month or two he never addressed a word to his wife or children; and that his resolution was only broken down by a severe illness in the winter of 1714?

Mr. Aitken on Mr. Wright's hypothesis.

Mr. Aitken,.[B] who has handled this hypothesis of Mr. Wright's, brings several arguments against it, which, taken together, seem to me quite conclusive. To begin with, several children were born to Defoe during this period. He paid much attention to their education, and in 1713, the penultimate year of this supposed silence, we find his sons helping him in his work. Again, in 1703 Mrs. Defoe was interceding for her husband's release from Newgate. Let me add that it was an age in which personalities were freely used in public controversy; that Defoe was continuously occupied with public controversy during these twenty-eight years, and managed to make as many enemies as any man within the four seas; and I think the silence of his adversaries upon a matter which, if proved, would be discreditable in the extreme, is the best of all evidence that Mr. Wright's hypothesis cannot be sustained. Nor do I see how Mr. Wright makes it square with his own conception of Defoe's character. "Of a forgiving temper himself," says Mr. Wright on p. 86, "he (Defoe) was quite incapable of understanding how another person could nourish resentment." This of a man whom the writer asserts to have sulked in absolute silence with his wife and family for twenty-eight years, two months, and nineteen days!

An inherent improbability.

At all events it will not square with *our* conception of Defoe's character. Those of us who have an almost unlimited admiration for Defoe as a master of narrative, and next to no affection for him as a man, might pass the heartlessness of such conduct. "At first sight," Mr. Wright admits, "it may appear monstrous that a man should for so long a time abstain from speech with his own family." Monstrous, indeed—but I am afraid we could have passed that. Mr. Wright, who has what I may call a purfled style, tells us that—

"To narrate the career of Daniel Defoe is to tell a tale of wonder and daring, of high endeavour and marvellous success. To dwell upon it is to take courage and to praise God for the splendid possibilities of life.... Defoe is always the hero; his career is as thick with events as a cornfield with corn; his fortunes change as quickly and as completely as the shapes in a kaleidoscope—he is up, he is down, he is courted, he is spurned; it is shine, it is shower, it is *couleur de rose*, it is Stygian night. Thirteen times he was rich and poor. Achilles was not more audacious, Ulysses more subtle, Æneas more pious."

That is one way of putting it. Here is another way (as the cookery books say):—"To narrate the career of Daniel Defoe is to tell a tale of a hosier and pantile maker, who had a hooked nose and wrote tracts indefatigably—he was up, he was down, he was in the Pillory, he was at Tooting; it was *poule de soie*, it was leather and prunella; and it was always tracts. Æneas was not so pious a member of the Butchers' Company; and there are a few milestones on the Dover Road; but Defoe's life was as thick with tracts as a cornfield with corn." These two estimates may differ here and there; but on one point they agree—that Defoe was an extremely restless, pushing, voluble person, who could as soon have stood on his head for twenty-eight years, two months, and nineteen days as have kept silence for that period with any man or woman in whose company he found himself frequently alone. Unless we have entirely misjudged his character—and, I may add, unless Mr. Wright has completely misrepresented the rest of his life—it simply was not *in* the man to keep this foolish vow for twenty-four hours.

No, I am afraid Mr. Wright's hypothesis will not do. And yet his plan of adding twenty-seven years to each important date in Crusoe's history has revealed so many coincident events in the life of Defoe that we cannot help feeling he is "hot," as they say in the children's game; that the wreck upon the island and Crusoe's twenty-eight years odd of solitude do really correspond with some great event and important period of Defoe's life. The wreck is dated 30th September, 1659. Add the twenty-seven years, and we come to September 30th, 1686. Where was Defoe at that date, and what was he doing? Mr. Wright has to confess that of his movements in 1686 and the two following years "we know little that is definite." Certainly we know of nothing that can correspond with Crusoe's shipwreck.

A suggestion.

But wait a moment—The *original* editions of *Robinson Crusoe* (and most, if not all, later editions) give the date of Crusoe's departure from the island as December 19th, 1686, instead of 1687. Mr. Wright suggests that this is a misprint; and, to be sure, it does not agree with the statement respecting the length of Crusoe's stay on the island, *if we assume the date of the wreck to be correct.* But, (as Mr. Aitken points out) the mistake must be the author's, not the printer's, because in the next paragraph we are told that Crusoe reached England in June, 1687, not 1688. I agree with Mr. Aitken; and I suggest *that the date of Crusoe's arrival at the island, not the date of his departure, is the date misprinted.* Assume for a moment that the date of departure (December 19th, 1686) is correct. Subtract the twenty-eight years, two months, and nineteen days of Crusoe's stay on the island, and we get September 30th, 1658, as the date of the wreck and his arrival at the island. Now add the twenty-seven years which separate Crusoe's experiences from Defoe's, and we come to September 30th, 1685. What was happening in England at the close of September, 1685? Why, Jeffreys was carrying through his Bloody Assize.

"Like many other Dissenters," says Mr. Wright on p. 21, "Defoe sympathised with Monmouth; and, to his misfortune, took part in the rising." His comrades perished in it, and he himself, in Mr. Wright's words, "probably had to lie low." There is no doubt that the Monmouth affair was the beginning of Defoe's troubles: and I suggest that certain passages in the story of Crusoe's voyage (*e.g.* the "secret proposal" of the three merchants who came to Crusoe) have a peculiar significance if read in this connection. I also think it possible there may be a particular meaning in the several waves, so carefully described, through which Crusoe made his way to dry land; and in the simile of the reprieved malefactor (p. 50 in Mr. Aitken's delightful edition); and in the several visits to the wreck.

I am no specialist in Defoe, but put this suggestion forward with the utmost diffidence. And yet, right or wrong, I feel it has more plausibility than Mr. Wright's. Defoe undoubtedly took part in the Monmouth rising, and was a survivor of that wreck "on the south side of the island": and undoubtedly it formed the turning-point of his career. If we could discover how he escaped Kirke and Jeffreys, I am inclined to believe we should have a key to the whole story of the shipwreck. I should not be sorry to find this hypothesis upset; for the story of Robinson Crusoe is quite good enough for me as it stands, and without any sub-intention. But whatever be the true explanation of the parable, if time shall discover it, I confess I expect it will be a trifle less recondite than Mr. Wright's, and a trifle more creditable to the father of the English novel.[C]

FOOTNOTES:

[A] "The Life of Daniel Defoe." By Thomas Wright, Principal of Cowper School, Olney. London: Cassell & Co.

[B] *Romances and Narratives by Daniel Defoe*. Edited by George A. Aitken. Vols. i., ii., and iii. Containing the Life and Adventures, Farther Adventures, and Serious Reflections of Robinson Crusoe. With a General Introduction by the Editor. London: J.M. Dent & Co.

[C] Upon this suggestion Mr. Aitken, in a postscript to his seventh volume of the *Romances and Narratives*, has since remarked as follows:—

"In a discussion in *The Speaker* upon Defoe's supposed period of 'silence,' published since the appearance of the first volume of this edition, Mr. Quiller Couch, while agreeing, for the reasons I have given (vol. i. p. lvii.), that there is no mistake in the date of Robinson Crusoe's departure from his island (December, 1686), has suggested that perhaps the error in the chronology lies, not in the length of time Crusoe is said to have lived on the island, but in the date given for his landing (September, 1659). That this suggestion is right appears from a passage which has hitherto escaped notice. Crusoe was born in 1632, and Defoe makes him say (vol. i. p. 147), 'The same day of the year I was born on, viz. the 30th of September, that same day I had my life so miraculously saved twenty-six years after, when I was cast ashore on this island.' Crusoe must, therefore, have reached his island on September 30, 1658, not 1659, as twice stated by Defoe; and by adding twenty-eight years to 1658 we get 1686, the date given for Crusoe's departure.

"It is, however, questionable whether this rectification helps us to interpret the allegory in *Robinson Crusoe*. It is true that if, in accordance with the 'key' suggested by Mr. Wright, we add twenty-seven years to the date of the shipwreck (1658) in order to find the corresponding event in Defoe's life, we arrive at September, 1685, when Jeffreys was sentencing many of those who—like Defoe—took part in Monmouth's rising. But we have no evidence that Defoe suffered seriously in consequence of the part he took in this rebellion; and the addition of twenty-seven years to the date of Crusoe's departure from the island (December, 1686) does not bring us to any corresponding event in Defoe's own story. Those who are curious will find the question discussed at greater length in *The Speaker* for April 13 and 20, and May 4, 1895."

LAWRENCE STERNE

Dec. 10, 1891. Sterne and Thackeray.

It is told by those who write scraps of Thackeray's biography that a youth once ventured to speak disrespectfully of Scott in his presence. "You and I, sir," said the great man, cutting him short, "should lift our hats at the mention of that great name."

An admirable rebuke!—if only Thackeray had remembered it when he sat down to write those famous Lectures on the English Humorists, or at least before he stood up in Willis's Rooms to inform a polite audience concerning his great predecessors. Concerning their work? No. Concerning their genius? No. Concerning the debt owed to them by mankind? Not a bit of it. Concerning their *lives*, ladies and gentlemen; and whether their lives were pure and respectable and free from scandal and such as men ought to have led whose works you would like your sons and daughters to handle. Mr. Frank T. Marzials, Thackeray's latest biographer, finds the matter of these Lectures "excellent":—

"One feels in the reading that Thackeray is a peer among his peers—a sort of elder brother,[A] kindly, appreciative and tolerant—as he discourses of Addison, Steele, Swift, Pope, Sterne, Fielding, Goldsmith. I know of no greater contrast in criticism—a contrast, be it said, not to the advantage of the French critic—than Thackeray's treatment of Pope and that of M. Taine. What allowance the Englishman makes for the physical ills that beset the 'gallant little cripple'; with what a gentle hand he touches the painful places in that poor twisted body! M. Taine, irritated apparently that Pope will not fit into his conception of English literature, exhibits the same deformities almost savagely."

I am sorry that I cannot read this kindliness, this appreciation, this tolerance, into the Lectures—into those, for instance, of Sterne and Fielding: that the simile of the "elder brother" carries different suggestions for Mr. Marzials and for me: and that the lecturer's attitude is to me less suggestive of a peer among his peers than of a tall "bobby"—a volunteer constable—determined to warn his polite hearers what sort of men these were whose books they had hitherto read unsuspectingly.

And even so—even though the lives and actions of men who lived too early to know Victorian decency must be held up to shock a crowd in Willis's Rooms, yet it had been but common generosity to tell the whole truth. Then the story of Fielding's *Voyage to Lisbon* might have touched the heart to sympathy even for the purely fictitious low comedian whom Thackeray presented: and Sterne's latest letters might have infused so much pity into the polite audience that they, like his own Recording Angel, might have blotted out his faults with a tear. But that was not Thackeray's way. Charlotte Brontë found "a finished taste and ease" in the Lectures, a "something high bred." Motley describes their style as "hovering," and their method as "the perfection of lecturing to high-bred audiences." Mr. Marzials quotes this expression "hovering" as admirably descriptive. It is. By judicious selection, by innuendo, here a pitying aposiopesis, there an indignant outburst, the charges are heaped up. Swift was a toady at heart, and used Stella vilely for the sake of that hussy Vanessa. Congreve had captivating manners—of course he had, the dog! And we all know what that meant in those days. Dick Steele drank and failed to pay his creditors. Sterne—now really I know what Club life is, ladies and gentlemen, and I might tell you a thing or two if I would: but really, speaking as a gentleman before a polite audience, I warn you against Sterne.

I do not suppose for a moment that Thackeray consciously defamed these men. The weaknesses, the pettinesses of humanity interested him, and he treated them with gusto, even as he spares us nothing of that horrible scene between Mrs. Mackenzie and Colonel Newcome. And of course poor Sterne was the easiest victim. The fellow was so full of his confounded sentiments. You ring a choice few of these on the counter and prove them base metal. You assume that the rest of the bag is of equal value. You "go one better" than Sir Peter Teazle and damn all sentiment, and lo! the fellow is no better than a smirking jester, whose antics you can expose till men and women, who had foolishly laughed and wept as he moved them, turn from him, loathing him as a swindler. So it is that although *Tristram Shandy* continues one of the most popular classics in the language, nobody dares to confess his debt to Sterne except in discreet terms of apology.

But the fellow wrote the book. You can't deny *that*, though Thackeray may tempt you to forget it. (What proportion does my Uncle Toby hold in that amiable Lecture?) The truth is that the elemental simplicity of Captain Shandy and Corporal Trim did not appeal to the author of *The Book of Snobs* in the same degree as the pettiness of the man Sterne appealed to him: and his business in Willis's Rooms was to talk, not of Captain Shandy, but of the man Sterne, to whom his hearers were to feel themselves superior as members of society. I submit that this was not a worthy task for a man of letters who was also a man of genius. I submit that it was an inversion of the true critical method to wreck Sterne's *Sentimental Journey* at the outset by picking Sterne's life to pieces, holding up the shreds and warning the reader that any nobility apparent in his book will be nothing better than a sham. Sterne is scarcely arrived at Calais and in conversation with the Monk before you are cautioned how you listen to the impostor. "Watch now," says the critic; "he'll be at his tricks in a moment. Hey, *paillasse*! There!—didn't I tell you?" And yet I am as sure that the opening pages of the *Sentimental Journey* are full of genuine feeling as I am that if Jonathan Swift had entered the room while the Lecture upon him was going forward, he would have eaten William Makepeace Goliath, white waistcoat and all.

Frenchmen, who either are less awed than we by lecturers in white waistcoats, or understand the methods of criticism somewhat better, cherish the *Sentimental Journey* (in spite of its indifferent French) and believe in the genius that created it. But the Briton reads it with shyness, and the British critic speaks of Sterne with bated breath, since Thackeray told it in Gath that Sterne was a bad man, and the daughters of Philistia triumphed.

October 6, 1894. Mr. Whibley's Edition of "Tristram Shandy."

We are a strenuous generation, with a New Humor and a number of interesting by-products; but a new *Tristram Shandy* stands not yet among our achievements. So Messrs. Henley and Whibley have made the best of it and given us a new edition of the old *Tristram*—two handsome volumes, with shapely pages, fair type, and an Introduction. Mr. Whibley supplies the Introduction, and that he writes lucidly and forcibly needs not to be said. His position is neither that so unfairly taken up by Thackeray; nor that of Allibone, who, writing for Heaven knows how many of Allibone's maiden aunts, summed up Sterne thus:—

"A standing reproach to the profession which he disgraced, grovelling in his tastes, indiscreet, if not licentious, in his habits, he lived unhonoured and died unlamented, save by those who found amusement in his wit or countenance in his immorality."[B]

But though he avoids these particular excesses; though he goes straight for the book, as a critic should; Mr. Whibley cannot get quit of the bad tradition of patronizing Sterne:—

"He failed, as only a sentimentalist can fail, in the province of pathos.... There is no trifle, animate or inanimate, he will not bewail, if he be but in the mood; nor does it shame him to dangle before the public gaze those poor shreds of sensibility he calls his feelings. Though he seldom deceives the reader into sympathy, none will turn from his choicest agony without a thrill of disgust. The *Sentimental Journey*, despite its interludes of tacit humour and excellent narrative, is the last extravagance of irrelevant grief.... Genuine sentiment was as strange to Sterne the writer as to Sterne the man; and he conjures up no tragic figure that is not stuffed with sawdust and tricked out in the rags of the green-room. Fortunately, there is scant opportunity for idle tears in

Tristram Shandy.... Yet no occasion is lost.... Yorick's death is false alike to nature and art. The vapid emotion is properly matched with commonness of expression, and the bad taste is none the more readily excused by the suggestion of self-defence. Even the humour of My Uncle Toby is something: degraded by the oft-quoted platitude: 'Go, poor devil,' says he, to an overgrown fly which had buzzed about his nose; 'get thee gone. Why should I hurt thee? This world surely is big enough to hold both thee and me.'"

But here Mr. Whibley's notorious hatred of sentiment leads him into confusion. That the passage has been over-quoted is no fault of Sterne's. Of My Uncle Toby, if of any man, it might have been predicted that he would not hurt a fly. To me this trivial action of his is more than merely sentimental. But, be this as it may, I am sure it is honestly characteristic.

Still, on the whole Mr. Whibley has justice. Sterne *is* a sentimentalist. Sterne *is* indecent by reason of his reticence—more indecent than Rabelais, because he uses a hint where Rabelais would have said what he meant, and prints a dash where Rabelais would have plumped out with a coarse word and a laugh. Sterne *is* a convicted thief. On a famous occasion Charles Reade drew a line between plagiary and justifiable borrowing. To draw material from a heterogeneous work—to found, for instance, the play of *Coriolanus* upon Plutarch's *Life*—is justifiable: to take from a homogeneous work—to enrich your drama from another man's drama—is plagiary. But even on this interpretation of the law Sterne must be condemned; for in decking out *Tristram* with feathers from the history of Gargantua he was pillaging a homogeneous work. Nor can it be pleaded in extenuation that he improved upon his originals—though it can, I think, be pleaded that he made his borrowings his own. I do not think much of Mr. Whibley's instance of Servius Sulpicius' letter. No doubt Sterne took his translation of it from Burton; but the letter is a very well known one, and Burton's translation happened to be uncommonly good, and the borrowing of a good rendering without acknowledgment was not, as far as I know, then forbidden by custom. In any case, the whole passage is intended merely to lead up to the beautiful perplexity of My Uncle Toby. And that is Sterne's own, and could never have been another man's. "After all," says Mr. Whibley, "all the best in Sterne is still Sterne's own."

But the more I agree with Mr. Whibley's strictures the more I desire to remove them from an Introduction to *Tristram Shandy*, and to read them in a volume of Mr. Whibley's collected essays. Were it not better, in reading *Tristram Shandy*, to take Sterne for once (if only for a change) at his own valuation, or at least to accept the original postulates of the story? If only for the entertainment he provides we owe him the effort. There will be time enough afterwards to turn to the cold judgment of this or that critic, or to the evidence of this or that thief-taker. For the moment he claims to be heard without prejudice; he has genius enough to make it worth our while to listen without prejudice; and the most lenient "appreciation" of his sins, if we read it beforehand, is bound to raise prejudice and infect our enjoyment as we read. And, as a corollary of this demand, let us ask that he shall be allowed to present his book to us exactly as he chooses. Mr. Whibley says, "He set out upon the road of authorship with a false ideal: 'Writing,' said he, 'when properly managed, is but a different name for conversation.' It would be juster to assert that writing is never properly managed, unless it be removed from conversation as far as possible." Very true; or, at least, very likely. But since Sterne *had* this ideal, let us grant him full liberty to make his spoon or spoil his horn, and let us judge afterwards concerning the result. The famous blackened page and the empty pages (all omitted in this new edition) are part of Sterne's method. They may seem to us trick-work and foolery; but, if we consider, they link on to his notion that writing is but a name for conversation; they are included in his demand that in writing a book a man should be allowed to "go cluttering away like hey-go mad." "You may take my word"—it is Sterne who speaks, and in his very first chapter—

"You may take my word that nine parts in ten of a man's sense or his nonsense, his success and miscarriages in this world, depend upon their motions and activity, and the different tracks and trains you put them into, so that when they are once set going—whether right or wrong, 'tis not a halfpenny matter—away they go cluttering like hey-go mad; and by treading the same steps over and over again, they presently make a road of it, as plain and smooth as a garden walk, which, when once they are used to, the devil himself sometimes shall not be able to drive them off it."

This, at any rate, is Sterne's own postulate. And I had rather judge him with all his faults after reading the book than be prepared beforehand to make allowances.

Nov. 12, 1895. Sterne's Good-nature.

Let one thing be recorded to the credit of this much-abused man. He wrote two masterpieces of fiction (one of them a work of considerable length), and in neither will you find an ill-natured character or an ill-natured word. On the admission of all critics My Father, My Mother, My Uncle Toby, Corporal Trim, and Mrs. Wadman are immortal creations. To the making of them there has gone no single sour or uncharitable thought. They are essentially amiable: and the same may be said of all the minor characters and of the author's disquisitions. Sterne has given us a thousand occasions to laugh, but never an occasion to laugh on the wrong side of the mouth. For savagery or bitterness you will search his books in vain. He is obscene, to be sure. But who, pray, was ever the worse for having read him? Alas, poor Yorick! He had his obvious and deplorable failings. I never heard that he communicated them. Good-humor he has been communicating now for a hundred and fifty years.

FOOTNOTES:

[A] But why "elder"?

[B] "Pan might *indeed* be proud if ever he begot
Such an Allibone . . . " *Spenser (revised)*.

SCOTT AND BURNS

Dec. 9, 1893. Scott's Letters.

"*All Balzac's novels occupy one shelf. The new edition fifty volumes long*"

—says Bishop Blougram. But for Scott the student will soon have to hire a room. The novels and poems alone stretch away into just sixty volumes in Cadell's edition; and this is only the beginning. At this very moment two new editions (one of which, at least, is indispensable) are unfolding their magnificent lengths, and report says that Messrs. Hodder and Stoughton already project a third, with introductory essays by Mr. Barrie. Then the Miscellaneous Prose Works by that untiring hand extend to some twenty-eight or thirty volumes. And when Scott stops, his biographer and his commentators begin, and all with like liberal notions of space and time. Nor do they deceive themselves. We take all they give, and call for more. Three years ago, and fifty-eight from the date of Scott's death, his Journal was published; and although Lockhart had drawn upon it for one of the fullest biographies in the language, the little that Lockhart had left unused was sufficient to make its publication about the most important literary event of the year 1890.

And now Mr. David Douglas, the publisher of the "Journal," gives us in two volumes a selection from the familiar letters preserved at Abbotsford. The period covered by this correspondence is from 1797, the year of Sir Walter's marriage, to 1825, when the "Journal" begins—"covered," however, being too large a word for the first seven years, which are represented by seven letters only; it is only in 1806 that we start upon something like a consecutive story. Mr. Douglas speaks modestly of his editorial work. "I have done," he says, "little more than arrange the correspondence in chronological order, supplying where necessary a slight thread of continuity by annotation and illustration." It must be said that Mr. Douglas has done this exceedingly well. There is always a note where a note is wanted, and never where information would be superfluous. On the taste and judgment of his selection one who has not examined the whole mass of correspondence at Abbotsford can only speak on *a priori* grounds. But it is unlikely that the writer of these exemplary footnotes has made many serious mistakes in compiling his text.

Man's perennial and pathetic curiosity about virtue has no more striking example than the public eagerness to be acquainted with every detail of Scott's life. For what, as a mere story, is that life?—a level narrative of many prosperous years; a sudden financial crash; and the curtain falls on the struggle of a tired and dying gentleman to save his honor. Scott was born in 1771 and died in 1832, and all that is special in his life belongs to the last six years of it. Even so the materials for the story are of the simplest—enough, perhaps, under the hand of an artist to furnish forth a tale of the length of Trollope's *The Warden*. In picturesqueness, in color, in wealth of episode and περιπέτεια, Scott's career will not compare for a moment with the career of Coleridge, for instance. Yet who could endure to read the life of Coleridge in six volumes? De Quincey, in an essay first published the other day by Dr. Japp, calls the story of the Coleridges "a perfect romance ... a romance of beauty, of intellectual power, of misfortune suddenly illuminated from heaven, of prosperity suddenly overcast by the waywardness of the individual." But the "romance" has been written twice and thrice, and desperately dull reading it makes in each case. Is it then an accident that Coleridge has been unhappy in his biographers, while Lockhart succeeded once for all, and succeeded so splendidly?

It is surely no accident. Coleridge is an ill man to read about just as certainly as Scott is a good man to read about; and the secret is just that Scott had character and Coleridge had not. In writing of the man of the "graspless hand," the biographer's own hand in time grows graspless on the pen; and in reading of him our hands too grow graspless on the page. We pursue the man and come upon group after group of his friends; and each as we demand "What have you done with Coleridge?" answers "He was here just now, and we helped him forward a little way." Our best biographies are all of men and women of character—and, it may be added, of beautiful character—of Johnson, Scott, and Charlotte Brontë.

There are certain people whose biographies *ought* to be long. Who could learn too much concerning Lamb? And concerning Scott, who will not agree with Lockhart's remark in the preface to his abridged edition of 1848:—"I should have been more willing to produce an enlarged edition; for the interest of Sir Walter's history lies, I think, peculiarly in its minute details"? You may explore here, and explore there, and still you find pure gold; for the man was gold right through.

So in the present volume every line is of interest because we refer it to Scott's known character and test it thereby. The result is always the same; yet the employment does not weary. In themselves the letters cannot stand, as mere writing, beside the letters of Cowper, or of Lamb. They are just the common-sense epistles of a man who to his last day remained too modest to believe in the extent of his own genius. The letters in this collection which show most acuteness on literary matters are not Scott's, but Lady Louisa Stuart's, who appreciated the Novels on their appearance (their faults as well as their merits) with a judiciousness quite wonderful in a contemporary. Scott's literary observations (with the exception of one passage where the attitude of an English gentleman towards literature is stated thus—"he asks of it that it shall arouse him from his habitual contempt of what goes on about him") are much less amusing; and his letters to Joanna Baillie the dullest in the volume, unless it be the answers which Joanna Baillie sent. Best of all, perhaps, is the correspondence (scarcely used by Lockhart) between Scott and Lady Abercorn, with its fitful intervals of warmth and reserve. This alone would justify Mr. Douglas's volumes. But, indeed, while nothing can be found now to alter men's conception of Scott, any book about him is justified, even if it do no more than heap up superfluous testimony to the beauty of his character.

June 15, 1895. A racial disability.

Since about one-third of the number of my particular friends happen to be Scotsmen, it has always distressed and annoyed me that, with the best will in the world, I have never been able to understand on what principle that perfervid race conducts its enthusiasms. Mine is a racial disability, of course; and the converse has been noted by no less a writer than Stevenson, in the story of his journey "Across the Plains":—

"There were no emigrants direct from Europe—save one German family and a knot of Cornish miners who kept grimly by themselves, one reading the New Testament all day long through steel spectacles, the rest discussing privately the secrets of their old-world mysterious race. Lady Hester Stanhope believed she could make something great of the Cornish; for my part I can make nothing of them at all. A division of races, older and more original than that of Babel, keeps this close, esoteric family apart from neighbouring Englishmen."

The loss on my side, to be sure, would be immensely the greater, were it not happily certain that I *can* make something of Scotsmen; can, and indeed do, make friends of them.

The Cult of Burns.

All the same, this disability weighs me down with a sense of hopeless obtuseness when I consider the deportment of the average intelligent Scot at a Burns banquet, or a Burns *conversazione*, or a Burns festival, or the unveiling of a Burns statue, or the putting up of a pillar on some spot made famous by Burns. All over the world—and all under it, too, when their time comes—Scotsmen are preparing after-dinner speeches about Burns. The great globe swings round out of the sun into the dark; there is always midnight somewhere; and always in this shifting region the eye of imagination sees orators gesticulating over Burns; companies of heated exiles with crossed arms shouting "Auld Lang Syne"; lesser groups—if haply they be lesser—reposing under tables, still in honor of Burns. And as the vast continents sweep "eastering out of the high shadow which reaches beyond the moon," and as new nations, with *their* cities and villages, their mountains and seashores, rise up on the morning-side, lo! fresh troops, and still fresh troops, and yet again fresh troops, wend or are carried out of action with the dawn.

Scott and Burns.

None but a churl would wish this enthusiasm abated. But why is it all lavished on Burns? That is what gravels the Southron. Why Burns? Why not Sir Walter? Had I the honor to be a fellow-countryman of Scott, and had I command of the racial tom-tom, it seems to me that I would tund upon it in honor of that great man until I dropped. To me, a Southron, Scott is the most imaginative, and at the same time the justest, writer of our language since Shakespeare died. To say this is not to suggest that he is comparable with Shakespeare. Scott himself, sensible as ever, wrote in his *Journal*, "The blockheads talk of my being like Shakespeare—not fit to tie his brogues." "But it is also true," said Mr. Swinburne, in his review of the *Journal*, "that if there were or could be any man whom it would not be a monstrous absurdity to compare with Shakespeare as a creator of men and inventor of circumstance, that man could be none other than Scott." Greater poems than his have been written; and, to my mind, one or two novels better than his best. But when one considers the huge mass of his work, and its quality in the mass; the vast range of his genius, and its command over that range; who shall be compared with him?

These are the reflections which occur, somewhat obviously, to the Southron. As for character, it is enough to say that Scott was one of the best men who ever walked on this planet; and that Burns was not. But Scott was not merely good: he was winningly good: of a character so manly, temperate, courageous that men read his Life, his Journal, his Letters with a thrill, as they might read of Rorke's Drift or Chitral. How then are we to account for the undeniable fact that his countrymen, in public at any rate, wax more enthusiastic over Burns? Is it that the *homeliness* of Burns appeals to them as a wandering race? Is it because, in farthest exile, a line of Burns takes their hearts straight back to Scotland?—as when Luath the collie, in "The Twa Dogs," describes the cotters' New Year's Day:—

"That merry day the year begins,
They bar the door on frosty winds;
The nappy reeks wi' mantling ream,
An' sheds a heart-inspirin' steam;
The luntin' pipe an' sneeshin' mill
Are handed round wi' richt guid will;
The cantie auld folks crackin' crouse,
The young anes rantin' through the house,—
My heart has been sae fain to see them,
That I for joy hae barkit wi' them."

That is one reason, no doubt. But there is another, I suspect. With all his immense range Scott saw deeply into character; but he did not, I think, see very deeply into feeling. You may extract more of the *lacrimæ rerum* from the story of his own life than from all his published works put together. The pathos of Lammermoor is taken-for-granted pathos. If you deny this, you will not deny, at any rate, that the pathos of the last scene of *Lear* is quite beyond his scope. Yet this is not more certainly beyond his scope than is the feeling in many a single line or stanza of Burns'. Verse after verse, line after line, rise up for quotation—

"Thou'lt break my heart, thou bonnie bird
That sings beside thy mate;
For sae I sat, and sae I sang,
And wist na o' my fate."

Or,

"O pale, pale now, those rosy lips
I aft hae kissed sae fondly!
And closed for aye the sparkling glance
That dwelt on me sae kindly!
And mouldering now in silent dust
The heart that lo'ed me dearly—
But still within my bosom's core
Shall live my Highland Mary."

Or,

"Had we never loved sae kindly,
Had we never loved sae blindly,
Never met—or never parted,
We had ne'er been broken-hearted."

Scott left an enormous mass of writing behind him, and almost all of it is good. Burns left very much less, and among it a surprising amount of inferior stuff. But such pathos as the above Scott cannot touch. I can understand the man who holds that these deeps of pathos should not be probed in literature: and am not sure that I wholly disagree with him. The question certainly is discutable and worth discussing. But such pathos, at any rate, is immensely popular: and perhaps this will account for the hold which Burns retains on the affections of a race which has a right to be at least thrice as proud of Scott.

However, if Burns is honored at the feast, Scott is read by the fireside. Hardly have the rich Dryburgh and Border editions issued from the press before Messrs. Archibald Constable and Co. are bringing out their reprint of the famous 48-volume edition of the Novels; and Mr. Barrie is supposed to be meditating another, with introductory notes of his own upon each Novel. In my own opinion nothing has ever beaten, or come near to beat, the 48-volume "Waverley" of 1829; and Messrs. Constable and Co. were happily inspired when they decided to make this the basis of their new edition. They have improved upon it in two respects. The paper is lighter and better. And each novel is kept within its own covers, whereas in the old editions a volume would contain the end of one novel and beginning of another. The original illustrations, by Wilkie, Landseer, Leslie, Stanfield, Bonington, and the rest, have been retained, in order to make the reprint complete. But this seems to me a pity; for a number of them were bad to begin with, and will be worse than ever now, being reproduced (as I understand) from impressions of the original plates. To do without illustrations were a counsel of perfection. But now that the novels have become historical, surely it were better to illustrate them with authentic portraits of Scott, pictures of scenery, facsimiles of MSS., and so on, than with (*e.g.*) a worn reproduction of what Mr. F.P. Stephanoff thought that Flora Mac-Ivor looked like while playing the harp and introducing a few irregular strains which harmonized well with the distant waterfall and the soft sigh of the evening breeze in the rustling leaves of an aspen which overhung the fair harpress—especially as F.P. Stephanoff does not seem to have known the difference between an aspen and a birch.

In short, did it not contain the same illustrations, this edition would probably excel even that of 1828. As it is, after many disappointments, we now have a cheap Waverley on what has always been the best model.

A Protest.

'SIR,—In your 'Literary Causerie' of last week ... the question is discussed why the name of Burns raises in Scotsmen such unbounded enthusiasm while that of Scott falls comparatively flat. This question has puzzled many another Englishman besides 'A.T.Q.C.' And yet the explanation is not far to seek: Burns appeals to the hearts and feelings of the masses in a way Scott never does. 'A.T.Q.C.' admits this, and gives quotations in support. These quotations, however excellent in their way, are not those that any Scotsman would trust to in support of the above proposition. A Scotsman would at once appeal to 'Scots wha hae,' 'Auld Lang Syne,' and 'A man's a man for a' that.' The very familiarity of these quotations has bred the proverbial contempt. Think of the soul-inspiring, 'fire-eyed fury' of 'Scots wha hae'; the glad, kind, ever fresh greeting of 'Auld Lang Syne'; the manly, sturdy independence of 'A man's a man for a' that,' and who can wonder at the ever-increasing enthusiasm for Burns' name?

Is there for honest poverty
That hangs his head and a' that?
The coward slave we pass him by—

We dare be poor for a' that.'
*   *   *   *   *
'The rank is but the guinea stamp—
The man's the gowd for a' that.'

"Nor is it in his patriotism, independence, and conviviality alone that Burns touches every mood of a Scotsman's heart. There is an enthusiasm of humanity about Burns which you will hardly find equalled in any other author, and which most certainly does not exist in Scott.

'Man's inhumanity to man
Makes countless thousands mourn.'
*   *   *   *   *
'Why has man this will and power
To make his fellow mourn?'

"These quotations might be multiplied were it necessary; but I think enough has been said to explain what puzzles 'A.T.Q.C.' I have an unbounded admiration of Sir W. Scott—quite as great as 'A.T.Q.C.' Indeed, I think him the greatest of all novelists; but, as a Scot, somewhat Anglicised by a residence in London of more than a quarter of a century, I unhesitatingly say that I would rather be the author of the above three lyrics of Burns' than I would be the author of all Scott's novels. Certain I am that if immortality were my aim I should be much surer of it in the one case than the other. I cannot conceive 'Scots wha hae,' 'Auld Lang Syne,' etc., ever dying. Are there any of Scott's writings of which the same could be said? I doubt it....

—I am yours, etc.,   "J.B.
"London, June 18th, 1895."

The hopelessness of the difficulty is amusingly, if rather distressingly, illustrated by this letter. Here again you have the best will in the world. Nothing could be kindlier than "J.B.'s" tone. As a Scot he has every reason to be impatient of stupidity on the subject of Burns: yet he takes real pains to set me right. Alas! his explanations leave me more than ever at sea, more desperate than ever of understanding *what exactly it is* in Burns that kindles this peculiar enthusiasm in Scotsmen and drives them to express it in feasting and oratory.

After casting about for some time, I suggested that Burns—though in so many respects immeasurably inferior to Scott—frequently wrote with a depth of feeling which Scott could not command. On second thoughts, this was wrongly put. Scott may have *possessed* the feeling, together with notions of his own, on the propriety of displaying it in his public writings. Indeed, after reading some of his letters again, I am sure he did possess it. Hear, for instance, how he speaks of Dalkeith Palace, in one of his letters to Lady Louisa Stuart:—

"I am delighted my dear little half god-daughter is turning out beautiful. I was at her christening, poor soul, and took the oaths as representing I forget whom. That was in the time when Dalkeith was Dalkeith; how changed alas! I was forced there the other day by some people who wanted to see the house, and I felt as if it would have done me a great deal of good to have set my manhood aside, to get into a corner and cry like a schoolboy. Every bit of furniture, now looking old and paltry, had some story and recollections about it, and the deserted gallery, which I have seen so happily filled, seemed waste and desolate like Moore's

'Banquet hall deserted,
Whose flowers are dead,
Whose odours fled,
And all but I departed.'

But it avails not either sighing or moralising; to have known the good and the great, the wise and the witty, is still, on the whole, a pleasing reflection, though saddened by the thought that their voices are silent and their halls empty."

Yes, indeed, Scott possessed deep feelings, though he did not exhibit them to the public.

Now Burns does exhibit his deep feelings, as I demonstrated by quotations. And I suggested that it is just his strength of emotion, his command of pathos and readiness to employ it, by which Burns appeals to the mass of his countrymen. On this point "J.B." expressly agrees with me; but—he will have nothing to do with my quotations! "However excellent in their way" these quotations may be, they "are not those that any Scotsman would trust to in support of the above proposition"; the above proposition being that "Burns appeals to the hearts and feelings of the masses in a way that Scott never does."

You see, I have concluded rightly; but on wrong evidence. Let us see, then, what evidence a Scotsman will call to prove that Burns is a writer of deep feeling. "A Scotsman," says "J.B." "would at once appeal to "Scots wha hae," "Auld Lang Syne," and "A man's a man for a' that." ... Think of the soul-inspiring, 'fire-eyed fury' of 'Scots wha hae'; the glad, kind, ever fresh greeting of 'Auld Lang Syne'; the manly, sturdy independence of 'A man's a man for a' that,' and who can wonder at the ever-increasing enthusiasm for Burns' name?... I would rather," says "J.B.," "be the author of the above three lyrics than I would be the author of all Scott's novels."

Here, then, is the point at which I give up my attempts, and admit my stupidity to be incurable. I grant "J.B." his "Auld Lang Syne." I grant the poignancy of—

"We twa hae paidl't i' the burn,
Frae morning sun till dine:
But seas between us braid hae roar'd
Sin auld lang syne."

I see poetry and deep feeling in this. I can see exquisite poetry and deep feeling in "Mary Morison"—

"Yestreen when to the trembling string,
The dance ga'ed thro' the lighted ha',
To thee my fancy took its wing,
I sat, but neither heard nor saw:
Tho' this was fair, and that was braw,
And yor the toast a' the town,
I sigh'd and said amang them a'
'Ye are na Mary Morison.'"

I see exquisite poetry and deep feeling in the Lament for the Earl of Glencairn—

"The bridegroom may forget the bride
Was made his wedded wife yestreen;
The monarch may forget the crown
That on his head an hour has been;
The mother may forget the child
That smiles sae sweetly on her knee;
But I'll remember thee, Glencairn,
And a' that thou hast done for me!"

But—it is only honest to speak one's opinion and to hope, if it be wrong, for a better mind—I do *not* find poetry of any high order either in "Scots wha hae" or "A man's a man for a' that." The former seems to me to be very fine rant—inspired rant, if you will—hovering on the borders of poetry. The latter, to be frank, strikes me as rather poor rant, neither inspired nor even quite genuine, and in no proper sense poetry at all. And "J.B." simply bewilders my Southron intelligence when he quotes it as an instance of deeply emotional song.

"Ye see yon birkie, ca'd a lord,
Wha struts, and stares, and a' that;
Tho' hundreds worship at his word,
He's but a coof for a' that:
For a' that, and a' that,

His riband, star and a' that.
The man of independent mind,
He looks and laughs at a' that."

The proper attitude, I should imagine, for a man "of independent mind" in these circumstances—assuming for the moment that ribands and stars *are* bestowed on imbeciles—would be a quiet disdain. The above stanza reminds me rather of ill-bred barking. People of assured self-respect do not call other people "birkies" and "coofs," or "look and *laugh* at a' that"—at least, not so loudly. Compare these verses of Burns with Samuel Daniel's "Epistle to the Countess of Cumberland," and you will find a higher manner altogether—

"He that of such a height hath built his mind,
And reared the dwelling of his thoughts so strong,
As neither fear nor hope can shake the frame
Of his resolved powers; nor all the wind
Of vanity and malice pierce to wrong
His settled peace, or to disturb the same;
What a fair seat hath he, from whence he may
The boundless wastes and wilds of men survey?

"And with how free an eye doth he look down
Upon these lower regions of turmoil?" ...

As a piece of thought, "A man's a man for a' that" unites the two defects of obviousness and inaccuracy. As for the deep feeling, I hardly see where it comes in—unless it be a feeling of wounded and blatant but militant self-esteem. As for the *poetry*—well, "J.B." had rather have written it than have written one-third of Scott's novels. Let us take him at less than his word: he would rather have written "A man's a man for a' that" than "Ivanhoe," "Redgauntlet," and "The Heart of Midlothian."

Ma sonties!

CHARLES READE

March 10, 1894. "The Cloister and the Hearth."

There is a venerable proposition—I never heard who invented it—that an author is finally judged by his best work. This would be comforting to authors if true: but is it true? A day or two ago I picked up on a railway bookstall a copy of Messrs. Chatto & Windus's new sixpenny edition of *The Cloister and the Hearth*, and a capital edition it is. I think I must have worn out more copies of this book than of any other; but somebody robbed me of the pretty "Elzevir edition" as soon as it came out, and so I have only just read Mr. Walter Besant's Introduction, which the publishers have considerately reprinted and thrown in with one of the cheapest sixpennyworths that ever came from the press. Good wine needs no bush, and the bush which Mr. Besant hangs out is a very small one. But one sentence at least has challenged attention.

"I do not say that the whole of life, as it was at the end of the fourteenth century, may be found in the *Cloister and the Hearth*; but I do say that there is portrayed so vigorous, lifelike, and truthful a picture of a time long gone by, and differing, in almost every particular from our own, that the world has never seen its like. To me it is a picture of the past more faithful than anything in the works of Scott."

This last sentence—if I remember rightly—was called a very bold one when it first appeared in print. To me it seems altogether moderate. Go steadily through Scott, and which of the novels can you choose to compare with the *Cloister* as a "vigorous, lifelike, and truthful picture of a time long gone by"?

Is it *Ivanhoe*?—a gay and beautiful romance, no doubt; but surely, as the late Mr. Freeman was at pains to point out, not a "lifelike and truthful picture" of any age that ever was. Is it *Old Mortality*? Well, but even if we here get something more like a "vigorous, lifelike, and truthful picture of a time gone by," we are bound to consider the scale of the two books. Size counts, as Aristotle pointed out, and as we usually forget. It is the whole of Western Europe that Reade reconstructs for the groundwork of his simple story.

Mr. Besant might have said more. He might have pointed out that no novel of Scott's approaches the *Cloister* in lofty humanity, in sublimity of pathos. The last fifty pages of the tale reach an elevation of feeling that Scott never touched or dreamed of touching. And the sentiment is sane and honest, too: the author reaches to the height of his great argument easily and without strain. It seems to me that, as an appeal to the feelings, the page that tells of Margaret's death is the finest thing in fiction. It appeals for a score of reasons, and each reason is a noble one. We have brought together in that page extreme love, self-sacrifice, resignation, courage, religious feeling: we have the end of a beautiful love-tale, the end of a good woman, and the last earthly trial of a good man. And with all this, there is no vulgarization of sacred ground, no cheap parade of the heart's secrets; but a deep sobriety relieved with the most delicate humor. Moreover, the language is Charles Reade's at its best—which is almost as good as at its worst it is abominable.

That Scott could never reach the emotional height of Margaret's death-scene, or of the scene in Clement's cave, is certain. Moreover in the *Cloister* Reade challenges comparison with Scott on Scott's own ground—the ground of sustained adventurous narrative—and the advantage is not with Scott. Once more, take all the Waverley Novels and search them through for two passages to beat the adventures of Gerard and Denis the Burgundian (1) with the bear and (2) at "The Fair Star" Inn, by the Burgundian Frontier. I do not think you will succeed, even then. Indeed, I will go so far as to say that to match these adventures of Gerard and Denis you must go again to Charles Reade, to the homeward voyage of the *Agra* in *Hard Cash*. For these and for sundry other reasons which, for lack of space, cannot be unfolded here, *The Cloister and the Hearth* seems to me a finer achievement than the finest novel of Scott's.

And now we come to the proposition that an author must be judged by his best work. If this proposition be true, then I must hold Reade to be a greater novelist than Scott. But do I hold this? Does anyone hold this? Why, the contention would be an absurdity.

Reade wrote some twenty novels beside *The Cloister and the Hearth*, and not one of the twenty approaches it. One only—*Griffith Gaunt*—is fit to be named in the same day with it; and *Griffith Gaunt* is marred by an insincerity in the plot which vitiates, and is at once felt to vitiate, the whole work. On everything he wrote before and after *The Cloister* Reade's essential vulgarity of mind is written large. That he shook it off in that great instance is one of the miracles of literary history. It may be that the sublimity of his theme kept him throughout in a state of unnatural exaltation. If the case cannot be explained thus, it cannot be explained at all. Other of his writings display the same, or at any rate a like, capacity for sustained narrative. *Hard Cash* displays it; parts of *It is Never Too Late to Mend* display it. But over much of these two novels lies the trail of that defective taste which makes *A Simpleton*, for instance, a prodigy of cheap ineptitude.

But if Reade be hopelessly Scott's inferior in manner and taste, what shall we say of the invention of the two men? Mr. Barrie once affirmed very wisely in an essay on Robert Louis Stevenson, "Critics have said enthusiastically—for it is difficult to write of Mr. Stevenson without enthusiasm—that Alan Breck is as good as anything in Scott. Alan Breck is certainly a masterpiece, quite worthy of the greatest of all story-tellers, *who, nevertheless, it should be remembered, created these rich side characters by the score, another before dinner-time.*" Inventiveness, is, I suppose, one of the first qualities of a great novelist: and to Scott's invention there was no end. But set aside *The Cloister*, and Reade's invention will be found to be extraordinarily barren. Plot after plot turns on the same old tiresome trick. Two young people are in love: by the villainy of a third person they are separated for a while, and one of the lovers is persuaded that the other is dead. The missing one may be kept missing by various devices; but always he is supposed to be dead, and always evidence is brought of his death, and always he turns up in the end. It is the same in *The Cloister*, in *It is Never Too Late to Mend*, in *Put Yourself in His Place*, in *Griffith Gaunt*, in *A Simpleton*. Sometimes, as in *Hard Cash* and *A Terrible Temptation*, he is wrongfully incarcerated as a madman; but this is obviously a variant only on the favorite trick. Now the device is good enough in a tale of the fourteenth century, when news travelled slowly, and when by the suppression of a letter, or by a piece of false news, two lovers, the one in Holland, the other in Rome, could easily be kept apart. But in a tale of modern life no trick could well be stagier. Besides the incomparable Margaret—of whom it does one good to hear Mr. Besant say, "No heroine in fiction is more dear to me"—Reade drew some admirable portraits of women; but his men, to tell the truth—and especially his priggish young heroes—seem remarkably ill invented. Again, of course, I except *The Cloister*. Omit that book, and you would say that such a character as Bailie Nicol Jarvie or Dugald Dalgetty were altogether beyond Reade's range. Open *The Cloister* and you find in Denis the Burgundian a character as good as the Bailie and Dalgetty rolled into one.

Other authors have been lifted above themselves. But was there ever a case of one sustained at such an unusual height throughout a long, intricate and arduous work?

HENRY KINGSLEY

Feb. 9, 1895. Henry Kingsley.

Mr. Shorter begins his Memoir of the author of *Ravenshoe* with this paragraph:—

"The story of Henry Kingsley's life may well be told in a few words, because that life was on the whole a failure. The world will not listen very tolerantly to a narrative of failure unaccompanied by the halo of remoteness. To write the life of Charles Kingsley would be a quite different task. Here was success, victorious success, sufficient indeed to gladden the heart even of Dr. Smiles—success in the way of Church preferment, success in the way of public veneration, success, above all, as a popular novelist, poet, and preacher. Canon Kingsley's life has been written in two substantial volumes containing abundant letters and no indiscretions. In this biography the name of Henry Kingsley is absolutely ignored. And yet it is not too much to say that, when time has softened his memory for us, as it has softened for us the memories of Marlowe and Burns and many another, the public interest in Henry Kingsley will be stronger than in his now more famous brother."[A]

A prejudice confessed.

I almost wish I could believe this. If one cannot get rid of a prejudice, the wisest course is to acknowledge it candidly: and therefore I confess myself as capable of jumping over the moon as of writing fair criticism on Charles or Henry Kingsley. As for Henry, I worshipped his books as a boy; to-day I find them full of faults—often preposterous, usually ill-constructed, at times unnatural beyond belief. John Gilpin never threw the Wash about on both sides of the way more like unto a trundling mop or a wild goose at play than did Henry Kingsley the decent flow of fiction when the mood was on him. His notion of constructing a novel was to take equal parts of wooden melodrama and low comedy and stick them boldly together in a paste of impertinent drollery and serious but entirely irrelevant moralizing. And yet each time I read *Ravenshoe*—and I must be close upon "double figures"—I like it better. Henry did my green unknowing youth engage, and I find it next to impossible to give him up, and quite impossible to choose the venerated Charles as a substitute in my riper age. For here crops up a prejudice I find quite ineradicable. To put it plainly, I cannot like Charles Kingsley. Those who have had opportunity to study the deportment of a certain class of Anglican divine at a foreign *table d'hôte* may perhaps understand the antipathy. There was almost always a certain sleek offensiveness about Charles Kingsley when he sat down to write. He had a knack of using the most insolent language, and attributing the vilest motives to all poor foreigners and Roman Catholics and other extra-parochial folk, and would exhibit a pained and completely ludicrous surprise on finding that he had hurt the feelings of these unhappy inferiors—a kind of indignant wonder that Providence should have given them any feelings to hurt. At length, encouraged by popular applause, this very second-rate man attacked a very first-rate man. He attacked with every advantage and with utter unscrupulousness; and the first-rate man handled him; handled him gently, scrupulously, decisively; returned him to his parish; and left him there, a trifle dazed, feeling his muscles.

Charles and Henry.

Still, one may dislike the man and his books without thinking it probable that his brother Henry will supersede him in the public interest; nay, without thinking it right that he should. Dislike him as you will, you must acknowledge that Charles Kingsley had a lyrical gift that—to set all his novels aside—carries him well above Henry's literary level. It is sufficient to say that Charles wrote "The Pleasant Isle of Avès" and "When all the world is young, lad," and the first two stanzas of "The Sands of Dee." Neither in prose nor in verse could Henry come near such excellence. But we may go farther. Take the novels of each, and, novel for novel, you must acknowledge—I say it regretfully—that Charles carries the heavier guns. If you ask me whether I prefer *Westward Ho!* or *Ravenshoe*, I answer without difficulty that I find *Ravenshoe* almost wholly delightful, and *Westward Ho!* as detestable in some parts as it is admirable in others; that I have read *Ravenshoe* again and again merely for pleasure, and that I can never read a dozen pages of *Westward Ho!* without wishing to put the book in the fire. But if you ask me which I consider the greater novel, I answer with equal readiness that *Westward Ho!* is not only the greater, but much the greater. It is a truth too seldom recognized that in literary criticism, as in politics, one may detest a man's work while admitting his greatness. Even in his episodes it seems to me that Charles stands high above Henry. Sam Buckley's gallop on Widderin in *Geoffry Hamlyn* is (I imagine) Henry Kingsley's finest achievement in vehement narrative: but if it can be compared for one moment with Amyas Leigh's quest of the Great Galleon then I am no judge of narrative. The one point—and it is an important one—in which Henry beats Charles as an artist is his sustained vivacity. Charles soars far higher at times; but Charles is often profoundly dull. Now, in all Henry's books I have not found a single dull page. He may be trivial, inconsequent, irrelevant, absurd; but he never wearies. It is a great merit: but it is not enough in itself to place a novelist even in the second rank. In a short sketch of Henry Kingsley, contributed by his nephew, Mr. Maurice Kingsley, to Messrs. Scribner's paper, *The Bookbuyer*, I find that the younger brother was considered at home "undoubtedly the novelist of the family; the elder being more of the poet, historian, and prophet." (Prophet!) "My father only wrote one novel pure and simple—viz. *Two Years Ago*—his other works being either historical novels or 'signs of the times.'" Now why an "historical novel" should not be a "novel pure and simple," and what kind of literary achievement a "sign of the times" may be, I leave the reader to guess. The whole passage seems to suggest a certain confusion in the Kingsley family with regard to the fundamental divisions of literature. And it seems clear that the Kingsley family considered novel-writing "pure and simple"—in so far as they differentiated this from other kinds of novel-writing—to be something not entirely respectable.

Their opinion of Henry Kingsley in particular is indicated in no uncertain manner. In Mrs. Charles Kingsley's life of her husband, Henry's existence is completely ignored. The briefest biographical note was furnished forth for Mr. Leslie Stephen's *Dictionary of National Biography*: and Mr. Stephen dismisses our author with a few curt lines. This disposition to treat Henry as an awful warning and nothing more, while sleek Charles is patted on the back for a saint, inclines one to take up arms on the other side and assert, with Mr. Shorter, that "when time has softened his memory for us, the public interest in Henry Kingsley will be stronger than in his now more famous brother." But can we look forward to this reversal of the public verdict? Can we consent with it if it ever comes? The most we can hope is that future generations will read Henry Kingsley, and will love him in spite of his faults.

Henry, the third son of the Rev. Charles Kingsley, was born in Northamptonshire on the 2nd of January, 1830, his brother Charles being then eleven years old. In 1836 his father became rector of St. Luke's Church, Chelsea—the church of which such effective use is made in *The Hillyars and the Burtons*—and his boyhood was passed in that famous old suburb. He was educated at King's College School and Worcester College, Oxford, where he became a famous oarsman, rowing bow of his College boat; also bow of a famous light-weight University "four," which swept everything before it in its time. He wound up his racing career by winning the Diamond Sculls at Henley. From 1853 to 1858 his life was passed in Australia, whence after some variegated experiences he returned to Chelsea in 1858, bringing back nothing but good "copy," which he worked into *Geoffry Hamlyn*, his first romance. *Ravenshoe* was written in 1861; *Austin Elliot* in 1863; *The Hillyars and the Burtons* in 1865; *Silcote of Silcotes* in 1867; *Mademoiselle Mathilde* (admired by few, but a favorite of mine) in 1868. He was married in 1864, and settled at Wargrave-on-Thames. In 1869 he went north to edit the *Edinburgh Daily Review*, and made a mess of it; in 1870 he represented that journal as field-correspondent in the Franco-Prussian War, was present at Sedan, and claimed to have been the first Englishman to enter Metz. In 1872 he returned to London and wrote novels in which his powers appeared to deteriorate steadily. He removed to Cuckfield, in Sussex, and there died in May, 1876.

Hardly a man of letters followed him to the grave, or spoke, in print, a word in his praise.

And yet, by all accounts, he was a wholly amiable ne'er-do-well—a wonderful flyfisher, an extremely clever amateur artist, a lover of horses and dogs and children (surely, if we except a chapter of Victor Hugo's, the children in *Ravenshoe* are the most delightful in fiction), and a joyous companion.

"To us children," writes Mr. Maurice Kingsley, "Uncle Henry's settling in Eversley was a great event.... At times he fairly bubbled over with humour; while his knowledge of slang—Burschen, Bargee, Parisian, Irish, Cockney, and English provincialisms—was awful and wonderful. Nothing was better than to get our uncle on his 'genteel behaviour,' which, of course, meant exactly the opposite, and brought forth inimitable stories, scraps of old songs and impromptu conversations, the choicest of which were between children, Irishwomen, or cockneys. He was the only man, I believe, who ever knew by heart the famous *Irish Court Scenes*—naughtiest and most humorous of tales—unpublished, of course, but handed down from generation to generation of the faithful. Most delightful was an interview between his late Majesty George the Fourth and an itinerant showman, which ended up with, 'No, George the Fourth, you shall not have my Rumptifoozle!' What said animal was, or the authenticity of the story, he never would divulge."

I think it is to the conversational quality of their style—its ridiculous and good-humored impertinences and surprises—that his best books owe a great deal of their charm. The footnotes are a study in themselves, and range from the mineral strata of Australia to the best way of sliding down banisters. Of the three tales already republished in this pleasant edition, *Ravenshoe* has always seemed to me the best in every respect; and in spite of its feeble plot and its impossible lay-figures—Erne, Sir George Hillyar, and the painfully inane Gerty—I should rank *The Hillyars and the Burtons* above the more terrifically imagined and more neatly constructed *Geoffry Hamlyn*. But this is an opinion on which I lay no stress.

FOOTNOTES:

[A] *The Recollections of Geoffry Hamlyn.* By Henry Kingsley. New Edition, with a Memoir by Clement Shorter. London: Ward, Lock & Bowden.

ALEXANDER WILLIAM KINGLAKE

January 10, 1891. His Life.

Alexander William Kinglake was born in 1812, the son of a country gentleman—Mr. W. Kinglake, of Wilton House, Taunton—and received a country gentleman's education at Eton and Trinity College, Cambridge. From college he went to Lincoln's Inn, and in 1837 was called to the Chancery Bar, where he practised with fair but not eminent success. In 1844 he published *Eothen*, and having startled the town, quietly resumed his legal work and seemed willing to forget the achievement. Ten years later he accompanied his friend, Lord Raglan, to the Crimea. He retired from the Bar in 1856, and entered Parliament next year as member for Bridgwater. Re-elected in 1868, he was unseated on petition in 1869, and thenceforward gave himself up to the work of his life. He had consented, after Lord Raglan's death, to write a history of the Invasion of the Crimea. The two first volumes appeared in 1863; the last was published but two years before he succumbed, in the first days of 1891, to a slow incurable disease. In all, the task had occupied thirty years. Long before these years ran out, the world had learnt to regard the Crimean struggle in something like its true perspective; but over Kinglake's mind it continued to loom in all its original proportions. To adapt a phrase of M. Jules Lemaître's, "*le monde a changé en trente ans: lui ne bouge; il ne lève plus de dessus son papier à copie sa face congestionné.*" And yet Kinglake was no cloistered scribe. Before his last illness he dined out frequently, and was placed by many among the first half-a-dozen talkers in London. His conversation, though delicate and finished, brimmed full of interest in life and affairs: but let him enter his study, and its walls became a hedge. Without, the world was moving: within, it was always 1854, until by slow toiling it turned into 1855.

Style.

His style is hard, elaborate, polished to brilliance. Its difficult labor recalls Thucydides. In effect it charms at first by its accuracy and vividness: but with continuous perusal it begins to weigh upon the reader, who feels the strain, the unsparing effort that this glittering fabric must have cost the builder, and at length ceases to sympathize with the story and begins to sympathize with the author. Kinglake started by disclaiming "composition." "My narrative," he says, in the famous preface to *Eothen*, "conveys not those impressions which *ought to have been* produced upon any well-constituted mind, but those which were really and truly received, at the time of his rambles, by a headstrong and not very amiable traveller.... As I have felt, so I have written."

"Eothen."

For all this, page after page of *Eothen* gives evidence of deliberate calculation of effect. That book is at once curiously like and curiously unlike Borrows' *Bible in Spain*. The two belong to the same period and, in a sense, to the same fashion. Each combines a tantalizing personal charm with a strong, almost fierce, coloring of circumstance. The central figure in each is unmistakably an Englishman, and quite as unmistakably a singular Englishman. Each bears witness to a fine eye for theatrical arrangement. But whereas Borrow stood for ever fortified by his wayward nature and atrocious English against the temptation of writing as he ought, Kinglake commenced author with a respect for "composition," ingrained perhaps by his Public School and University training. Borrow arrays his page by instinct, Kinglake by study. His irony (as in the interview with the Pasha) is almost too elaborate; his artistic judgment (as in the Plague chapter) almost too sure; the whole book almost too clever. The performance was wonderful; the promise a trifle dangerous.

The "Invasion."

"Composition" indeed proved the curse of the *Invasion of the Crimea*: for Kinglake was a slow writer, and composed with his eye on the page, the paragraph, the phrase, rather than on the whole work. Force and accuracy of expression are but parts of a good prose style; indeed are, strictly speaking, inseparable from perspective, balance, logical connection, rise and fall of emotion. It is but an indifferent landscape that contains no pedestrian levels: and his desire for the immediate success of each paragraph as it came helped Kinglake to miss the broad effect. He must always be vivid; and when the strain told, he exaggerated and sounded—as Matthew Arnold accused him of sounding—the note of provinciality. There were other causes. He was, as we have seen, an English country gentleman—*avant tout je suis gentilhomme anglais*, as the Duke of Wellington wrote to Louis XVIII. His admiration of the respectable class to which he belonged is revealed by a thousand touches in his narrative—we can find half a score in the description of Codrington's assault on the Great Redoubt in the battle of the Alma; nor, when some high heroic action is in progress, do we often miss an illustration, or at least a metaphor, from the hunting-field. Undoubtedly he had the distinction of his class; but its narrowness was his as surely. Also the partisanship of the eight volumes grows into a weariness. The longevity of the English Bench is notorious; but it comes of hearing both sides of every question.

After all, he was a splendid artist. He tamed that beautiful and dangerous beast, the English sentence, with difficulty indeed, but having tamed, worked it to high achievements. The great occasion always found him capable, and his treatment of it is not of the sort to be forgotten: witness the picture of the Prince President cowering in an inner chamber during the bloodshed of the *Coup d'État*, the short speech of Sir Colin Campbell to his Highlanders before the Great Redoubt (given in the exact manner of Thucydides), or the narrative of the Heavy Brigade's charge at Balaclava, culminating thus—

"The difference that there was in the temperaments of the two comrade regiments showed itself in the last moments of the onset. The Scots Greys gave no utterance except to a low, eager, fierce moan of rapture—the moan of outbursting desire. The Inniskillings went in with a cheer. With a rolling prolongation of clangour which resulted from the bends of a line now deformed by its speed, the 'three hundred' crashed in upon the front of the column."

C.S.C. and J.K.S.

Dec. 5, 1891. Cambridge Baras.

What I am about to say will, no doubt, be set down to tribal malevolence; but I confess that if Cambridge men appeal to me less at one time than another it is when they begin to talk about their poets. The grievance is an old one, of course—at least as old as Mr. Birrell's "*Obiter Dicta*": but it has been revived by the little book of verse ("*Quo Musa Tendis?*") that I have just been reading. I laid it down and thought of Mr. Birrell's essay on Cambridge Poets, as he calls them: and then of another zealous gentleman, hailing from the same University, who arranged all the British bards in a tripos and brought out the Cambridge men at the top. This was a very characteristic performance: but Mr. Birrell's is hardly less so in these days when (to quote the epistolary parent) so much prominence is given to athleticism in our seats of learning. For he picks out a team of lightblue singers as though he meant to play an inter-University match, and challenges Oxford to "come on." He gives Milton a "blue," and says we oughtn't to play Shelley because Shelley isn't in residence.

Now to me this is as astonishing as if my butcher were to brag about Kirke White. My doctor might retort with Keats; and my scrivener—if I had one—might knock them both down with the name of Milton. It would be a pretty set-to; but I cannot see that it would affect the relative merits of mutton and laudanum and the obscure products of scrivenage. Nor, conversely (as they say at Cambridge), is it certain, or even likely, that the difference between a butcher or a doctor is the difference between Kirke White and Keats. And this talk about "University" poets seems somewhat otiose unless it can be shown that Cambridge and Oxford directly encourage poesy, or aim to do so. I am aware that somebody wins the Newdigate every year at Oxford, and that the same thing happens annually at Cambridge with respect to the Chancellor's Prize. But—to hark back to the butcher and apothecary—verses are perennially made upon Mr. Lipton's Hams and Mrs. Allen's Hair Restorer. Obviously some incentive is needed beyond a prize for stanzas on a given subject. I can understand Cambridge men when they assert that they produce more Wranglers than Oxford: that is a justifiable boast. But how does Cambridge encourage poets?

Calverley.

Oxford expelled Shelley: Cambridge whipped Milton.[A]*Facit indignatio versus.* If we press this misreading of Juvenal, Oxford erred only on the side of thoroughness. But that, notoriously, is Oxford's way. She expelled Landor, Calverley, and some others. My contention is that to expel a man is—however you look at it—better for his poesy than to make a don of him.

Oxford says, "You are a poet; therefore this is no place for you. Go elsewhere; we set your aspiring soul at large." Cambridge says: "You are a poet. Let us employ you to fulfil other functions. Be a don." She made a don of Gray, of Calverley. Cambridge men are for ever casting Calverley in our teeth; whereas, in truth, he is specially to be quoted against them. As everybody knows, he was at both Universities, so over him we have a fair chance of comparing methods. As everybody knows, he went to Balliol first, and his ample cabin'd spirit led him to climb a wall, late at night. Something else caused him to be discovered, and Blaydes—he was called Blaydes then—was sent down.

Nobody can say what splendid effect this might have had upon his poetry. But he changed his name and went to Cambridge. And Cambridge made a don of him. If anybody thinks this was an intelligent stroke, let him consider the result. Calverley wrote a small amount of verse that, merely as verse, is absolutely faultless. To compare great things with little, you might as well try to alter a line of Virgil's as one of Calverley's. Forget a single epithet and substitute another, and the result is certain disaster. He has the perfection of the phrase—and there it ends. I cannot remember a single line of Calverley's that contains a spark of human feeling. Mr. Birrell himself has observed that Calverley is just a bit inhuman. But the cause of it does not seem to have occurred to him. Nor does the biography explain it. If we are to believe the common report of all who knew Calverley, he was a man of simple mind and sincere, of quick and generous emotions. His biographers tell us also that he was one who seemed to have the world at his feet, one who had only to choose a calling to excel in it. Yet he never fulfilled his friends' high expectations. What was the reason of it all?

The accident that cut short his career is not wholly to blame, I think. At any rate, it will not explain away the exception I have taken to his verse. Had that been destined to exhibit the humanity which we seek, some promise of it would surely be discoverable; for he was a full-grown man at the time of that unhappy tumble on the ice. But there is none. It is all sheer wit, impish as a fairy changeling's, and always barren of feeling. Mr. Birrell has not supplied the explanatory epithet, so I will try to do so. It is "donnish." Cambridge, fondly imagining that she was showing right appreciation of Calverley thereby, gave him a Fellowship. Mr. Walter Besant, another gentleman from Calverley's college, complained, the other day, that literary distinction was never marked with a peerage. It is the same sort of error. And now Cambridge, having made Calverley a don, claims him as a Cambridge poet; and the claim is just, if the epithet be intended to mark the limitations imposed by that University on his achievement.

"J.K.S."

Of "J.K.S.," whose second volume, *Quo Musa Tendis?* (Macmillan & Bowles), has just come from the press, it is fashionable to say that he follows after Calverley, at some distance. To be sure, he himself has encouraged this belief by coming from Cambridge and writing about Cambridge, and invoking C.S.C. on the first page of his earlier volume, *Lapsus Calami*. But, except that J.K.S. does his talent some violence by constraining it to imitate Calverley's form, the two men have little in common. The younger has a very different wit. He is more than academical. He thinks and feels upon subjects that were far outside Calverley's scope. Among the dozen themes with which he deals under the general heading of *Paullo Majora Canamus*, there is not one which would have interested his "master" in the least. Calverley appears to have invited his soul after this fashion—"Come, let us go into the King's Parade and view the undergraduate as he walks about having no knowledge of good or evil. Let us make a jest of the books he admires and the schools for which he is reading." And together they manage it excellently. They talk Cambridge "shop" in terms of the wittiest scholarship. But of the very existence of a world of grown-up men and women they seem to have no inkling, or, at least, no care.

The problems of J.K.S. are very much more grown-up. You have only to read *Paint and Ink* (a humorous, yet quite serious, address to a painter upon the scope of his art) or *After the Golden Wedding* (wherein are given the soliloquies of the man and the woman who have been married for fifty years) to assure yourself that if J.K.S. be not Calverley's equal, it is only because his mind is vexed with problems bigger than ever presented themselves to the Cambridge don. To C.S.C., Browning was a writer of whose eccentricities of style delicious sport might be made. J.K.S. has parodied Browning too; but he has also perpended Browning, and been moulded by him. There are many stanzas in this small volume that, had Browning not lived, had never been written. Take this, from a writer to a painter:—

"So I do dare claim to be kin with you,
And I hold you higher than if your task
Were doing no more than you say you do:
We shall live, if at all, we shall stand or fall,
As men before whom the world doffs its mask
And who answer the questions our fellows ask."

Many such lines prove our writer's emancipation from servitude to the Calverley fetish, a fetish that, I am convinced, has done harm to many young men of parts. It is pretty, in youth, to play with style as a puppy plays with a bone, to cut teeth upon it. But words are, after all, a poor thing without matter. J.K.S.'s emancipation has come somewhat late; but he has depths in him which he has not sounded yet, and it is quite likely that when he sounds them he may astonish the world rather considerably. Now, if we may interpret the last poem in his book, he is turning towards prose. "I go," he says—

"I go to fly at higher game:
At prose as good as I can make it;
And though it brings nor gold nor fame,
I will not, while I live, forsake it."

It is no disparagement to his verse to rejoice over this resolve of his. For a young man who begins with epic may end with good epic; but a young man who begins with imitating Calverley will turn in time to prose if he means to write in earnest. And J.K.S. may do well or ill, but that he is to be watched has been evident since the days when he edited the *Reflector*.[B]

FOOTNOTES:

[A] I am bound to admit that the only authority for this is a note written into the text of Aubrey's *Lives*.

[B] The reader will refer to the date at the head of this paper:—
"Heu miserande puer! signa fata aspera rumpas,
Tu Marcellus eris.
*   *   *   *   *   *
Sed nox atra caput tristi circumvolat umbra."

ROBERT LOUIS STEVENSON

April 15, 1893. The "Island Nights' Entertainments."

I wish Mr. Stevenson had given this book another title. It covers but two out of the three stories in the volume; and, even so, it has the ill-luck to be completely spoilt by its predecessor, the *New Arabian Nights*.

The *New Arabian Nights* was in many respects a parody of the Eastern book. It had, if we make a few necessary allowances for the difference between East and West, the same, or very near the same, atmosphere of gallant, extravagant, intoxicated romance. The characters had the same adventurous irresponsibility, and exhibit the same irrelevancies and futilities. The Young Man with the Cream Cakes might well have sprung from the same brain as the facetious Barmecide, and young Scrymgeour sits helpless before his destiny as sat that other young man while the inexorable Barber sang the song and danced the dance of Zantout. Indeed Destiny in these books resembles nothing so much as a Barber with forefinger and thumb nipping his victims by the nose. It is as omnipotent, as irrational, as humorous and almost as cruel in the imitation as in the original. Of course I am not comparing these in any thing but their general presentment of life, or holding up *The Rajah's Diamond* against *Aladdin*. I am merely pointing out that life is presented to us in Galland and in Mr. Stevenson's first book of tales under very similar conditions—the chief difference being that Mr. Stevenson has to abate something of the supernatural, or to handle it less frankly.

But several years divide the *New Arabian Nights* from the *Island Nights' Entertainments*; and in the interval our author has written *The Master of Ballantrae* and his famous *Open Letter* on Father Damien. That is to say, he has grown in his understanding of the human creature and in his speculations upon his creature's duties and destinies. He has travelled far, on shipboard and in emigrant trains; has passed through much sickness; has acquired property and responsibility; has mixed in public affairs; has written *A Footnote to History*, and sundry letters to the *Times*; and even, as his latest letter shows, stands in some danger of imprisonment. Therefore, while the title of his new volume would seem to refer us once more to the old Arabian models, we are not surprised to find this apparent design belied by the contents. The third story, indeed, *The Isle of Voices*, has affinity with some of the Arabian tales—with Sindbad's adventures, for instance. But in the longer *Beach of Falesá* and *The Bottle Imp* we are dealing with no debauch of fancy, but with the problems of real life.

For what is the knot untied in the *Beach of Falesá*? If I mistake not, our interest centres neither in Case's dirty trick of the marriage, nor in his more stiff-jointed trick of the devil-contraptions. The first but helps to construct the problem, the second seems a superfluity. The problem is (and the author puts it before us fair and square), How is Wiltshire a fairly loose moralist with some generosity of heart, going to treat the girl he has wronged? And I am bound to say that as soon as Wiltshire answers that question before the missionary—an excellent scene and most dramatically managed—my interest in the story, which is but halftold at this point, begins to droop. As I said, the "devil-work" chapter strikes me as stiff, and the conclusion but rough-and-tumble. And I feel certain that the story itself is to blame, and neither the scenery nor the persons, being one of those who had as lief Mr. Stevenson spake of the South Seas as of the Hebrides, so that he speak and I listen. Let it be granted that the Polynesian names are a trifle hard to distinguish at first—they are easier than Russian by many degrees—yet the difficulty vanishes as you read the *Song of Rahéro*, or the *Footnote to History*. And if it comes to habits, customs, scenery, etc., I protest a man must be exacting who can find no romance in these while reading Melville's *Typee*. No, the story itself is to blame.

But what is the human problem in *The Bottle Imp*? (Imagine Scheherazadé with a human problem!) Nothing less, if you please than the problem of Alcestis—nothing less and even something more; for in this case when the wife has made her great sacrifice of self, it is no fortuitous god but her own husband who wins her release, and at a price no less fearful than she herself has paid. Keawe being in possession of a bottle which must infallibly bring him to hell-flames unless he can dispose of it at a certain price, Kokua his wife by a stratagem purchases the bottle from him, and stands committed to the doom he has escaped. She does her best to hide this from Keawe, but he, by accident discovering the truth, by another stratagem wins back the curse upon his own head, and is only rescued by a *deus ex machinâ* in the shape of a drunken boatswain.

Two or three reviewers have already given utterance upon this volume; and they seem strangely unable to determine which is the best of its three tales. I vote for *The Bottle Imp* without a second's doubt; and, if asked my reasons, must answer (1), that it deals with a high and universal problem, whereas in *The Isle of Voices* there is no problem at all, and in the *Beach of Falesá* the problem is less momentous and perhaps (though of this I won't be sure) more closely restricted by the accidents of circumstance and individual character; (2) as I have hinted, the *Beach of Falesá* has faults of construction, one of which is serious, if not vital, while *The Isle of Voices*, though beautifully composed, is tied down by the triviality of its subject. But *The Bottle Imp* is perfectly constructed: the last page ends the tale, and the tale is told with a light grace, sportive within restraint, that takes nothing from the seriousness of the subject. Some may think this extravagant praise for a little story which, after all (they will say), is flimsy as a soap bubble. But let them sit down and tick off on their fingers the names of living authors who could have written it, and it may begin to dawn on them that a story has other dimensions than length and thickness.

Sept. 9, 1893. First thoughts on "Catriona."

Some while ago Mr. Barrie put together in a little volume eleven sketches of eleven men whose fame has travelled far beyond the University of Edinburgh. For this reason, I believe, he called them "An Edinburgh Eleven"—as fond admirers speak of Mr. Arthur Shrewsbury (upon whose renown it is notorious that the sun never sets) as "the Notts Professional," and of a yet more illustrious cricketer by his paltry title of "Doctor"—

"Not so much honouring thee,
As giving it a hope that there
It could not wither'd be."

Of the Eleven referred to, Mr. Robert Louis Stevenson was sent in at eighth wicket down to face this cunning "delivery":—"He experiments too long; he is still a boy wondering what he is going to be. With Cowley's candor he tells us that he wants to write something by which he may be for ever known. His attempts in this direction have been in the nature of trying different ways, and he always starts off whistling. Having gone so far without losing himself, he turns back to try another road. Does his heart fail him, despite his jaunty bearing, *or is it because there is no hurry?* ... But it is quite time the great work was begun."

I have taken the liberty to italicise a word or two, because in them Mr. Barrie supplied an answer to his question. "The lyf so short, the craft so long to lerne!" is not an exhortation to hurry: and in Mr. Stevenson's case, at any rate, there was not the least need to hurry. There was, indeed, a time when Mr. Stevenson had not persuaded himself of this. In *Across the Plains* he tells us how, at windy Anstruther and an extremely early age, he used to draw his chair to the table and pour forth literature "at such a speed, and with such intimations of early death and immortality, as I now look back upon with wonder. Then it was that I wrote *Voces Fidelium*, a series of dramatic monologues in verse; then that I indited the bulk of a Covenanting novel—like so many others, never finished. Late I sat into the night, toiling (as I thought) under the very dart of death, toiling to leave a memory behind me. I feel moved to thrust aside the curtain of the years, to hail that poor feverish idiot, to bid him go to bed and clap *Voces Fidelium* on the fire before he goes, so clear does he appear to me, sitting there between his candles in the rose-scented room and the late night; so ridiculous a picture (to my elderly wisdom) does the fool present!"

There was no hurry then, as he now sees: and there never was cause to hurry, I repeat. "But how is this? Is, then, the great book written?" I am sure I don't know. Probably not: for human experience goes to show that *The* Great Book (like *The* Great American Novel) never gets written. But that *a* great story has been written is certain enough: and one of the curious points about this story is its title.

It is not *Catriona*; nor is it *Kidnapped*. *Kidnapped* is a taking title, and *Catriona* beautiful in sound and suggestion of romance: and *Kidnapped* (as everyone knows) is a capital tale, though imperfect; and *Catriona* (as the critics began to point out, the day after its issue) a capital tale with an awkward fissure midway in it. "It is the fate of sequels"—thus Mr. Stevenson begins his Dedication—"to disappoint those who have waited for them"; and it is possible that the boys of Merry England (who, it may be remembered, thought more of *Treasure Island* than of *Kidnapped*) will take but lukewarmly to *Catriona*, having had five years in which to forget its predecessor. No: the title of the great story is *The Memoirs of David Balfour*. Catriona has a prettier name than David, and may give it to the last book of her lover's adventures: but the Odyssey was not christened after Penelope.

Put *Kidnapped* and *Catriona* together within the same covers, with one title-page, one dedication (here will be the severest loss) and one table of contents, in which the chapters are numbered straight away from I. to LX.: and—this above all things—read the tale right through from David's setting forth from the garden gate at Essendean to his homeward voyage, by Catriona's side, on the Low Country ship. And having done this, be so good as to perceive how paltry are the objections you raised against the two volumes when you took them separately. Let me raise again one or two of them.

(1.) *Catriona* is just two stories loosely hitched together—the one of David's vain attempt to save James Stewart, the other of the loves of David and Catriona: and in case the critic should be too stupid to detect this, Mr. Stevenson has been at the pains to divide his book into Part I. and Part II. Now this, which is a real fault in a book called *Catriona*, is no fault at all in *The Memoirs of David Balfour*, which by its very title claims to be constructed loosely. In an Odyssey the road taken by the wanderer is all the nexus required; and the continuity of his presence (if the author know his business) is warrant enough for the continuity of our interest in his adventures. That the history of Gil Blas of Santillane consists chiefly of episodes is not a serious criticism upon Lesage's novel.

(2.) In *Catriona* more than a few of the characters are suffered to drop out of sight just as we have begun to take an interest in them. There is Mr. Rankeillor, for instance, whose company in the concluding chapter of *Kidnapped* was too good to be spared very easily; and there is Lady Allardyce—a wonderfully clever portrait; and Captain Hoseason—we tread for a moment on the verge of re-acquaintance, but are disappointed; and Balfour of Pilrig; and at the end of Part I. away into darkness goes the Lord Advocate Preston-grange, with his charming womenkind.

Well, if this be an objection to the tale, it is one urged pretty often against life itself—that we scarce see enough of the men and women we like. And here again that which may be a fault in *Catriona* is no fault at all in *The Memoirs of David Balfour*. Though novelists may profess in everything they write to hold a mirror up to life, the reflection must needs be more artificial in a small book than in a large. In the one, for very clearness, they must isolate a few human beings and cut off the currents (so to speak) bearing upon them from the outside world: in the other, with a larger canvas they are able to deal with life more frankly. Were the Odyssey cut down to one episode—say that of Nausicäa—we must round it off and have everyone on the stage and provided with his just portion of good and evil before we ring the curtain down. As it is, Nausicäa goes her way. And as it is, Barbara Grant must go her way at the end of Chapter XX.; and the pang we feel at parting with her is anything rather than a reproach against the author.

(3.) It is very certain, as the book stands, that the reader must experience some shock of disappointment when, after 200 pages of the most heroical endeavoring, David fails in the end to save James Stewart of the Glens. Were the book concerned wholly with James Stewart's fate, the cheat would be intolerable: and as a great deal more than half of *Catriona* points and trembles towards his fate like a magnetic needle, the cheat is pretty bad if we take *Catriona* alone. But once more, if we are dealing with *The Memoirs of David Balfour*—if we bear steadily in mind that David Balfour is our concern—not James Stewart—the disappointment is far more easily forgiven. Then, and then only, we get the right perspective of David's attempt, and recognize how inevitable was the issue when this stripling engaged to turn back the great forces of history.

It is more than a lustre, as the Dedication reminds us, since David Balfour, at the end of the last chapter of *Kidnapped*, was left to kick his heels in the British Linen Company's office. Five years have a knack of making people five years older; and the wordy, politic intrigue of *Catriona* is at least five years older than the rough-and-tumble intrigue of *Kidnapped*; of the fashion of the *Vicomte de Bragelonne* rather than of the *Three Musketeers*. But this is as it should be; for older and astuter heads are now mixed up in the case, and Prestongrange is a graduate in a very much higher school of diplomacy than was Ebenezer Balfour. And if no word was said in *Kidnapped* of the love of women, we know now that this matter was held over until the time came for it to take its due place in David Balfour's experience. Everyone knew that Mr. Stevenson would draw a woman beautifully as soon as he was minded. Catriona and her situation have their foreshadowing in *The Pavilion on the Links*. But for all that she is a surprise. She begins to be a surprise—a beautiful surprise—when in Chapter X. she kisses David's hand "with a higher passion than the common kind of clay has any sense of;" and she is a beautiful surprise to the end of the book. The loves of these two make a moving story—old, yet not old: and I pity the heart that is not tender for Catriona when she and David take their last walk together in Leyden, and "the knocking of her little shoes upon the way sounded extraordinarily pretty and sad."

Nov. 3, 1894. "The Ebb Tide."

A certain Oxford lecturer, whose audience demurred to some trivial mistranslation from the Greek, remarked: "I perceive, gentlemen, that you have been taking a mean advantage of me. You have been looking it out in the Lexicon."

The pleasant art of reasoning about literature on internal evidence suffers constant discouragement from the presence and activity of those little people who insist upon "looking it out in the Lexicon." Their brutal methods will upset in two minutes the nice calculations of months. Your logic, your taste, your palpitating sense of style, your exquisite ear for rhythm and cadence—what do these avail against the man who goes straight to Stationers' Hall or the Parish Register?

"Two thousand pounds of education
Drops to a ten-rupee jezail,"

as Mr. Kipling sings. The answer, of course, is that the beauty of reasoning upon internal evidence lies in the process rather than the results. You spend a month in studying a poet, and draw some conclusion which is entirely wrong: within a week you are set right by some fellow with a Parish Register. Well, but meanwhile you have been reading poetry, and he has not. Only the uninstructed judge criticism by its results alone.

If, then, after studying Messrs. Stevenson and Osbourne's *The Ebb-Tide* (London: Heinemann) I hazard a guess or two upon its authorship; and if somebody take it into his head to write out to Samoa and thereby elicit the information that my guesses are entirely wrong—why then we shall have been performing each of us his proper function in life; and there's an end of the matter.

Let me begin though—after reading a number of reviews of the book—by offering my sympathy to Mr. Lloyd Osbourne. Very possibly he does not want it. I guess him to be a gentleman of uncommonly cheerful heart. I hope so, at any rate: for it were sad to think that indignation had clouded even for a minute the gay spirit that gave us *The Wrong Box*—surely the funniest book written in the last ten years. But he has been most shamefully served. Writing with him, Mr. Stevenson has given us *The Wrecker* and *The Ebb-Tide*. Faults may be found in these, apart from the criticism that they are freaks in the development of Mr. Stevenson's genius. Nobody denies that they are splendid tales: nobody (I imagine) can deny that they are tales of a singular and original pattern. Yet no reviewer praises them on their own merits or points out their own defects. They are judged always in relation to Mr. Stevenson's previous work, and the reviewers concentrate their censure upon the point that they are freaks in Mr. Stevenson's development—that he is not continuing as the public expected him to continue.

Now there are a number of esteemed novelists about the land who earn comfortable incomes by doing just what the public expects of them. But of Mr. Stevenson's genius—always something wayward—freaks might have been predicted from the first. A genius so consciously artistic, so quick in sympathy with other men's writings, however diverse, was bound from the first to make many experiments. Before the public took his career in hand and mapped it out for him, he made such an experiment with *The Black Arrow*; and it was forgiven easily enough. But because he now takes Mr. Osbourne into partnership for a new set of experiments, the reviewers—not considering that these, whatever their faults, are vast improvements on *The Black Arrow*—ascribe all those faults to the new partner.

But that is rough criticism. Moreover it is almost demonstrably false. For the weakness of *The Wrecker*, such as it was, lay in the Paris and Barbizon business and the author's failure to make this of one piece with the main theme, with the romantic histories of the *Currency Lass* and the *Flying Scud*. But which of the two partners stands responsible for this Paris-Barbizon business? Mr. Stevenson beyond a doubt. If you shut your eyes to Mr. Stevenson's confessed familiarity with the Paris and the Barbizon of a certain era; if you choose to deny that he wrote that chapter on Fontainebleau in *Across the Plains*; if you go on to deny that he wrote the opening of Chapter XXI. of *The Wrecker*; why then you are obliged to maintain that it was Mr. Osbourne, and not Mr. Stevenson, who wrote that famous chapter on the Roussillon Wine—which is absurd. And if, in spite of its absurdity, you stick to this also, why, then you are only demonstrating that Mr. Lloyd Osbourne is one of the greatest living writers of fiction: and your conception of him as a mere imp of mischief jogging the master's elbow is wider of the truth than ever.

No; the vital defect of *The Wrecker* must be set down to Mr. Stevenson's account. Fine story as that was, it failed to assimilate the Paris-Barbizon business. *The Ebb-Tide*, on the other hand, is all of one piece. It has at any rate one atmosphere, and one only. And who can demand a finer atmosphere of romance than that of the South Pacific?

The Ebb-Tide, so far as atmosphere goes, is all of one piece. And the story, too, is all of one piece—until we come to Attwater: I own Attwater beats me. As Mr. Osbourne might say, "I have no use for" that monstrous person. I wish, indeed, Mr. Osbourne *had* said so: for again I cannot help feeling that the offence of Attwater lies at Mr. Stevenson's door. He strikes me as a bad dream of Mr. Stevenson's—a General Gordon out of the *Arabian Nights*. Do you remember a drawing of Mr. du Maurier's in *Punch*, wherein, seizing upon a locution of Miss Rhoda Broughton's, he gave us a group of "magnificently ugly" men? I seem to see Attwater in that group.

But if Mr. Stevenson is responsible for Attwater, surely also he contributed the two splendid surprises of the story. I am the more certain because they occur in the same chapter, and within three pages of each other. I mean, of course, Captain Davis's sudden confession about his "little Adar," and the equally startling discovery that the cargo of the *Farallone* schooner, supposed to be champagne, is mostly water. These are the two triumphant surprises of the book: and I shall continue to believe that only one living man could have contrived them, until somebody writes to Samoa and obtains the assurance that they are among Mr. Osbourne's contributions to the tale.

Two small complaints I have to make. The first is of the rather inartistically high level of profanity maintained by the speech of Davis and Huish. It is natural enough, of course; but that is no excuse if the frequency of the swearing prevent its making its proper impression in the right place. And the name "Robert Herrick," bestowed on one of the three beach-loafers, might have been shunned. You may call an ordinary negro "Julius Cæsar": for out of such extremes you get the legitimately grotesque. But the Robert Herrick, loose writer of the lovely *Hesperides*, and the Robert Herrick, shameful haunter of Papeete beach, are not extremes: and it was so very easy to avoid the association of ideas.

Dec. 22, 1894. R.L.S. In Memorium.

The Editor asks me to speak of Stevenson this week: because, since the foundation of THE SPEAKER, as each new book of Stevenson's appeared, I have had the privilege of writing about it here. So this column, too, shall be filled; at what cost ripe journalists will understand, and any fellow-cadet of letters may guess.

For when the telegram came, early on Monday morning, what was our first thought, as soon as the immediate numbness of sorrow passed and the selfish instinct began to reassert itself (as it always does) and whisper "What have *I* lost? What is the difference to *me*?" Was it not something like this—"Put away books and paper and pen. Stevenson is dead. Stevenson is dead, and now there is nobody left to write for." Our children and grandchildren shall rejoice in his books; but we of this generation possessed in the living man something that they will not know. So long as he lived, though it were far from Britain—though we had never spoken to him and he, perhaps, had barely heard our names—we always wrote our best for Stevenson. To him each writer amongst us—small or more than small—had been proud to have carried his best. That best might be poor enough. So long as it was not slipshod, Stevenson could forgive. While he lived, he moved men to put their utmost even into writings that quite certainly would never meet his eye. Surely another age will wonder over this curiosity of letters—that for five years the needle of literary endeavor in Great Britain has quivered towards a little island in the South Pacific, as to its magnetic pole.

Yet he founded no school, though most of us from time to time have poorly tried to copy him. He remained altogether inimitable, yet never seemed conscious of his greatness. It was native in him to rejoice in the successes of other men at least as much as in his own triumphs. One almost felt that, so long as good books were written, it was no great concern to him whether he or others wrote them. Born with an artist's craving for beauty of expression, he achieved that beauty with infinite pains. Confident in romance and in the beneficence of joy, he cherished the flame of joyous romance with more than Vestal fervor, and kept it ardent in a body which Nature, unkind from the beginning, seemed to delight in visiting with more unkindness—a "soul's dark cottage, battered and decayed" almost from birth. And his books leave the impression that he did this chiefly from a sense of duty: that he labored and kept the lamp alight chiefly because, for the time, other and stronger men did not.

Had there been another Scott, another Dumas—if I may change the image—to take up the torch of romance and run with it, I doubt if Stevenson would have offered himself. I almost think in that case he would have consigned with Nature and sat at ease, content to read of new Ivanhoes and new D'Artagnans: for—let it be said again—no man had less of the ignoble itch for merely personal success. Think, too, of what the struggle meant for him: how it drove him unquiet about the world, if somewhere he might meet with a climate to repair the constant drain upon his feeble vitality; and how at last it flung him, as by a "sudden freshet," upon Samoa—to die "far from Argos, dear land of home."

And then consider the brave spirit that carried him—the last of a great race—along this far and difficult path; for it is the man we must consider now, not, for the moment, his writings. Fielding's voyage to Lisbon was long and tedious enough; but almost the whole of Stevenson's life has been a voyage to Lisbon, a voyage in the very penumbra of death. Yet Stevenson spoke always as gallantly as his great predecessor. Their "cheerful stoicism," which allies his books with the best British breeding, will keep them classical as long as our nation shall value breeding. It shines to our dim eyes now, as we turn over the familiar pages of *Virginibus Puerisque*, and from page after page—in sentences and fragments of sentences—"It is not altogether ill with the invalid after all" ... "Who would project a serial novel after Thackeray and Dickens had each fallen in mid-course." [*He* had two books at least in hand and uncompleted, the papers say.] "Who would find heart enough to begin to live, if he dallied with the consideration of death?" ... "What sorry and pitiful quibbling all this is!" ... "It is better to live and be done with it, than to die daily in the sick-room. By all means begin your folio; even if the doctor does not give you a year, even if he hesitates over a month, make one brave push and see what can be accomplished in a week.... For surely, at whatever age it overtake the man, this is to die young.... The noise of the mallet and chisel is scarcely quenched, the trumpets are hardly done blowing, when, trailing with him clouds of glory, this happy-starred, full-blooded spirit shoots into the spiritual land."

As it was in *Virginibus Puerisque*, so is it in the last essay in his last book of essays:—

"And the Kingdom of Heaven is of the childlike, of those who are easy to please, who love and who give pleasure. Mighty men of their hands, the smiters, and the builders, and the judges, have lived long and done sternly, and yet preserved this lovely character; and among our carpet interests and two-penny concerns, the shame were indelible if *we* should lose it. *Gentleness and cheerfulness, these come before all morality; they are the perfect duties....*"

I remember now (as one remembers little things at such times) that, when first I heard of his going to Samoa, there came into my head (Heaven knows why) a trivial, almost ludicrous passage from his favorite, Sir Thomas Browne: a passage beginning "He was fruitlessly put in hope of advantage by change of Air, and imbibing the pure Aerial Nitre of those Parts; and therefore, being so far spent, he quickly found Sardinia in Tivoli, and the most healthful air of little effect, where Death had set her Broad Arrow...." A statelier sentence of the same author occurs to me now—

"To live indeed, is to be again ourselves, which being not only a hope, but an evidence in noble believers, it is all one to lie in St. Innocent's Churchyard, as in the sands of Egypt. Ready to be anything in the ecstacy of being ever, and as content with six foot as the *moles* of Adrianus."

This one lies, we are told, on a mountain-top, overlooking the Pacific. At first it seemed so much easier to distrust a News Agency than to accept Stevenson's loss. "O captain, my captain!" ... One needs not be an excellent writer to feel that writing will be thankless work, now that Stevenson is gone. But the papers by this time leave no room for doubt. "A grave was dug on the summit of Mount Vaea, 1,300 feet above the sea. The coffin was carried up the hill by Samoans with great difficulty, a track having to be cut through the thick bush which covers the side of the hill from the base to the peak." For the good of man, his father and grandfather planted the high sea-lights upon the Inchcape and the Tyree Coast. He, the last of their line, nursed another light and tended it. Their lamps still shine upon the Bell Rock and the Skerryvore; and—though in alien seas, upon a rock of exile—this other light shall continue, unquenchable by age, beneficent, serene.

Nov. 2, 1895. The "Vailima Letters."

Eagerly as we awaited this volume, it has proved a gift exceeding all our hopes—a gift, I think, almost priceless. It unites in the rarest manner the value of a familiar correspondence with the value of an intimate journal: for these Samoan letters to his friend Mr. Sidney Colvin form a record, scarcely interrupted, of Stevenson's thinkings and doings from month to month, and often from day to day, during the last four romantic years of his life. The first is dated November 2nd, 1890, when he and his household were clearing the ground for their home on the mountain-side of Vaea: the last, October 6th, 1894, just two months before his grave was dug on Vaea top. During his Odyssey in the South Seas (from August, 1888, to the spring of 1890) his letters, to Mr. Colvin at any rate, were infrequent and tantalizingly vague; but soon after settling on his estate in Samoa, "he for the first time, to my infinite gratification, took to writing me long and regular monthly budgets as full and particular as heart could wish; and this practice he maintained until within a few weeks of his death." These letters, occupying a place quite apart in Stevenson's correspondence, Mr. Colvin has now edited with pious care and given to the public.

But the great, the happy surprise of the *Vailima Letters* is neither their continuity nor their fulness of detail—although on each of these points they surpass our hopes. The great, the entirely happy surprise is their intimacy. We all knew—who could doubt it?—that Stevenson's was a clean and transparent mind. But we scarcely allowed for the innocent zest (innocent, because wholly devoid of vanity or selfishness) which he took in observing its operations, or for the child-like confidence with which he held out the crystal for his friend to gaze into.

One is at first inclined to say that had these letters been less open-hearted they had made less melancholy reading—the last few of them, at any rate. For, as their editor says, "the tenor of these last letters of Stevenson's to me, and of others written to several of his friends at the same time, seemed to give just cause for anxiety. Indeed, as the reader will have perceived, a gradual change had during the past months been coming over the tone of his correspondence.... To judge by these letters, his old invincible spirit of cheerfulness was beginning to give way to moods of depression and overstrained feeling, although to those about him, it seems, his charming, habitual sweetness and gaiety of temper were undiminished." Mr. Colvin is thinking, no doubt, of passages such as this, from the very last letter:—

"I know I am at a climacteric for all men who live by their wits, so I do not despair. But the truth is, I am pretty nearly useless at literature.... Were it not for my health, which made it impossible, I could not find it in my heart to forgive myself that I did not stick to an honest, commonplace trade when I was young, which might have now supported me during these ill years. But do not suppose me to be down in anything else; only, for the nonce, my skill deserts me, such as it is, or was. It was a very little dose of inspiration, and a pretty little trick of style, long lost, improved by the most heroic industry. So far, I have managed to please the journalists. But I am a fictitious article, and have long known it. I am read by journalists, by my fellow-novelists, and by boys; with these *incipit et explicit* my vogue."

I appeal to all who earn their living by pen or brush—Who does not know moods such as this? Who has not experience of those dark days when the ungrateful canvas refuses to come right, and the artist sits down before it and calls himself a fraud? We may even say that these fits of incapacity and blank despondency are part of the cost of all creative work. They may be intensified by terror for the family exchequer. The day passes in strenuous but futile effort, and the man asks himself, "What will happen to me and mine if this kind of thing continues?" Stevenson, we are allowed to say (for the letters tell us), did torment himself with these terrors. And we may say further that, by whatever causes impelled, he certainly worked too hard during the last two years of his life. With regard to the passage quoted, what seems to me really melancholy is not the baseless self-distrust, for that is a transitory malady most incident to authorship; but that, could a magic carpet have transported Stevenson at that moment to the side of the friend he addressed—could he for an hour or two have visited London—all this apprehension had been at once dispelled. He left England before achieving his full conquest of the public heart, and the extent of that conquest he, in his exile, never quite realized. When he visited Sydney, early in 1893, it was to him a new and disconcerting experience—but not, I fancy altogether unpleasing—*digito monstrari*, or, as he puts it elsewhere, to "do the affable celebrity life-sized." Nor do I think he quite realized how large a place he filled in the education, as in the affections, of the younger men—the Barries and Kiplings, the Weymans, Doyles and Crocketts—whose courses began after he had left these shores. An artist gains much by working alone and away from chatter and criticism and adulation: but his gain has this corresponding loss, that he must go through his dark hours without support. Even a master may take benefit at times—if it be only a physical benefit—from some closer and handier assurance than any letters can give of the place held by his work in the esteem of "the boys."

We must not make too much of what he wrote in this dark mood. A few days later he was at work on *Weir of Hermiston*, laboring "at the full pitch of his powers and in the conscious happiness of their exercise." Once more he felt himself to be working at his best. The result the world has not yet been allowed to see: for the while we are satisfied and comforted by Mr. Colvin's assurances. "The fragment on which he wrought during the last month of his life gives to my mind (as it did to his own) for the first time the true measure of his powers; and if in the literature of romance there is to be found work more masterly, of more piercing human insight and more concentrated imaginative wisdom, I do not know it."

On the whole, these letters from Vailima give a picture of a serene and—allowance being made for the moods—a contented life. It is, I suspect, the genuine Stevenson that we get in the following passage from the letter of March, 1891:—

"Though I write so little, I pass all my hours of field-work in continual converse and imaginary correspondence. I scarce pull up a weed, but I invent a sentence on the matter to yourself; it does not get written; *autant en emportent les vents*; but the intent is there, and for me (in some sort) the companionship. To-day, for instance, we had a great talk. I was toiling, the sweat dripping from my nose, in the hot fit after a squall of rain; methought you asked me—frankly, was I happy? Happy (said I); I was only happy once; that was at Hyères; it came to an end from a variety of reasons—decline of health, change of place, increase of money, age with his stealing steps; since then, as before then, I know not what it means. But I know pleasures still; pleasure with a thousand faces and none perfect, a thousand tongues all broken, a thousand hands, and all of them with scratching nails. High among these I place the delight of weeding out here alone by the garrulous water, under the silence of the high wood, broken by incongruous sounds of birds. And take my life all through, look at it fore and back, and upside down—I would not change my circumstances, unless it were to bring you here. And yet God knows perhaps this intercourse of writing serves as well; and I wonder, were you here indeed, would I commune so continually with the thought of you. I say 'I wonder' for a form; I know, and I know I should not."

In a way the beauty of these letters is this, that they tell us so much of Stevenson that is new, and nothing that is strange—nothing that we have difficulty in reconciling with the picture we had already formed in our own minds. Our mental portraits of some other writers, drawn from their deliberate writings, have had to be readjusted, and sometimes most cruelly readjusted, as soon as their private correspondence came to be published. If any of us dreamed of this danger in Stevenson's case (and I doubt if anyone did), the danger at any rate is past. The man of the letters is the man of the books—the same gay, eager, strenuous, lovable spirit, curious as ever about life and courageous as ever in facing its chances. Profoundly as he deplores the troubles in Samoa, when he hears that war has been declared he can hardly repress a boyish excitement. "War is a huge *entraînement*," he writes in June, 1893; "there is no other temptation to be compared to it, not one. We were all wet, we had been five hours in the saddle, mostly riding hard; and we came home like schoolboys, with such a lightness of spirits, and I am sure such a brightness of eye, as you could have lit a candle at."

And that his was not by any means mere "literary" courage one more extract will prove. One of his boys, Paatalise by name, had suddenly gone mad:—

"I was busy copying David Balfour, with my left hand—a most laborious task—Fanny was down at the native house superintending the floor, Lloyd down in Apia, and Bella in her own house cleaning, when I heard the latter calling on my name. I ran out on the verandah; and there on the lawn beheld my crazy boy with an axe in his hand and dressed out in green ferns, dancing. I ran downstairs and found all my house boys on the back verandah, watching him through the dining-room. I asked what it meant?—'Dance belong his place,' they said.—'I think this is no time to dance,' said I. 'Has he done his work?'—'No,' they told me, 'away bush all morning.' But there they all stayed in the back verandah. I went on alone through the dining-room and bade him stop. He did so, shouldered the axe, and began to walk away; but I called him back, walked up to him, and took the axe out of his unresisting hands. The boy is in all things so good, that I can scarce say I was afraid; only I felt it had to be stopped ere he could work himself up by dancing to some craziness. Our house boys protested they were not afraid; all I know is they were all watching him round the back door, and did not follow me till I had the axe. As for the out-boys, who were working with Fanny in the native house, they thought it a bad business, and made no secret of their fears."

But indeed all the book is manly, with the manliness of Scott's *Journal* or of Fielding's *Voyage to Lisbon*. "To the English-speaking world," concludes Mr. Colvin, "he has left behind a treasure which it would be vain as yet to attempt to estimate; to the profession of letters one of the most ennobling and inspiriting of examples; and to his friends an image of memory more vivid and more dear than are the presences of almost any of the living." Very few men of our time have been followed out of this world with the same regret. None have repined less at their own fate—

"This be the verse you grave for me:—
'Here he lies where he longed to be;
Home is the sailor, home from the sea,
And the hunter home from the hill.'"

M. ZOLA

Sept. 23, 1892. La Débâcle.

To what different issues two men will work the same notion! Imagine this world to be a flat board accurately parcelled out into squares, and you have the basis at once of *Alice through the Looking-Glass* and of *Les Rougon-Macquart*. But for the mere fluke that the Englishman happened to be whimsical and the Frenchman entirely without humor (and the chances were perhaps against this), we might have had the Rougon-Macquart family through the looking-glass, and a natural and social history of Alice in *parterres* of existence labelled *Drink, War, Money*, etc. As it is, in drawing up any comparison of these two writers we should remember that Mr. Carroll sees the world in sections because he chooses, M. Zola because he cannot help it.

If life were a museum, M. Zola would stand a reasonable chance of being a Balzac. But I invite the reader who has just laid down *La Débâcle* to pick up *Eugénie Grandet* again and say if that little Dutch picture has not more sense of life, even of the storm and stir and big furies of life, than the detonating *Débâcle*. The older genius

"Saw life steadily and saw it whole"

—No matter how small the tale, he draws no curtain around it; it stands in the midst of a real world, set in the white and composite light of day. M. Zola sees life in sections and by one or another of those colors into which daylight can be decomposed by the prism. He is like a man standing at the wings with a limelight apparatus. The rays fall now here, now there, upon the stage; are luridly red or vividly green; but neither mix nor pervade.

I am aware that the tone of the above paragraph is pontifical and its substance a trifle obvious, and am eager to apologize for both. Speaking as an impressionist, I can only say that *La Débâcle* stifles me. And this is the effect produced by all his later books. Each has the exclusiveness of a dream; its subject—be it drink or war or money—possesses the reader as a nightmare possesses the dreamer. For the time this place of wide prospect, the world, puts up its shutters; and life becomes all drink, all war, all money, while M. Zola (adaptable Bacchanal!) surrenders his brain to the intoxication of his latest theme. He will drench himself with ecclesiology, or veterinary surgery, or railway technicalities—everything by turns and everything long; but, like the gentleman in the comic opera, he "never mixes." Of late he almost ceased to add even a dash of human interest.

Mr. George Moore, reviewing *La Débâcle* in the *Fortnightly* last month, laments this. He reminds us of the splendid opportunity M. Zola has flung away in his latest work.

"Jean and Maurice," says Mr. Moore, "have fought side by side; they have alternately saved each other's lives; war has united them in a bond of inseparable friendship; they have grasped each other's hands, and looked in each other's eyes, overpowered with a love that exceeds the love that woman ever gave to man; now they are ranged on different sides, armed one against the other. The idea is a fine one, and it is to be deeply regretted that M. Zola did not throw history to the winds and develop the beautiful human story of the division of friends in civil war. Never would history have tempted Balzac away from the human passion of such a subject...."

But it is just fidelity to the human interest of every subject that gives the novelist his rank; that makes—to take another instance—a page or two of Balzac, when Balzac is dealing with money, of more value than the whole of *l'Argent*.

Of Burke it has been said by a critic with whom it is a pleasure for once in a way to agree, that he knew how the whole world lived.

"It was Burke's peculiarity and his glory to apply the imagination of a poet of the first order to the facts and business of life.... Burke's imagination led him to look over the whole land: the legislator devising new laws, the judge expounding and enforcing old ones, the merchant despatching all his goods and extending his credit, the banker advancing the money of his customers upon the credit of the merchant, the frugal man slowly accumulating the store which is to support him in old age, the ancient institutions of Church and University with their seemly provisions for sound learning and true religion, the parson in his pulpit, the poet pondering his rhymes, the farmer eyeing his crops, the painter covering his canvases, the player educating the feelings. Burke saw all this with the fancy of a poet, and dwelt on it with the eye of a lover."

Now all this, which is true of Burke, is true of the very first literary artists— of Shakespeare and Balzac. All this, and more—for they not only see all this immense activity of life, but the emotions that animate each of the myriad actors.

Suppose them to treat of commerce: they see not only the goods and money changing hands, but the ambitions, dangers, fears, delights, the fierce adventures by desert and seas, the slow toil at home, upon which the foundations of commerce are set. Like the Gods,

"They see the ferry
On the broad, clay-laden
Lone Chorasmian stream;—thereon,
With snort and strain,

"Two horses, strongly swimming, tow
The ferry-boat, with woven ropes
To either bow
Firm-harness'd by the mane; a chief,
With shout and shaken spear,
Stands at the prow, and guides them; but astern
The cowering merchants, in long robes,
Sit pale beside their wealth...."

Like the Gods, they see all this; but, unlike the Gods, they must feel also:—

"They see the merchants
On the Oxus stream;—*but care
Must visit first them too, and make them pale.
Whether, through whirling sand,
A cloud of desert robber-horse have burst
Upon their caravan; or greedy kings,
In the wall'd cities the way passes through,
Crush'd them with tolls; or fever-airs,
On some great river's marge,
Mown them down, far from home.*"

Mr. Moore speaks of M. Zola's vast imagination. It is vast in the sense that it sees one thing at a time, and sees it a thousand times as big as it appears to most men. But can the imagination that sees a whole world under the influence of one particular fury be compared with that which surveys this planet and sees its inhabitants busy with a million diverse occupations? Drink, Money, War—these may be usefully personified as malignant or beneficent angels, for pulpit purposes. But the employment of these terrific spirits in the harrying of the Rougon-Macquart family recalls the announcement that

"The Death-Angel smote Alexander McGlue...."

while the methods of the *Roman Expérimental* can hardly be better illustrated than by the rest of the famous stanza—

"—And gave him protracted repose:
He wore a check shirt and a Number 9 shoe,
And he had a pink wart on his nose."

SELECTION

May 4, 1895. Hazlitt.

"Coming forward and seating himself on the ground in his white dress and tightened turban, the chief of the Indian jugglers begins with tossing up two brass balls, which is what any of us could do, and concludes with keeping up four at the same time, which is what none of us could do to save our lives." ... You remember Hazlitt's essay on the Indian Jugglers, and how their performance shook his self-conceit. "It makes me ashamed of myself. I ask what there is that I can do as well as this. Nothing..... Is there no one thing in which I can challenge competition, that I can bring as an instance of exact perfection, in which others cannot find a flaw? The utmost I can pretend to is to write a description of what this fellow can do. I can write a book; so can many others who have not even learned to spell. What abortions are these essays! What errors, what ill-pieced transitions, what crooked reasons, what lame conclusions! How little is made out, and that little how ill! Yet they are the best I can do."

Nevertheless a play of Shakespeare's, or a painting by Reynolds, or an essay by Hazlitt, imperfect though it be, is of more rarity and worth than the correctest juggling or tight-rope walking. Hazlitt proceeds to examine why this should be, and discovers a number of good reasons. But there is one reason, omitted by him, or perhaps left for the reader to infer, on which we may profitably spend a few minutes. It forms part of a big subject, and tempts to much abstract talk on the universality of the Fine Arts; but I think we shall be putting it simply enough if we say that an artist is superior to an "artiste" because he does well what ninety-nine people in a hundred are doing poorly all their lives.

Selection.

When people compare fiction with "real life," they start with asserting "real life" to be a conglomerate of innumerable details of all possible degrees of pertinence and importance, and go on to show that the novelist selects from this mass those which are the most important and pertinent to his purpose. (I speak here particularly of the novelist, but the same is alleged of all practitioners of the fine arts.) And, in a way, this is true enough. But who (unless in an idle moment, or with a view to writing a treatise in metaphysics) ever takes this view of the world? Who regards it as a conglomerate of innumerable details? Critics say that the artist's difficulty lies in selecting the details proper to his purpose, and his justification rests on the selection he makes. But where lives the man whose difficulty and whose justification do not lie just here?—who is not consciously or unconsciously selecting from morning until night? You take the most ordinary country walk. How many millions of leaves and stones and blades of grass do you pass without perceiving them at all? How many thousands of others do you perceive, and at once allow to slip into oblivion? Suppose you have walked four miles with the express object of taking pleasure in country sights. I dare wager the objects that have actually engaged your attention for two seconds are less than five hundred, and those that remain in your memory, when you reach home, as few as a dozen. All the way you have been, quite unconsciously, selecting and rejecting. And it is the brain's bedazzlement over this work, I suggest, and not merely the rhythmical physical exertion, that lulls the more ambitious walker and induces that phlegmatic mood so prettily described by Stevenson—the mood in which

"we can think of this or that, lightly or laughingly, as a child thinks, or as we think in a morning doze; we can make puns or puzzle out acrostics, and trifle in a thousand ways with words and rhymes; but when it comes to honest work, when we come to gather ourselves together for an effort, we may sound the trumpet as long and loud as we please; the great barons of the mind will not rally to the standard, but sit, each one at home, warming his hands over his own fire and brooding on his own private thought!"

Again, certain critics never seem tired of pelting the novelist with comparisons drawn between painting and photography. "Mr. So-and-So's fidelity to life suggests the camera rather than the brush and palette"; and the implication is that Mr. So-and-So and the camera resemble each other in their tendency to reproduce irrelevant detail. The camera, it is assumed, repeats this irrelevant detail. The photographer does not select. But is this true? I have known many enthusiasts in photography whose enthusiasm I could not share. But I never knew one, even among amateurs, who wished to photograph everything he saw, from every possible point of view. Even the amateur selects—wrongly as a rule: still he selects. The mere act of setting up a camera in any particular spot implies a process of selection. And when the deed is done, the scenery has been libelled. Our eyes behold the photograph, and go through another process of selection. In short, whatever they look upon, men and women are selecting ceaselessly.

The artist therefore does well and consciously, and for a particular end, what every man or woman does poorly, and unconsciously, and casually. He differs in the photographer in that he has more licence to eliminate. When once the camera is set up, it's owner's power over the landscape has come to an end. The person who looks on the resultant photograph must go through the same process of choosing and rejecting that he would have gone through in contemplating the natural landscape. The sole advantage is that the point of view has been selected for him, and that he can enjoy it without fatigue in any place and at any time.

The truth seems to be that the human brain abhors the complexity—the apparently aimless complexity—of nature and real life, and is for ever trying to get away from it by selecting this and ignoring that. And it contrives so well that I suppose the average man is not consciously aware twice a year of that conglomerate of details which the critics call real life. He holds one stout thread, at any rate, to guide him through the maze—the thread of self-interest.

The justification of the poet or the novelist is that he discovers a better thread. He follows up a universal where the average man follows only a particular. But in following it, he does but use those processes by which the average man arrives, or attempts to arrive, at pleasure.

EXTERNALS

Nov. 18, 1893. Story and Anecdote.

I suppose I am no more favored than most people who write stories in receiving from unknown correspondents a variety of suggestions, outlines of plots, sketches of situations, characters, and so forth. One cannot but feel grateful for all this spontaneous beneficence. The mischief is that in ninety-nine cases out of a hundred (the fraction is really much smaller) these suggestions are of no possible use.

Why should this be? Put briefly, the reason is that a story differs from an anecdote. I take the first two instances that come into my head: but they happen to be striking ones, and, as they occur in a book of Mr. Kipling's, are safe to be well known to all my correspondents. In Mr. Kipling's fascinating book, *Life's Handicap, On Greenhow Hill* is a story; *The Lang Men o' Larut* is an anecdote. *On Greenhow Hill* is founded on a study of the human heart, and it is upon the human heart that the tale constrains one's interest. *The Lang Men o' Larut* is just a yarn spun for the yarn's sake: it informs us of nothing, and is closely related (if I may use some of Mr. Howells' expressive language for the occasion) to "the lies swapped between men after the ladies have left the table." And the reason why the story-teller, when (as will happen at times) his invention runs dry, can take no comfort in the generous outpourings of his unknown friends, is just this—that the plots are merely plots, and the anecdotes merely anecdotes, and the difference between these and a story that shall reveal something concerning men and women is just the difference between bad and good art.

Let us go a step further. At first sight it seems a superfluous contention that a novelist's rank depends upon what he can see and what he can tell us of the human heart. But, as a matter of fact, you will find that four-fifths at least of contemporary criticism is devoted to matters quite different—to what I will call Externals, or the Accidents of Story-telling: and that, as a consequence, our novelists are spending a quite unreasonable proportion of their labor upon Externals. I wrote "as a consequence" hastily, because it is always easier to blame the critics. If the truth were known, I dare say the novelists began it with their talk about "documents," "the scientific method," "observation and experiment," and the like.

The Fallacy of "Documents."

Now you may observe a man until you are tired, and then you may begin and observe him over again: you may photograph him and his surroundings: you may spend years in studying what he eats and drinks: you may search out what his uncles died of, and the price he pays for his hats, and—know nothing at all about him. At least, you may know enough to insure his life or assess him for Income Tax: but you are not even half-way towards writing a novel about him. You are still groping among externals. His unspoken ambitions; the stories he tells himself silently, at midnight, in his bed; the pain he masks with a dull face and the ridiculous fancies he hugs in secret—these are the Essentials, and you cannot get them by Observation. If you can discover these, you are a Novelist born: if not, you may as well shut up your note-book and turn to some more remunerative trade. You will never surprise the secret of a soul by accumulating notes upon Externals.

Local Color.

Then, again, we have Local Color, an article inordinately bepraised just now; and yet an External. For human nature, when every possible allowance has been made for geographical conditions, undergoes surprisingly little change as we pass from one degree of latitude or longitude to another. The Story of Ruth is as intelligible to an Englishman as though Ruth had gleaned in the stubble behind Tess Durbeyfield. Levine toiling with the mowers, Achilles sulking in his tent, Iphigeneia at the altar, Gil Blas before the Archbishop of Granada have as close a claim on our sympathy as if they lived but a few doors from us. Let me be understood. I hold it best that a novelist should be intimately acquainted with the country in which he lays his scene. But, none the less, the study of local color is not of the first importance. And the critic who lavishes praise upon a writer for "introducing us to an entirely new atmosphere," for "breaking new ground," and "wafting us to scenes with which the jaded novel-reader is scarcely acquainted," and for "giving us work which bears every trace of minute local research," is praising that which is of secondary importance. The works of Richard Jefferies form a considerable museum of externals of one particular kind; and this is possibly the reason why the Cockney novelist waxes eloquent over Richard Jefferies. He can now import the breath of the hay-field into his works at no greater expense of time and trouble than taking down the *Gamekeeper at Home* from his club bookshelf and perusing a chapter or so before settling down to work. There is not the slightest harm in his doing this: the mistake lies in thinking local color (however acquired) of the first importance.

In judging fiction there is probably no safer rule than to ask one's self, How far does the pleasure excited in me by this book depend upon the transitory and trivial accidents that distinguish this time, this place, this character, from another time, another place, another character? And how far upon the abiding elements of human life, the constant temptations, the constant ambitions, and the constant nobility and weakness of the human heart? These are the essentials, and no amount of documents or local color can fill their room.

Sept. 30, 1893. The Country as "Copy."

The case of a certain small volume of verse in which I take some interest, and its treatment at the hands of the reviewers, seems to me to illustrate in a sufficiently amusing manner a trick that the British critic has been picking up of late. In a short account of Mr. Hosken, the postman poet, written by way of preface to his *Verses by the Way* (Methuen & Co.), I took occasion to point out that he is not what is called in the jargon of these days a "nature-poet"; that his poetic bent inclines rather to meditation than to description; and that though his early struggles in London and elsewhere have made him acquainted with many strange people in abnormal conditions of life, his interest has always lain, not in these striking anomalies, but in the destiny of humanity as a whole and its position in the great scheme of things.

These are simple facts. I found them, easily enough, in Mr. Hosken's verse—where anybody else may find them. They also seem to me to be, for a critic's purpose, ultimate facts. It is an ultimate fact that Publius Virgilius Maro wore his buskins somewhat higher in the heel than did Quintus Horatius Flaccus: and no critic, to my knowledge, has been impertinent enough to point out that, since Horace had some experience of the tented field, while Virgil was a stay-at-home courtier, therefore Horace should have essayed to tell the martial exploits of Trojan and Rutulian while Virgil contented himself with the gossip of the Via Sacra. Yet—to compare small things with great—this is the mistake into which our critics have fallen in Mr. Hosken's case; and I mention it because the case is typical. They try to get behind the ultimate facts and busy themselves with questions they have no proper concern with. Some ask petulantly why Mr. Hosken is not a "nature-poet." Some are gravely concerned that "local talent" (*i.e.* the talent of a man who happens to dwell in some locality other than the critic's) should not concern itself with local affairs; and remind him—

"To thine orchard edge belong
All the brass and plume of song."

As if a man may not concern himself with the broader problems of life and attack them with all the apparatus of recorded experience, unless he happen to live on one bank or other of the Fleet Ditch! If a man have the gift, he can find all the "brass and plume of song" in his orchard edge. If he have not, he may (provided he be a *bonâ fide* traveller) find it elsewhere. What, for instance, were the use of telling Keats: "To thy surgery belong all the brass and plume of song"? He couldn't find it there, so he betook himself to Chapman and Lempriere. If you ask, "What right has a country postman to be handling questions that vexed the brain of Plato?"—I ask in return, "What right had

John Keats, who knew no Greek, to busy himself with Greek mythology?" And the answer is that each has a perfect right to follow his own bent.

The assumption of many critics that only within the metropolitan cab radius can a comprehensive system of philosophy be constructed, and that only through the plate-glass windows of two or three clubs is it possible to see life steadily, and see it whole, is one that I have before now had occasion to dispute. It is joined in this case to another yet more preposterous—that from a brief survey of an author's circumstances we can dictate to him what he ought to write about, and how he ought to write it. And I have observed particularly that if a writer be a countryman, or at all well acquainted with country life, all kinds of odd entertainment is expected of him in the way of notes on the habits of birds, beasts, and fishes, on the growth of all kinds of common plants, on the proper way to make hay, to milk a cow, and so forth.

Richard Jefferies.

Now it is just the true countryman who would no more think of noting these things down in a book than a Londoner would think of stating in a novel that Bond Street joins Oxford Street and Piccadilly: simply because they have been familiar to him from boyhood. And to my mind it is a small but significant sign of a rather lamentable movement—of none other, indeed, than the "Rural Exodus," as Political Economists call it—that each and every novelist of my acquaintance, while assuming as a matter of course that his readers are tolerably familiar with the London Directory, should, equally as a matter of course, assume them to be ignorant of the commonest features of open-air life. I protest there are few things more pitiable than the transports of your Cockney critic over Richard Jefferies. Listen, for instance, to this kind of thing:—

"Here and there upon the bank wild gooseberry and currant bushes may be found, planted by birds carrying off ripe fruit from the garden. A wild gooseberry may sometimes be seen growing out of the decayed 'touchwood' on the top of a hollow withy-pollard. Wild apple trees, too, are not uncommon in the hedges.

"The beautiful rich colour of the horse-chestnut, when quite ripe and fresh from its prickly green shell, can hardly be surpassed; underneath the tree the grass is strewn with shells where they have fallen and burst. Close to the trunk the grass is worn away by the restless trampling of horses, who love the shade its foliage gives in summer. The oak apples which appear on the oaks in spring—generally near the trunk—fall off in summer, and lie shrivelled on the ground, not unlike rotten cork, or black as if burned. But the oak-galls show thick on some of the trees, light green, and round as a ball; they will remain on the branches after the leaves have fallen, turning brown and hard, and hanging there till the spring comes again."—*Wild Life in a Southern County*, pp. 224-5.

I say it is pitiable that people should need to read these things in print. Let me apply this method to some district of south-west London—say the Old Brompton Road:—

"Here and there along the street Grocery Stores and shops of Italian Warehousemen may be observed, opened here as branches of bigger establishments in the City. Three gilt balls may occasionally be seen hanging out under the first-floor windows of a 'pawnbroker's' residence. House-agents, too, are not uncommon along the line of route.

"The appearance of a winkle, when extracted from its shell with the aid of a pin, is extremely curious. There is a winkle-stall by the South Kensington Station of the Underground Railway. Underneath the stall the pavement is strewn with shells, where they have fallen and continue to lie. Close to the stall is a cab-stand, paved with a few cobbles, lest the road be worn overmuch by the restless trampling of cab-horses, who stand here because it is a cab-stand. The thick woollen goods which appear in the haberdashers' windows through the winter—generally *inside* the plate glass—give way to garments of a lighter texture as the summer advances, and are put away or exhibited at decreased prices. But collars continue to be shown, quite white and circular in form; they will probably remain, turning grey as the dust settles on them, until they are sold."

This is no travesty. It is a hasty, but I believe a pretty exact application of Jefferies' method. And I ask how it would look in a book. If the critics really enjoy, as they profess to, all this trivial country lore, why on earth don't they come into the fresh air and find it out for themselves? There is no imperative call for their presence in London. Ink will stain paper in the country as well as in town, and the Post will convey their articles to their editors. As it is, they do but overheat already overheated clubs. Mr. Henley has suggested concerning Jefferies' works that

"in years to be, when the whole island is one vast congeries of streets, and the fox has gone down to the bustard and the dodo, and outside museums of comparative anatomy the weasel is not, and the badger has ceased from the face of the earth, it is not doubtful that the *Gamekeeper* and *Wild Life* and the *Poacher*—epitomising, as they will, the rural England of certain centuries before—will be serving as material authority for historical descriptions, historical novels, historical epics, historical pictures, and will be honoured as the most useful stuff of their kind in being."

Let me add that the movement has begun. These books are already supplying the club-novelist with his open-air effects: and, therefore, the club-novelist worships them. From them he gathers that "wild apple-trees, too, are not uncommon in the hedges," and straightway he informs the public of this wonder. But it is hard on the poor countryman who, for the benefit of a street-bred reading public, must cram his books with solemn recitals of his A, B, C, and impressive announcements that two and two make four and a hedge-sparrow's egg is blue.

Aug. 18, 1894. A Defence of "Local Fiction."

Under the title "Three Years of American Copyright" the *Daily Chronicle* last Tuesday published an account of an interview with Mr. Brander Matthews, who holds (among many titles to distinction) the Professorship of Literature in Columbia College, New York. Mr. Matthews is always worth listening to, and has the knack of speaking without offensiveness even when chastising us Britons for our national peculiarities. His conversation with the *Daily Chronicle's* interviewer contained a number of good things; but for the moment I am occupied with his answer to the question "What form of literature should you say is at present in the ascendant in the United States?" "Undoubtedly," said Mr. Matthews, "what I may call local fiction."

"Every district of the country is finding its 'sacred poet.' Some of them have only a local reputation, but all possess the common characteristic of starting from fresh, original, and loving study of local character and manners. You know what Miss Mary E. Wilkins has done for New England, and you probably know, too, that she was preceded in the same path by Miss Sarah Orne Jewett and the late Mrs. Rose Terry Cooke. Mr. Harold Frederic is performing much the same service for rural New York, Miss Murfree (Charles Egbert Craddock) for the mountains of Tennessee, Mr. James Lane Allen for Kentucky, Mr. Joel Chandler Harris for Georgia, Mr. Cable for Louisiana, Miss French (Octave Thanet) for Iowa, Mr. Hamlin Garland for the western prairies, and so forth. Of course, one can trace the same tendency, more or less clearly, in English fiction...."

And Mr. Matthews went on to instance several living novelists, Scotch, Irish, and English to support this last remark.

The matter, however, is not in doubt. With Mr. Barrie in the North, and Mr. Hardy in the South; with Mr. Hall Caine in the Isle of Man, Mr. Crockett in Galloway, Miss Barlow in Lisconnell; with Mr. Gilbert Parker in the territory of the H.B.C., and Mr. Hornung in Australia; with Mr. Kipling scouring the wide world, but returning always to India when the time comes to him to score yet another big artistic success; it hardly needs elaborate proof to arrive at the conclusion that 'locality' is playing a strong part in current fiction.

The thing may possibly be overdone. Looking at it from the artistic point of view as dispassionately as I may, I think we are overdoing it. But that, for the moment, is not the point of view I wish to take. If for the moment we can detach ourselves from the prejudice of fashion and look at the matter from the historical point of view—if we put ourselves into the position of the conscientious gentleman who, fifty or a hundred years hence, will be surveying us and our works—I think we shall find this elaboration of "locality" in fiction to be but a swing-back of the pendulum, a natural revolt from the thin-spread work of the "carpet-bagging" novelist who takes the whole world for his province, and imagines he sees life steadily and sees it whole when he has seen a great deal of it superficially.

The "carpet-bagger" still lingers among us. We know him, with his "tourist's return" ticket, and the ready-made "plot" in his head, and his note-book and pencil for jotting down "local color." We still find him working up the scenery of Bolivia in the Reading Room of the British Museum. But he is going rapidly out of fashion; and it is as well to put his features on record and pigeon-hole them, if only that we may recognize him on that day when the pendulum shall swing him triumphantly back into our midst, and "locality" shall in its turn pass out of vogue.

I submit this simile of the pendulum with some diffidence to those eager theorists who had rather believe that their art is advancing steadily, but at a fair rate of speed, towards perfection. My own less cheerful—yet not altogether cheerless view—is that the various fashions in art swing to and fro upon intersecting curves. Some of the points of intersection are fortunate points—others are obviously the reverse; and generally the fortunate points lie near the middle of each arc, or the mean; while the less fortunate ones lie towards the ends, that is, towards excess upon one side or another. I have already said that, in the amount of attention they pay to locality just now, the novelists seem to be running into excess. If I must choose between one excess and the other—between the carpet-bagger and the writer of "dialect-stories," each at his worst—I unhesitatingly choose the latter. But that is probably because I happened to be born in the 'sixties.

Let us get back (I hear you implore) to the historical point of view, if possible: anywhere, anywhere, out of the *Poetics!* And I admit that a portion of the preceding paragraph reads like a bad parody of that remarkable work. Well, then, I believe that our imaginary historian—I suppose he will be a German: but we need not let our imagination dwell upon *that*—will find a dozen reasons in contemporary life to account for the attention now paid by novelists to "locality." He will find one of them, no doubt, in the development of locomotion by steam. He will point out that any cause which makes communication easier between two given towns is certain to soften the difference in the characteristics of their inhabitants: that the railway made communication easier and quicker year by year; and its tendency was therefore to obliterate local peculiarities. He will describe how at first the carpet-bagger went forth in railway-train and steamboat, rejoicing in his ability to put a girdle round the world in a few weeks, and disposed to ignore those differences of race and region which he had no time to consider and which he was daily softening into uniformity. He will then relate that towards the close of the nineteenth century, when these differences were rapidly perishing, people began to feel the loss of them and recognize their scientific and romantic value; and that a number of writers entered into a struggle against time and the carpet-bagger, to study these differences and place them upon record, before all trace of them should disappear. And then I believe our historian, though he may find that in 1894 we paid too much attention to the *minutiæ* of dialect, folk-lore and ethnic differences, and were inclined to overlay with these the more catholic principles of human conduct, will acknowledge that in our hour we did the work that was most urgent. Our hour, no doubt, is not the happiest; but, since this is the work it brings, there can be no harm in going about it zealously.

CLUB TALK

Nov. 12, 1892. Mr. Gilbert Parker.

Mr. Gilbert Parker's book of Canadian tales, "Pierre and His People" (Methuen and Co.), is delightful for more than one reason. To begin with, the tales themselves are remarkable, and the language in which they are told, though at times it overshoots the mark by a long way and offends by what I may call an affected virility, is always distinguished. You feel that Mr. Parker considers his sentences, not letting his bolts fly at a venture, but aiming at his effects deliberately. It is the trick of promising youth to shoot high and send its phrases in parabolic curves over the target. But a slight wildness of aim is easily corrected, and to see the target at all is a more conspicuous merit than the public imagines. Now Mr. Parker sees his target steadily; he has a thoroughly good notion of what a short story ought to be: and more than two or three stories in his book are as good as can be.

Open Air v. Clubs.

But to me the most pleasing quality in the book is its open-air flavor. Here is yet another young author, and one of the most promising, joining the healthy revolt against the workshops. Though for my sins I have to write criticism now and then, and use the language of the workshops, I may claim to be one of the rebels, having chosen to pitch a small tent far from cities and to live out of doors: and it rejoices me to see the movement growing, as it undoubtedly has grown during the last few years, and find yet one more of the younger men refusing, in Mr. Stevenson's words, to cultivate restaurant fat, to fall in mind "to a thing perhaps as low as many types of *bourgeois*—the implicit or exclusive artist." London is an alluring dwelling-place for an author, even for one who desires to write about the country. He is among the paragraph-writers, and his reputation swells as a cucumber under glass. Being in sight of the newspaper men, he is also in their mind. His prices will stand higher than if he go out into the wilderness. Moreover, he has there the stimulating talk of the masters in his profession, and will be apt to think that his intelligence is developing amazingly, whereas in fact he is developing all on one side; and the end of him is—the Exclusive Artist:—

> "*When the flicker of London sun falls faint on the
> Club-room's green and gold
> The sons of Adam sit them down and scratch with their
> pens in the mould—
> They scratch with their pens in the mould of their
> graves and the ink and the anguish start,
> For the Devil mutters behind the leaves: 'It's pretty,
> but is it Art?'*"

The spirit of our revolt is indicated clearly enough on that page of Mr. Stevenson's "Wrecker," from which I have already quoted a phrase:—

"That was a home word of Pinkerton's, deserving to be writ in letters of gold on the portico of every School of Art: 'What I can't see is why you should want to do nothing else.' The dull man is made, not by the nature, but by the degree of his immersion in a single business. And all the more if that be sedentary, uneventful, and ingloriously safe. More than half of him will then remain unexercised and undeveloped; the rest will be distended and deformed by over-nutrition, over-cerebration and the heat of rooms. And I have often marvelled at the impudence of gentlemen who describe and pass judgment on the life of man, in almost perfect ignorance of all its necessary elements and natural careers. Those who dwell in clubs and studios may paint excellent pictures or write enchanting novels. There is one thing that they should not do: they should pass no judgment on man's destiny, for it is a thing with which they are unacquainted. Their own life is an excrescence of the moment, doomed, in the vicissitude of history, to pass and disappear. The eternal life of man, spent under sun and rain and in rude physical effort, lies upon one side, scarce changed since the beginning."

A few weeks ago our novelists were discussing the reasons why they were novelists and not playwrights. The discussion was sterile enough, in all conscience: but one contributor—it was "Lucas Malet"—managed to make it clear that English fiction has a character to lose. "If there is one thing," she said, "which as a nation we understand, it is *out-of-doors* by land and sea." Heaven forbid that, with only one Atlantic between me and Mr. W.D. Howells, I should enlarge upon any merit of the English novel: but I do suggest that this open-air quality is a characteristic worth preserving, and that nothing is so likely to efface it as the talk of workshops. It is worth preserving because it tends to keep us in sight of the elemental facts of human nature. After all, men and women depend for existence on the earth and on the sky that makes earth fertile; and man's last act will be, as it was his first, to till the soil. All empires, cities, tumults, civil and religious wars, are transitory in comparison. The slow toil of the farm-laborer, the endurance of the seaman, outlast them all.

Open Air in Criticism.

That studio-talk tends to deaden this sense of the open-air is just as certain. It runs not upon Nature, but upon the presentation of Nature. I am almost ready to assert that it injures a critic as surely as it spoils a creative writer. Certainly I remember that the finest appreciation of Carlyle—a man whom every critic among English-speaking races had picked to pieces and discussed and reconstructed a score of times—was left to be uttered by an inspired loafer in Camden, New Jersey. I love to read of Whitman dropping the newspaper that told him of Carlyle's illness, and walking out under the stars—

"Every star dilated, more vitreous, larger than usual. Not as in some clear nights when the larger stars entirely outshine the rest. Every little star or cluster just as distinctly visible and just as high. Berenice's hair showing every gem, and new ones. To the north-east and north the Sickle, the Goat and Kids, Cassiopeia, Castor and Pollux, and the two Dippers. While through the whole of this silent indescribable show, inclosing and bathing my whole receptivity, ran the thought of Carlyle dying."

In such a mood and place—not in a club after a dinner unearned by exercise—a man is likely, if ever, to utter great criticism as well as to conceive great poems. It is from such a mood and place that we may consider the following fine passage fitly to issue:—

"The way to test how much he has left his country were to consider, or try to consider, for a moment the array of British thought, the resultant *ensemble* of the last fifty years, as existing to-day, *but with Carlyle left out*. It would be like an army with no artillery. The show were still a gay and rich one—Byron, Scott, Tennyson, and many more—horsemen and rapid infantry, and banners flying—but the last heavy roar so dear to the ear of the trained soldier, and that settles fate and victory, would be lacking."

For critic and artist, as for their fellow-creatures, I believe an open-air life to be the best possible. And that is why I am glad to read in certain newspaper paragraphs that Mr. Gilbert Parker is at this moment on the wide seas, and bound for Quebec, where he starts to collect material for a new series of short stories. His voyage will loose him, in all likelihood, from the little he retains of club art.

Of course, a certain proportion of our novelists must write of town life: and to do this fitly they must live in town. But they must study in the town itself, not in a club. Before anyone quotes Dickens against me, let him reflect, first on the immensity of Dickens' genius, and next on the conditions under which Dickens studied London. If every book be a part of its writer's autobiography I invite the youthful author who now passes his evenings in swapping views about Art with his fellow cockneys to pause and reflect if he is indeed treading in Dickens' footsteps or stands in any path likely to lead him to results such as Dickens achieved.

EXCURSIONISTS IN POETRY

Nov. 5, 1892. An Itinerary.

Besides the glorious exclusiveness of it, there is a solid advantage just now, in not being an aspirant for the Laureateship. You can go out into the wilderness for a week without troubling to leave an address. A week or so back I found with some difficulty a friend who even in his own judgment has no claim to the vacant office, and we set out together across Dartmoor, Exmoor, the Quantocks, by eccentric paths over the southern ranges of Wales to the Wye, and homewards by canoe between the autumn banks of that river. The motto of the voyage was Verlaine's line—

"Et surtout ne parlons pas littérature"

—especially poetry. I think we felt inclined to congratulate each other after passing the Quantocks in heroic silence; but were content to read respect in each other's eyes.

The Return to Literature.

On our way home we fell across a casual copy of the *Globe* newspaper, and picked up a scrap of information about the Blorenge, a mountain we had climbed three days before. It is (said the *Globe*) the only thing in the world that rhymes with orange. From this we inferred that the Laureate had not been elected during our wanderings, and that the Anglo-Saxon was still taking an interest in poetry. It was so.

Public Excursions in Verse.

The progress of this amusing epidemic may be traced in the *Times*. It started mildly and decorously with the death of a politician. The writer of Lord Sherbrooke's obituary notice happened to remember and transcribe the rather flat epigram beginning—

"Here lie the bones of Robert Lowe,
Where he's gone to I don't know...."

with Lowe's own Latin translation of the same. At once the *Times* was flooded with other versions by people who remembered the lines more or less imperfectly, who had clung each to his own version since childhood, who doubted if the epigram were originally written on Lord Sherbrooke, who had seen it on an eighteenth-century tombstone in several parts of England, and so on. London Correspondents took up the game and carried it into the provincial press. Then country clergymen bustled up and tried to recall the exact rendering; while others who had never heard of the epigram waxed emulous and produced translations of their own, with the Latin of which the local compositor made sport after his kind. For weeks there continued quite a pretty rivalry among these decaying scholars.

The gentle thunders of this controversy had scarcely died down when the *Times* quoted a four-lined epigram about Mr. Leech making a speech, and Mr. Parker making something darker that was dark enough without; and another respectable profession, which hitherto had remained cold, began to take fire and dispute with ardor. The Church, the Legislature, the Bar, were all excited by this time. They strained on the verge of surpassing feats, should the occasion be given. From men in this mood the occasion is rarely withheld. Lord Tennyson died. He had written at Cambridge a prize poem on Timbuctoo. Somebody else, at Cambridge or elsewhere, had also written about Timbuctoo and a Cassowary that ate a missionary with his this and his that and his hymn-book too. Who was this somebody? Did he write it at Cambridge (home of poets)? And what were the "trimmings," as Mr. Job Trotter would say, with which the missionary was eaten?

Poetry was in the air by this time. It would seem that those treasures which the great Laureate had kept close were by his death unlocked and spread over England, even to the most unexpected corners. "All have got the seed," and already a dozen gentlemen were busily growing the flower in the daily papers. It was not to be expected that our senators, barristers, stockbrokers, having proved their strength, would stop short at Timbuctoo and the Cassowary. Very soon a bold egregious wether jumped the fence into the Higher Criticism, and gave us a new and amazing interpretation of the culminating line in *Crossing the Bar*. The whole flock was quick upon his heels. "Allow me to remind the readers of your valuable paper that there are *two* kinds of pilot" is the sentence that now catches our eyes as we open the *Times*. And according to the *Globe* if you need a rhyme for orange you must use Blorenge. And the press exists to supply the real wants of the public.[A]

They talk of decadence. But who will deny the future to a race capable of producing, on the one hand, *Crossing the Bar*—and on the other, this comment upon it, signed "T.F.W." and sent to the *Times* from Cambridge, October 27th, 1892?—

" ... a poet so studious of fitness of language as Tennyson would hardly, I suspect, have thrown off such words on such an occasion haphazard. If the analogy is to be inexorably criticised, may it not be urged that, having in his mind not the mere passage 'o'er life's solemn main,' which we all are taking, with or without reflection, but the near approach to an unexploredocean beyond it, he was mentally assigning to the pilot in whom his confidence was fast the *status* of the navigator of old days, the sailing-master, on whose knowledge and care crews and captains engaged in expeditions alike relied? Columbus himself married the daughter of such a man, *un piloto Italiano famoso navigante*. Camoens makes the people of Mozambique offer Vasco da Gama a *piloto* by whom his fleet shall be deftly (*sabiamente*) conducted across the Indian Ocean. In the following century (1520-30) Sebastian Cabot, then in the service of Spain, commanded a squadron which was to pass through the Straits of Magellan to the Moluccas, having been appointed by Charles V. Grand Pilot of Castile. The French still call the mates of merchant vessels—that is, the officers who watch about, take charge of the deck—*pilotes*, and this designation is not impossibly reserved to them as representing the *pilote hauturier* of former times, the scientific guide of ships *dans la haute mer*, as distinguished from the *pilote côtier*, who simply hugged the shore. The last class of pilot, it is almost superfluous to observe, is still with us and does take our ships, inwards or outwards, across the bar, if there be one, and does no more. The *hauturier* has long been replaced in all countries by the captain, and it must be within the experience of some of us that when outward bound the captain as often as not has been the last man to come on board. We did not meet him until the ship, which until his arrival was in the hands of the *côtier*, was well out of harbour. Then our *côtier* left us."

Prodigious!

FOOTNOTES:

[A] *Note*, Oct. 21, 1893.—The nuisance revived again when Mr. Nettleship the younger perished on Mont Blanc. And again, the friend of Lowe and Nettleship, the great Master of Balliol, had hardly gone to his grave before a dispute arose, not only concerning his parentage (about which any man might have certified himself at the smallest expense of time and trouble), but over an unusually pointless epigram that was made at Cambridge many years ago, and neither on him, nor on his father, but on an entirely different Jowett, *Semper ego auditor tantum?*—

If a funny "Cantab" write a dozen funny rhymes,
Need a dozen "Cantabs" write about it to the *Times*?
Need they write, at any rate, a generation after,
Stating cause and date of joke and reasons for their laughter?

THE POPULAR CONCEPTION OF A POET

June 24, 1893. March 4, 1804. In what respect Remarkable.

What seems to me chiefly remarkable in the popular conception of a Poet is its unlikeness to the truth. Misconception in this case has been flattered, I fear, by the poets themselves:—

"The poet in a golden Clime was born,
With golden stars above;
Dowered with the hate of hate, the scorn of scorn,
The love of love.
He saw thro' life and death, thro' good and ill;
He saw thro' his own soul.
The marvel of the Everlasting Will,
An open scroll,
Before him lay...."

I should be sorry to vex any poet's mind with my shallow wit; but this passage always reminds me of the delusions of the respectable Glendower:—

"At my birth
The frame and huge foundation of the earth
Shak'd like a coward."

—and Hotspur's interpretation (slightly petulant, to be sure), "Why, so it would have done at the time if your mother's cat had but kittened, though you yourself had never been born." I protest that I reverence poetry and the poets: but at the risk of being warned off the holy ground as a "dark-browed sophist," must declare my plain opinion that the above account of the poet's birth and native gifts does not consist with fact.

Yet it consents with the popular notion, which you may find presented or implied month by month and week by week, in the reviews; and even day by day—for it has found its way into the newspapers. Critics have observed that considerable writers fall into two classes—

Two lines of Poetic Development.

(1) Those who start with their heads full of great thoughts, and are from the first occupied rather with their matter than with the manner of expressing it.

(2) Those who begin with the love of expression and intent to be artists in words, *and come through expression to profound thought.*

The Popular Type.

Now, for some reason it is fashionable just now to account Class 1 the more respectable; a judgment to which, considering that Virgil and Shakespeare belong to Class 2, I refuse my assent. It is fashionable to construct an imaginary figure out of the characteristics of Class 1, and set him up as the Typical Poet. The poet at whose nativity Tennyson assists in the above verses of course belongs to Class 1. A babe so richly dowered can hardly help his matter overcrowding his style; at least, to start with.

But this is not all. A poet who starts with this tremendous equipment can hardly help being something too much for the generation in which he is born. Consequently, the Typical Poet is misunderstood by his contemporaries, and probably persecuted. In his own age his is a voice crying in the wilderness; in the wilderness he speeds the "viewless arrows of his thought"; which fly far, and take root as they strike earth, and blossom; and so Truth multiplies, and in the end (most likely after his death) the Typical Poet comes by his own.

Such is the popular conception of the Typical Poet, and I observe that it fascinates even educated people. I have in mind the recent unveiling of Mr. Onslow Ford's Shelley Memorial at University College, Oxford. Those who assisted at that ceremony were for the most part men and women of high culture. Excesses such as affable Members of Parliament commit when distributing school prizes or opening free public libraries were clearly out of the question. Yet even here, and almost within the shadow of Bodley's great library, speaker after speaker assumed as axiomatic this curious fallacy—that a Poet is necessarily a thinker in advance of his age, and therefore peculiarly liable to persecution at the hands of his contemporaries.

How supported by History.

But logic, I believe, still flourishes in Oxford; and induction still has its rules. Now, however many different persons Homer may have been, I cannot remember that one of him suffered martyrdom, or even discomfort, on account of his radical doctrine. I seem to remember that Æchylus enjoyed the esteem of his fellow-citizens, sided with the old aristocratic party, and lived long enough to find his own tragedies considered archaic; that Sophocles, towards the end of a very prosperous life, was charged with senile decay and consequent inability to administer his estates—two infirmities which even his accusers did not seek to connect with advanced thinking; and that Euripides, though a technical innovator, stood hardly an inch ahead of the fashionable dialectic of his day, and suffered only from the ridicule of his comic contemporaries and the disdain of his wife—misfortunes incident to the most respectable. Pindar and Virgil were court favorites, repaying their patrons in golden song. Dante, indeed, suffered banishment; but his banishment was just a move in a political (or rather a family) game. Petrarch and Ariosto were not uncomfortable in their generations. Chaucer and Shakespeare lived happy lives and sang in the very key of their own times. Puritanism waited for its hour of triumph to produce its great poet, who lived unmolested when the hour of triumph passed and that of reprisals succeeded. Racine was a royal pensioner; Goethe a chamberlain and the most admired figure of his time. Of course, if you hold that these poets one and all pale their ineffectual fires before the radiant Shelley, our argument must go a few steps farther back. I have instanced them as acknowledged kings of song.

The Case of Tennyson.

Tennyson was not persecuted. He was not (and more honor to him for his clearness) even misunderstood. I have never met with the contention that he stood an inch ahead of the thought of his time. As for seeing through death and life and his own soul, and having the marvel of the everlasting will spread before him like an open scroll,—well, to begin with, I doubt if these things ever happened to any man. Heaven surely has been, and is, more reticent than the verse implies. But if they ever happened, Tennyson most certainly was not the man they happened to. What Tennyson actually sang, till he taught himself to sing better, was:—

"Airy, fairy Lilian,
Flitting fairy Lilian,
When I ask her if she love me,
Claps her tiny hands above me,
Laughing all she can;
She'll not tell me if she love me,
Cruel little Lilian."

There is not much of the scorn of scorn, or the love of love, or the open scroll of the everlasting will, about *Cruel Little Lilian*. But there *is* a distinct striving after style—a striving that, as everyone knows, ended in mastery: and through style Tennyson reached such heights of thought as he was capable of. To the end his thought remained inferior to his style: and to the end the two in him were separable, whereas in poets of the very first rank they are inseparable. But that towards the end his style lifted his thought to heights of which even *In Memoriam* gave no promise cannot, I think, be questioned by any student of his collected works.

Tennyson belongs, if ever poet belonged, to Class 2: and it is the prettiest irony of fate that, having unreasonably belauded Class 1, he is now being found fault with for not conforming to the supposed requirements of that Class. He, who spoke of the poet as of a seër "through life and death," is now charged with seeing but a short way beyond his own nose. The Rev. Stopford Brooke finds that he had little sympathy with the aspirations of the struggling poor; that he bore himself coldly towards the burning questions of the hour;

that, in short, he stood anywhere but in advance of his age. As if plenty of people were not interested in these things! Why, I cannot step out into the street without running against somebody who is in advance of the times on some point or another.

Of Virgil and Shakespeare.

Virgil and Shakespeare were neither martyrs nor preachers despised in their generation. I have said that as poets they also belong to Class 2. Will a champion of the Typical Poet (new style) dispute this, and argue that Virgil and Shakespeare, though they escaped persecution, yet began with matter that overweighted their style—with deep stuttered thoughts—in fine, with a Message to their Time? I think that view can hardly be maintained. We have the *Eclogues* before the *Æneid*; and *The Comedy of Errors* before *As You Like It*. Expression comes first; and through expression, thought. These are the greatest names, or of the greatest: and they belong to Class 2.

Of Milton.

Again, no English poetry is more thoroughly informed with thought than Milton's. Did he find big thoughts hustling within him for utterance? And did he at an early age stutter in numbers till his oppressed soul found relief? And was it thus that he attained the glorious manner of

"Seasons return, but not to me returns
Day, or the sweet approach of even or morn...."

—and so on. No, to be short, it was not. At the age of twenty-four, or thereabouts, he deliberately proposed to himself to be a great poet. To this end he practised and studied, and travelled unweariedly until his thirty-first year. Then he tried to make up his mind what to write about. He took some sheets of paper—they are to be seen at this day in the Library of Trinity College, Cambridge—and set down no less than ninety-nine subjects for his proposed *magnum opus*, before he could decide upon *Paradise Lost*. To be sure, when the *magnum opus* was written it fetched £5 only. But even this does not prove that Milton was before his age. Perhaps he was behind it. *Paradise Lost* appeared in 1667: in 1657 it might have fetched considerably more than £5.

If the Typical Poet have few points in common with Shakespeare or Milton, I fear that the Typical Poet begins to be in a bad way.

Of Coleridge.

Shall we try Coleridge? He had "great thoughts"—thousands of them. On the other hand, he never had the slightest difficulty in uttering them, in prose. His great achievements in verse—his *Genevieve*, his *Christabel*, his *Kubla Khan*, his *Ancient Mariner*—are achievements of expression. When they appeal from the senses to the intellect their appeal is usually quite simple.

"He prayeth best who loveth best
All things both great and small."

No, I am afraid Coleridge is not the Typical Poet.

On the whole I suspect the Typical Poet to be a hasty generalization from Shelley.

POETS ON THEIR OWN ART

May 11, 1895. A Prelude to Poetry.

"To those who love the poets most, who care most for their ideals, this little book ought to be the one indispensable book of devotion, the *credo* of the poetic faith." "This little book" is the volume with which Mr. Ernest Rhys prefaces the pretty series of Lyrical Poets which he is editing for Messrs. Dent & Co. He calls it *The Prelude to Poetry*, and in it he has brought together the most famous arguments stated from time to time by the English poets in defence and praise of their own art. Sidney's magnificent "Apologie" is here, of course, and two passages from Ben Jonson's "Discoveries," Wordsworth's preface to the second edition of "Lyrical Ballads," the fourteenth chapter of the "Biographia Literaria," and Shelley's "Defence."

Poets as Prose-writers.

What admirable prose these poets write! Southey, to be sure, is not represented in this volume. Had he written at length upon his art—in spite of his confession that, when writing prose, "of what is now called style not a thought enters my head at any time"—we may be sure the reflection would have been even more obvious than it is. But without him this small collection makes out a splendid case against all that has been said in disparagement of the prose style of poets. Let us pass what Hazlitt said of Coleridge's prose; or rather let us quote it once again for its vivacity, and so pass on—

"One of his (Coleridge's) sentences winds its 'forlorn way obscure' over the page like a patriarchal procession with camels laden, wreathed turbans, household wealth, the whole riches of the author's mind poured out upon the barren waste of his subject. The palm tree spreads its sterile branches overhead, and the land of promise is seen in the distance."

All this is very neatly malicious, and particularly the last co-ordinate sentence. But in the chapter chosen by Mr. Rhys from the "Biographia Literaria" Coleridge's prose is seen at its best—obedient, pertinent, at once imaginative and restrained—as in the conclusion—

"Finally, good sense is the body of poetic genius, fancy its drapery, motion its life, and imagination the soul that is everywhere, and in each; and forms all into one graceful and intelligent whole."

The prose of Sidney's *Apologie* is Sidney's best; and when that has been said, nothing remains but to economize in quoting. I will take three specimens only. First then, for beauty:—

"Nature never set forth the earth in so rich tapistry, as divers Poets have done, neither with plesant rivers, fruitful trees, sweet-smelling flowers: nor whatsoever else may make the too much loved earth more lovely. Her world is brasen, the Poets only deliver a golden: but let those things alone and goe to man, for whom as the other things are, so it seemeth in him her uttermost cunning is imployed, and know whether shee have brought forth so true a lover as *Theagines*, so constant a friende as *Pilades*, so valiant a man as *Orlando*, so right a Prince as *Xenophon's Cyrus*; so excellent a man every way as *Virgil's Aeneas*...."

Next for wit—roguishness, if you like the term better:—

"And therefore, if *Cato* misliked *Fulvius*, for carrying *Ennius* with him to the field, it may be answered, that if *Cato* misliked it, the noble *Fulvius* liked it, or else he had not done it."

And lastly for beauty and wit combined:—

"For he (the Poet) doth not only show the way, but giveth so sweete a prospect into the way, as will intice any man to enter into it. Nay he doth, as if your journey should lye through a fayre Vineyard, at the first give you a cluster of Grapes: that full of that taste, you may long to passe further. He beginneth not with obscure definitions, which must blur the margent with interpretations, and load the memory with doubtfulnesse: but he cometh to you with words set in delightful proportion, either accompanied with or prepared for the well inchanting skill of Musicke: and with a tale forsooth he cometh unto you: with a tale which holdeth children from play, and old men from the chimney corner."

"Is not this a glorious way to talk?" demanded the Rev. T.E. Brown of this last passage, when he talked about Sidney, the other day, in Mr. Henley's *New Review*. "No one can fail," said Mr. Brown, amiably assuming the fineness of his own ear to be common to all mankind—"no one can fail to observe the sweetness and the strength, the outspokenness, the downrightness, and, at the same time, the nervous delicacy of pausation, the rhythm all ripple and suspended fall, the dainty *but*, the daintier *and forsooth*, as though the pouting of a proud reserve curved the fine lip of him, and had to be atoned for by the homeliness of *the chimney-corner.*"

Everybody admires Sidney's prose. But how of this?—

"Poetry is the breath and finer spirit of all knowledge; it is the impassioned expression which is in the countenance of all science. Emphatically it may be said of the Poet, as Shakespeare has said of man, 'that he looks before and after.' He is the rock of defence of human nature; an upholder and preserver, carrying everywhere with him relationship and love. In spite of difference of soil and climate, of language and manners, of laws and customs, *in spite of things silently gone out of mind, and things violently destroyed*, the Poet binds together by passion and knowledge the vast empire of human society, as it is spread over the whole earth, and over all time."

It is Wordsworth who speaks—too rhetorically, perhaps. At any rate, the prose will not compare with Sidney's. But it is good prose, nevertheless; and the phrase I have ventured to italicise is superb.

Their high claims for Poesy.

As might be expected, the poets in this volume agree in pride of their calling. We have just listened to Wordsworth. Shelley quotes Tasso's proud sentence—"Non c'è in mondo chi merita nome di creatore, se non Iddio ed il Poeta": and himself says, "The jury which sits in judgment upon a poet, belonging as he does to all time, must be composed of his peers: it must be impanelled by Time from the selectest of the wise of many generations." Sidney exalts the poet above the historian and the philosopher; and Coleridge asserts that "no man was ever yet a great poet without being at the same time a profound philosopher." Ben Jonson puts it characteristically: "Every beggarly corporation affords the State a mayor or two bailiffs yearly; but *Solus rex, aut poeta, non quotannis nascitur*." The longer one lives, the more cause one finds to rejoice that different men have different ways of saying the same thing.

Inspiration not Improvisation.

The agreement of all these poets on some other matters is more remarkable. Most of them claim *inspiration* for the great practitioners of their art; but wonderful is the unanimity with which they dissociate this from *improvisation*. They are sticklers for the rules of the game. The Poet does not pour his full heart

"In profuse strains of *unpremeditated* art."

On the contrary, his rapture is the sudden result of long premeditation. The first and most conspicuous lesson of this volume seems to be that Poetry is an *art*, and therefore has rules. Next after this, one is struck with the carefulness with which these practitioners, when it comes to theory, stick to their Aristotle.

Poetry not mere Metrical Composition.

For instance, they are practically unanimous in accepting Aristotle's contention that it is not the metrical form that makes the poem. "Verse," says Sidney, "is an ornament and no cause to poetry, since there have been many most excellent poets that never versified, and now swarm many versifiers that need never answer to the name of poets." Wordsworth apologizes for using the word "Poetry" as synonymous with metrical composition. "Much confusion," he says, "has been introduced into criticism by this contradistinction of Poetry and Prose, instead of the more philosophical one of Poetry and Matter of Fact or Science. The only strict antithesis to Prose is Metre: nor is this, in truth, a *strict* antithesis, because lines and passages of metre so naturally occur in writing prose that it would be scarcely possible to avoid them, even were it desirable." And Shelley—"It is by no means essential that a poet should accommodate his language to this traditional form, so that the harmony, which is its spirit, be observed…. The distinction between poets and prose writers is a vulgar error." Shelley goes on to instance Plato and Bacon as true poets, though they wrote in prose. "The popular division into prose and verse," he repeats, "is inadmissible in accurate philosophy."

Its philosophic function.

Then again, upon what Wordsworth calls "the more philosophical distinction" between Poetry and Matter of Fact—quoting, of course, the famous Φιλοσοφώτερον καὶ σπουδαιότερον passage in the *Poetics*—it is wonderful with what hearty consent our poets pounce upon this passage, and paraphrase it, and expand it, as the great justification of their art: which indeed it is. Sidney gives the passage at length. Wordsworth writes, "Aristotle, I have been told, hath said that Poetry is the most philosophic of all writings: it is so." Coleridge quotes Sir John Davies, who wrote of Poesy (surely with an eye on the *Poetics*):

"From their gross matter she abstracts their forms,
And draws a kind of quintessence from things;
Which to her proper nature she transforms
To bear them light on her celestial wings.

"Thus does she, when from individual states
She doth abstract the universal kinds;
Which then reclothed in divers names and fates
Steal access through our senses to our minds."

And Shelley has a remarkable paraphrase, ending, "The story of particular facts is as a mirror which obscures and distorts that which should be beautiful: poetry is a mirror which makes beautiful that which is distorted."

In fine, this book goes far to prove of poetry, as it has been proved over and over again of other arts, that it is the men big enough to break the rules who accept and observe them most cheerfully.

THE ATTITUDE OF THE PUBLIC TOWARDS LETTERS

Sept. 29, 1894. The "Great Heart" of the Public.

I observe that our hoary friend, the Great Heart of the Public, has been taking his annual outing in September. Thanks to the German Emperor and the new head of the House of Orleans, he has had the opportunity of a stroll through the public press arm in arm with his old crony and adversary, the Divine Right of Kings. And the two have gone once more a-roaming by the light of the moon, to drop a tear, perchance, on the graves of the Thin End of the Wedge and the Stake in the Country. You know the unhappy story?—how the Wedge drove its thin end into the Stake, with fatal results: and how it died of remorse and was buried at the cross-roads with the Stake in its inside! It is a pathetic tale, and the Great Heart of the Public can always be trusted to discriminate true pathos from false.

Miss Marie Corelli's Opinion of it.

It was Mr. G.B. Burgin, in the September number of the *Idler*, who let the Great Heart loose this time—unwittingly, I am sure; for Mr. Burgin, when he thinks for himself (as he usually does), writes sound sense and capital English. But in the service of Journalism Mr. Burgin called on Miss Marie Corelli, the authoress of *Barabbas*, and asked what she thought of the value of criticism. Miss Corelli "idealised the subject by the poetic manner in which she mingled tea and criticism together." She said—

"I think authors do not sufficiently bear in mind the important fact that, in this age of ours, the public *thinks for itself* much more extensively than we give it credit for. It is a cultured public, and its great brain is fully capable of deciding things. It rather objects to be treated like a child and told 'what to read and what to avoid'; and, moreover, we must not fail to note that it mistrusts criticism generally, and seldom reads 'reviews.' And why? Simply 'logrolling.' It is perfectly aware, for instance, that Mr. Theodore Watts is logroller-in-chief to Mr. Swinburne; that Mr. Le Gallienne 'rolls' greatly for Mr. Norman Gale; and that Mr. Andrew Lang tumbles his logs along over everything for as many as his humour fits...."

—I don't know the proportion of tea to criticism in all this: but Miss Corelli can hardly be said to "idealise the subject" here:—

" ... The public is the supreme critic; and though it does not write in the *Quarterly* or the *Nineteenth Century*, it thinks and talks independently of everything and everybody, and on its thought and word alone depends the fate of any piece of literature."

Mr. Hall Caine's View.

Then Mr. Burgin called on Mr. Hall Caine, who "had just finished breakfast." Mr. Hall Caine gave reasons which compelled him to believe that "for good or bad, criticism is a tremendous force." But he, too, confessed that in his opinion the public is the "ultimate critic." "It often happens that the public takes books on trust from the professed guides of literature, but if the books are not *right*, it drops them." And he proceeded to make an observation, with which we may most cordially agree. "I am feeling," he said, "increasingly, day by day, that *rightness* in imaginative writing is more important than subject, or style, or anything else. If a story is right in its theme, and the evolution of its theme, it will live; if it is not right, it will die, whatever its secondary literary qualities."

In what sense the Public is the "Ultimate Critic."

I say that we may agree with this most cordially: and it need not cost us much to own that the public is the "ultimate critic," if we mean no more than this, that, since the public holds the purse, it rests ultimately with the public to buy, or neglect to buy, an author's books. That, surely, is obvious enough without the aid of fine language. But if Mr. Hall Caine mean that the public, without instruction from its betters, is the best judge of a book; if he consent with Miss Corelli that the general public is a cultured public with a great brain, and by the exercise of that great brain approves itself an infallible judge of the rightness or wrongness of a book, then I would respectfully ask for evidence. The poets and critics of his time united in praising Campion as a writer of lyrics: the Great Brain and Heart of the Public neglected him utterly for three centuries: then a scholar and critic arose and persuaded the public that Campion was a great lyrical writer: and now the public accepts him as such. Shall we say, then, the Great Heart of the Public is the "ultimate judge" of Campion's lyrics? Perhaps: but we might as well praise for his cleanliness a boy who has been held under the pump. When Martin Farquhar Tupper wrote, the Great Heart of the Public expanded towards him at once. The public bought his effusions by tens of thousands. Gradually the small voice of skilled criticism made itself heard, and the public grew ashamed of itself; and, at length, laughed at Tupper. Shall we, then, call the public the ultimate judge of Tupper? Perhaps: but we might as well praise the continence of a man who turns in disgust from drink on the morning after a drunken fit.[A]

What is "The Public"?

The proposition that the Man in the Street is a better judge of literature than the Critic—the man who knows little than the man who knows more—wears (to my mind, at least) a slightly imbecile air on the face of it. It also appears to me that people are either confusing thought or misusing language when they confer the title of "supreme critic" on the last person to be persuaded. And, again, what is "the public?" I gather that Miss Corelli's story of *Barabbas* has had an immense popular success. But so, I believe, has the *Deadwood Dick* series of penny dreadfuls. And the gifted author of *Deadwood Dick* may console himself (as I daresay he does) for the neglect of the critics by the thought that the Great Brain[B] of the Public is the supreme judge of literature. But obviously he and Miss Corelli will not have the same Public in their mind. If for "the Great Brain of the Public" we substitute "the Great Brain of that Part of the Public which subscribes to Mudie's," we may lose something of impressiveness, but we shall at least know what we are talking about.

June 17, 1893. Mr. Gosse's View.

Astounding as the statement must appear to any constant reader of the Monthly Reviews, it is mainly because Mr. Gosse happens to be a man of letters that his opinion upon literary questions is worth listening to. In his new book[C] he discusses a dozen or so: and one of them—the question, "What Influence has Democracy upon Literature?"—not only has a chapter to itself, but seems to lie at the root of all the rest. I may add that Mr. Gosse's answer is a trifle gloomy.

"As we filed slowly out of the Abbey on the afternoon of Wednesday, the 12th of October, 1892, there must have occurred to others, I think, as to myself, a whimsical and half-terrifying sense of the symbolic contrast between what we had left and what we had emerged upon. Inside, the grey and vitreous atmosphere, the reverberations of music moaning somewhere out of sight, the bones and monuments of the noble dead, reverence, antiquity, beauty, rest. Outside, in the raw air, a tribe of hawkers urging upon the edges of a dense and inquisitive crowd a large sheet of pictures of the pursuit of a flea by a 'lady,' and more insidious salesmen doing a brisk trade in what they falsely pretended to be 'Tennyson's last poem.' Next day we read in our newspapers affecting accounts of the emotion displayed by the vast crowd outside the Abbey—horny hands dashing away the tear, seamstresses holding 'the little green volumes' to their faces to hide their agitation. Happy for those who could see these with their fairy telescopes out of the garrets of Fleet Street. I, alas!—though I sought assiduously—could mark nothing of the kind."

Nothing of the kind was there. Why should anything of the kind be there? Her poetry has been one of England's divinest treasures: but of her population a very few understand it; and the shrine has always been guarded by the elect who happen to possess, in varying degrees, certain qualities of mind and ear. It is, as Mr. Gosse puts it, by a sustained effort of bluff on the part of these elect that English poetry is kept upon its high pedestal of honor. The worship of it as one of the glories of our birth and state is imposed upon the masses by a small aristocracy of intelligence and taste.

Mr. Gissing's Testimony.

What do the "masses" care for poetry? In an appendix Mr. Gosse prints a letter from Mr. George Gissing, who, as everyone knows, has studied the popular mind assiduously, and with startling results. Here are a few sentences from his letter:—

(1) "After fifteen years' observation of the poorer classes of English folk, chiefly in London and the south, I am pretty well assured that, whatever civilising agencies may be at work among the democracy, poetry is not one of them."

(2) "The custodian of a Free Library in a southern city informs me that 'hardly once in a month' does a volume of verse pass over his counter; that the exceptional applicant (seeking Byron or Longfellow) is generally 'the wife of a tradesman;' and that an offer of verse to man or woman who comes simply for 'a book' is invariably rejected; 'they won't even look at it.'"

(3) "It was needless folly to pretend that, because one or two of Tennyson's poems became largely known through popular recitation, therefore Tennyson was dear to the heart of the people, a subject of their pride whilst he lived, of their mourning when he died. My point is that *no* poet holds this place in the esteem of the English lower orders."

(4) "Some days before (the funeral) I was sitting in a public room, where two men, retired shopkeepers, exchanged an occasional word as they read the morning's news. 'A great deal here about Lord Tennyson' said one. The 'Lord' was significant. I listened anxiously for his companion's reply. 'Ah, yes.' The man moved uneasily, and added at once: 'What do you think about this long-distance ride?' In that room (I frequented it on successive days with this object) not a syllable did I hear regarding Tennyson save the sentence faithfully recorded."

Poetry not beloved by any one Class.

Mr. Gissing, be it observed, speaks only of the class which he has studied: but in talking of "demos," or, more loosely, of "democracy," we must be careful not to limit these terms to the "lower" and "lower-middle" classes.

For Poetry, who draws her priests and warders from all classes of society, is generally beloved of none. The average country magnate, the average church dignitary, the average professional man, the average commercial traveller—to all these she is alike unknown: at least, the insensibility of each is differentiated by shades so fine that we need not trouble ourselves to make distinctions. A public school and university education does as little for the Squire Westerns one meets at country dinner-tables as a three-guinea subscription to a circulating library for the kind of matron one comes upon at a *table d'hôte*. Five minutes after hearing the news of Browning's death I stopped an acquaintance in the street, a professional man of charming manner, and repeated it to him. He stared for a moment, and then murmured that he was sorry to hear it. Clearly he did not wish to hurt my feelings by confessing that he hadn't the vaguest idea who Browning might be. And if anybody think this an extreme case, let him turn to the daily papers and read the names of those who were at Newmarket on that same afternoon when our great poet was laid in the Abbey with every pretence of national grief. The pursuit of one horse by another is doubtless a more elevating spectacle than "the pursuit of a flea by a 'lady,'" but on that afternoon even a tepid lover of letters must have found an equal incongruity in both entertainments.

I do not say that the General Public hates Poetry. But I say that those who care about it are few, and those who know about it are fewer. Nor do these assert their right of interference as often as they might. Just once or twice in the last ten or fifteen years they have pulled up some exceptionally coarse weed on which the General Public had every disposition to graze, and have pitched it over the hedge to Lethe wharf, to root itself and fatten there; and terrible as those of Polydorus have been the shrieks of the avulsed root. But as a rule they have sat and piped upon the stile and considered the good cow grazing, confident that in the end she must "bite off more than she can chew."

The "Outsiders."

Still, the aristocracy of letters exists: and in it, if nowhere else, titles, social advantages, and commercial success alike count for nothing; while Royalty itself sits in the Court of the Gentiles. And I am afraid we must include in the crowd not only those affable politicians who from time to time open a Public Library and oblige us with their views upon literature, little realizing what Hecuba is to them, and still less what they are to Hecuba, but also those affable teachers of religion, philosophy, and science, who condescend occasionally to amble through the garden of the Muses, and rearrange its labels for us while drawing our attention to the rapid deterioration of the flowerbeds. The author of *The Citizen of the World* once compared the profession of letters in England to a Persian army, "where there are many pioneers, several suttlers, numberless servants, women and children in abundance, and but few soldiers." Were he alive to-day he would be forced to include the Volunteers.

FOOTNOTES:

[A] In a private letter, from which I am allowed to quote, Mr. Hall Caine (October 2nd, 1894) explains and (as I think) amends his position:—"If I had said *time* instead of *the public*, I should have expressed myself exactly. It is impossible for me to work up any enthusiasm for the service done to literature by criticism as a whole. I have, no doubt, the unenviable advantage over you of having wasted three mortal months in reading all the literary criticism extant of the first quarter of this century. It would be difficult to express my sense of its imbecility, its blundering, and its bad passions. But the good books it assailed are not lost, and the bad ones it glorified do not survive. It is not that the public has been the better judge, but that good work has the seeds of life, while bad work carries with it the seeds of dissolution. This is the key to the story of Wordsworth on the one hand, and to the story of Tupper on the other. Tupper did not topple down because James Hannay smote him. Fifty James Hannays had shouted him up before. And if there had not been a growing sense that the big mountain was a mockery, five hundred James Hannays would not have brought it down. The truth is that it is not the 'critic who knows' or the public which does not know that determines the ultimate fate of a book—the immediate fate they may both influence. The book must do that for itself. If it is right, it lives; if it is wrong, it dies. And the critic who re-establishes a neglected poet is merely articulating the growing sense. There have always been a few good critics, thank God ... but the finest critic is the untutored sentiment of the public, not of to-day or to-morrow or the next day, but of all days together—a sentiment which tells if a thing is right or wrong by holding on to it or letting it drop."

Of course, I agree that a book must ultimately depend for its fate upon its own qualities. But when Mr. Hall Caine talks of "a growing sense," I ask, In whom does this sense first grow? And I answer, In the cultured few who enforce it upon the many—as in this very case of Wordsworth. And I hold the credit of the result (apart from the author's share) belongs rather to those few persistent advocates than to those judges who are only "ultimate" in the sense that they are the last to be convinced.

[B] If the reader object that I am using the Great Heart and Great Brain of the Public as interchangeable terms, I would refer him to Mr. Du Maurier's famous Comic Alphabet, letter Z:—

"Z is a Zoophyte, whose heart's in his head,
And whose head's in his turn—rudimentary Z!"

[C] *Questions at Issue*; by Edmund Gosse. London: William Heinemann.

A CASE OF BOOKSTALL CENSORSHIP

March 16, 1895. The "Woman Who Did," and Mr. Eason who wouldn't.

"In the romantic little town of 'Ighbury,
My father kept a Succulating Libary...."

—and, I regret to say, gave himself airs on the strength of it.

The persons in my instructive little story are—

H.H. Prince Francis of Teck.

Mr. Grant Allen, author of *The Woman Who Did*.

Mr. W.T. Stead, Editor of *The Review of Reviews*.

Messrs. Eason & Son, booksellers and newsvendors, possessing on the railways of Ireland a monopoly similar to that enjoyed by Messrs. W.H. Smith & Son on the railways of Great Britain.

Mr. James O'Hara, of 18, Cope Street, Dublin.

A Clerk.

Now, on the appearance of Mr. Grant Allen's *The Woman Who Did*, Mr. Stead conceived the desire of criticising it as the "Book of the Month" in *The Review of Reviews* for February, 1895. He strongly dissents from the doctrine of *The Woman Who Did*, and he also believes that the book indicts, and goes far to destroy, its own doctrine. This opinion, I may say, is shared by many critics. He says "Wedlock is to Mr. Grant Allen *Nehushtan*. And the odd thing about it is that the net effect of the book which he has written with his heart's blood to destroy this said *Nehushtan* can hardly fail to strengthen the foundation of reasoned conviction upon which marriage rests." And again—"Those who do not know the author, but who take what I must regard as the saner view of the relations of the sexes, will rejoice at what might have been a potent force for evil has been so strangely overruled as to become a reinforcement of the garrison defending the citadel its author desires so ardently to overthrow. From the point of view of the fervent apostle of Free Love, this is a Boomerang of a Book."

Believing this—that the book would be its own best antidote—Mr. Stead epitomized it in his *Review*, printed copious extracts, and wound up by indicating his own views and what he deemed the true moral of the discussion. The *Review* was published and, so far as Messrs. W.H. Smith & Son were concerned, passed without comment. But to the Editor's surprise (he tells the story in the *Westminster Gazette* of the 2nd inst.), no sooner was it placed on the market in Ireland than he received word that every copy had been recalled from the bookstalls, and that Messrs. Eason had refused to sell a single copy. On telegraphing for more information, Mr. Stead was sent the following letter:—

"DEAR SIR,—Allen's book is an avowed defence of Free Love, and a direct attack upon the Christian view of marriage. Mr. Stead criticises Allen's views adversely, but we do not think the antidote can destroy the ill-effects of the poison, and we decline to be made the vehicle for the distribution of attacks upon the most fundamental institution of the Christian state.—Yours faithfully,

———."

Mr. Stead thereupon wrote to the managing Director of Messrs. Eason & Son, and received this reply:—

"DEAR SIR,—We have considered afresh the character of the February number of your *Review* so far as it relates to the notice of Grant Allen's book, and we are more and more confirmed in the belief that its influence has been, and is, most pernicious.

"Grant Allen is not much heard of in Ireland, and the laudations you pronounce on him as a writer, so far as we know him, appear wholly unmerited.

"At any rate, he appears in your *Review* as the advocate for Free Love, and it seems to us strange that you should place his work in the exaggerated importance of 'The Book of the Month,' accompanied by eighteen pages of comment and quotation, in which there is a publicity given to the work out of all proportion to its merits.

"I do not doubt that the topic of Free Love engages the attention of the corrupt Londoner. There are plenty of such persons who are only too glad to get the sanction of writers for the maintenance and practice of their evil thoughts, but the purest and best lives in all parts of the field of Christian philanthropy will mourn the publicity you have given to this evil book. It is not even improbable that the perusal of Grant Allen's book, which you have lifted into importance as 'The Book of the Month,' may determine the action of souls to their spiritual ruin.

"The problem of indirect influence is full of mystery, but, as the hour of our departure comes near, the possible consequences to other minds of the example and teaching of our lives may quicken our perceptions, and we may see and deeply regret our actions when not directed by the highest authority, the will of God.—We are, dear Sir, yours very truly (for Eason & Son, Limited),

"CHARLES EASON, Managing Director."

Exception may be taken to this letter on many points, some trivial and some important. Of the trivial points we may note with interest Mr. Eason's assumption that his opinion is wanted on the literary merits of the ware he vends; and, with concern, the rather slipshod manner in which he allows himself and his assistants to speak of a gentleman as "Allen," or "Grant Allen," without the usual prefix. But no one can fail to see that this is an honest letter—the production of a man conscious of responsibility and struggling to do his best in circumstances he imperfectly understands. Nor do I think this view of Mr. Eason need be seriously modified upon perusal of a letter received by Mr. Stead from a Mr. James O'Hara, of 18, Cope Street, Dublin, and printed in the *Westminster Gazette* of March 11th. Mr. O'Hara writes:—

Mr. Eason in Two Attitudes.

"DEAR SIR,—The following may interest you and your readers. I was a subscriber to the library owned by C. Eason & Co., Limited, and in December asked them for *Napoleon and the Fair Sex*, by Masson. The librarian informed me Mr. Eason had decided not to circulate it, as it contained improper details, which Mr. Eason considered immoral. A copy was also refused to one of the best-known pressmen in Dublin, a man of mature years and experience.

"Three days afterwards I saw a young man ask the librarian for the same book, and Eason's manager presented it to him with a low bow. I remarked on this circumstance to Mr. Charles Eason, who told me that he had issued it to this one subscriber only, because he was Prince Francis of Teck.

"I told him it was likely, from the description he had given me of it, to be more injurious to a young man such as Prince Francis of Teck than to me; but he replied: 'Oh, these high-up people *are different*. Besides, they are so influential we cannot refuse them. However, if you wish, you can now have the book.'

"I told Mr. Eason that I did not wish to read it ever since he had told me when I first applied for it that it was quite improper."

The two excuses produced by Mr. Eason do not agree very well together. The first gives us to understand that, in Mr. Eason's opinion, ordinary moral principles cannot be applied to persons of royal blood. The second gives us to understand that though, in Mr. Eason's opinion, ordinary moral principles *can* be applied to princes, the application would involve more risk than Mr. Eason cares to undertake. Each of his excuses, taken apart, is intelligible enough. Taken together they can hardly be called consistent. But the effects of royal and semi-royal splendor upon the moral eyesight are well known, and need not be dwelt on here. After all, what concerns us is not Mr. Eason's attitude towards Prince Francis of Teck, but Mr. Eason's attitude towards the reading public. And in this respect, from one point of view—which happens to be his own—Mr. Eason's attitude seems to me irreproachable. He is clearly alive to his responsibility, and is honestly concerned that the goods he purveys to the public shall be goods of which his conscience approves. Here is no grocer who sands his sugar before hurrying to family prayer. Here is a man who carries his religion into his business, and stakes his honor on the purity of his wares. I think it would be wrong in the extreme to deride Mr. Eason's action in the matter of *The Woman Who Did* and Mr. Stead's review. He is doing his best, as Mr. Stead cheerfully allows.

The reasonable Objection to Bookstall Censorship.

But, as I said above, he is doing his best under circumstances he imperfectly understands—and, let me add here, in a position which is unfair to him. That Mr. Eason imperfectly understands his position will be plain (I think) to anyone who studies his reply to Mr. Stead. But let me make the point clear; for it is the crucial point in the discussion of the modern Bookstall Censorship. A great deal may be said against setting up a censorship of literature. A great deal may be said in favor of a censorship. But if a censorship there must be, the censor should be deliberately chosen for his office, and, in exercising his power, should be directly responsible to the public conscience. If a censorship there must be, let the community choose a man whose qualifications have been weighed, a man in whose judgment it decides that it can rely. But that Tom or Dick or Harry, or Tom Dick Harry & Co. (Limited), by the process of collaring a commercial monopoly from the railway companies, should be exalted into the supreme arbiters of what men or women may or may not be allowed to read—this surely is unjustifiable by any argument? Mr. Eason may on the whole be doing more good than harm. He is plainly a very well-meaning man of business. If he knows a good book from a bad—and the public has no reason to suppose that he does—I can very well believe that when his moral and literary judgment came into conflict with his business interests, he would sacrifice his business interests. But the interests of good literature and profitable business cannot always be identical; and whenever they conflict they put Mr. Eason into a false position. As managing director of Messrs. Eason & Son, he must consider his shareholders; as supreme arbiter of letters, he stands directly answerable to the public conscience. I protest, therefore, that these functions should never be combined in one man. As readers of THE SPEAKER know, I range myself on the side of those who would have literature free. But even our opponents, who desire control, must desire a form of control such as reason approves.

THE POOR LITTLE PENNY DREADFUL

Oct. 5, 1895. Our "Crusaders."

The poor little Penny Dreadful has been catching it once more. Once more the British Press has stripped to its massive waist and solemnly squared up to this hardened young offender. It calls this remarkable performance a "Crusade."

I like these Crusades. They remind one of that merry passage in *Pickwick* (p. 254 in the first edition):—

"Whether Mr. Winkle was seized with a temporary attack of that species of insanity which originates in a sense of injury, or animated by this display of Mr. Weller's valour, is uncertain; but certain it is, that he no sooner saw Mr. Grummer fall, than *he made a terrific onslaught on a small boy who stood next to him*; whereupon Mr. Snodgrass—"

[Pay attention to Mr. Snodgrass, if you please, and cast your memories back a year or two, to the utterances of a famous Church Congress on the National Vice of Gambling.]

"—whereupon Mr. Snodgrass, in a truly Christian spirit, and in order that he might take no one unawares, announced in a very loud tone that he was going to begin, and proceeded to take off his coat with the utmost deliberation. He was immediately surrounded and secured; and it is but common justice both to him and to Mr. Winkle to say that they did not make the slightest attempt to rescue either themselves or Mr. Weller, who, after a most vigorous resistance, was overpowered by numbers and taken prisoner. The procession then reformed, the chairmen resumed their stations, and the march was re-commenced."

"The chairmen resumed their stations, and the march was re-commenced." Is it any wonder that Dickens and Labiche have found no fit successors? One can imagine the latter laying down his pen and confessing himself beaten at his own game; for really this periodical "crusade" upon the Penny Dreadful has all the qualities of the very best vaudeville—the same bland exhibition of *bourgeois* logic, the same wanton appreciation of evidence, the same sententious alacrity in seizing the immediate explanation—the more trivial the better—the same inability to reach the remote cause, the same profound unconsciousness of absurdity.

You remember *La Grammaire*? Caboussat's cow has eaten a piece of broken glass, with fatal results. Machut, the veterinary, comes:—

Caboussat. "Un morceau de verre ... est-ce drole? Une vache de quatre ans."

Machut. "Ah! monsieur, les vaches ... ça avale du verre à tout âge. J'en ai connu une qui a mangé une éponge à laver les cabriolets ... à sept ans! Elle en est morte."

Caboussat. "Ce que c'est que notre pauvre humanité!"

Penny Dreadfuls and Matricide.

Our friends have been occupied with the case of a half-witted boy who consumed Penny Dreadfuls and afterwards went and killed his mother. They infer that he killed his mother because he had read Penny Dreadfuls (*post hoc ergo propter hoc*) and they conclude very naturally that Penny Dreadfuls should be suppressed. But before roundly pronouncing the doom of this—to me unattractive—branch of fiction, would it not be well to inquire a trifle more deeply into cause and effect? In the first place matricide is so utterly unnatural a crime that there must be something abominably peculiar in a form of literature that persuades to it. But a year or two back, on the occasion of a former crusade, I took the pains to study a considerable number of Penny Dreadfuls. My reading embraced all those—I believe I am right in saying all—which were reviewed, a few days back, in the *Daily Chronicle*; and some others. I give you my word I could find nothing peculiar about them. They were even rather ostentatiously on the side of virtue. As for the bloodshed in them, it would not compare with that in many of the five-shilling adventure stories at that time read so eagerly by boys of the middle and upper classes. The style was ridiculous, of course: but a bad style excites nobody but a reviewer, and does not even excite him to deeds of the kind we are now trying to account for. The reviewer in the *Daily Chronicle* thinks worse of these books than I do. But he certainly failed to quote anything from them that by the wildest fancy could be interpreted as sanctioning such a crime as matricide.

The Cause to be sought in the Boy rather than in the Book.

Let us for a moment turn our attention from the Penny Dreadful to the boy—from the *éponge á laver les cabriolets* to *notre pauvre humanité*. Now—to speak quite seriously—it is well known to every doctor and every schoolmaster (and should be known, if it is not, to every parent), that all boys sooner or later pass through a crisis in growth during which absolutely nothing can be predicted of their behavior. At such times honest boys have given way to lying and theft, gentle boys have developed an unexpected savagery, ordinary boys—"the small apple-eating urchins whom we know"—have fallen into morbid brooding upon unhealthy subjects. In the immense majority of cases the crisis is soon over and the boy is himself again; but while it lasts, the disease will draw its sustenance from all manner of things—things, it may be, in themselves quite innocent. I avoid particularizing for many reasons; but any observant doctor will confirm what I have said. Now the moderately affluent boy who reads five-shilling stories of adventure has many advantages at this period over the poor boy who reads Penny Dreadfuls. To begin with, the crisis has a tendency to attack him later. Secondly, he meets it fortified by a better training and more definite ideas of the difference between right and wrong, virtue and vice. Thirdly (and this is very important), he is probably under school discipline at the time—which means, that he is to some extent watched and shielded. When I think of these advantages, I frankly confess that the difference in the literature these two boys read seems to me to count for very little. I myself have written "adventure-stories" before now: stories which, I suppose—or, at any rate, hope—would come into the class of "Pure Literature," as the term is understood by those who have been writing on this subject in the newspapers. They were, I hope, better written than the run of Penny Dreadfuls, and perhaps with more discrimination of taste in the choice of adventures. But I certainly do not feel able to claim that their effect upon a perverted mind would be innocuous.

Fallacy of the "Crusade."

For indeed it is not possible to name any book out of which a perverted mind will not draw food for its disease. The whole fallacy lies in supposing literature the cause of the disease. Evil men are not evil because they read bad books: they read bad books because they are evil: and being evil, or diseased, they are quickly able to extract evil or disease even from very good books. There is talk of disseminating the works of our best authors, at a cheap rate, in the hope that they will drive the Penny Dreadful out of the market. But has good literature at the cheapest driven the middle classes from their false gods? And let it be remembered, to the credit of these poor boys, that they do buy their books. The middle classes take *their* poison on hire or exchange.

But perhaps the full enormity of the cant about Penny Dreadfuls can best be perceived by travelling to and fro for a week between London and Paris and observing the books read by those who travel with first-class tickets. I think a fond belief in Ivanhoe-within-the-reach-of-all would not long survive that experiment.

IBSEN'S "PEER GYNT"

Oct. 7, 1892. A Masterpiece.

"*Peer Gynt* takes its place, as we hold, on the summits of literature precisely because it means so much more than the poet consciously intended. Is not this one of the characteristics of the masterpiece, that everyone can read in it his own secret? In the material world (though Nature is very innocent of symbolic intention) each of us finds for himself the symbols that have relevance and value for him; and so it is with the poems that are instinct with true vitality."

I was glad to come across the above passage in Messrs. William and Charles Archer's introduction to their new translation of Ibsen's *Peer Gynt* (London: Walter Scott), because I can now, with a clear conscience, thank the writers for their book, even though I fail to find some of the things they find in it. The play's the thing after all. *Peer Gynt* is a great poem: let us shake hands over that. It will remain a great poem when we have ceased pulling it about to find what is inside or search out texts for homilies in defence of our own particular views of life. The world's literature stands unaffected, though Archdeacon Farrar use it for chapter-headings and Sir John Lubbock wield it as a mallet to drive home self-evident truths.

Not a Pamphlet.

Peer Gynt is an extremely modern story founded on old Norwegian folk-lore—the folk-lore which Asbjörnsen and Moe collected, and Dasent translated for our delight in childhood. Old and new are curiously mixed; but the result is piquant and not in the least absurd, because the story rests on problems which are neither old nor new, but eternal, and on emotions which are neither older nor newer than the breast of man. To be sure, the true devotee of Ibsen will not be content with this. You will be told by Herr Jaeger, Ibsen's biographer, that *Peer Gynt* is an attack on Norwegian romanticism. The poem, by the way, is romantic to the core—so romantic, indeed, that the culminating situation, and the page for which everything has been a preparation, have to be deplored by Messrs. Archer as "a mere commonplace of romanticism, which Ibsen had not outgrown when he wrote *Peer Gynt*." But your true votary is for ever taking his god off the pedestal of the true artist to set him on the tub of the hot-gospeller; even so genuine a specimen of impressionist work as *Hedda Gabler* being claimed by him for a sermon. And if ever you have been moved by *Ghosts*, or *Brand*, or *Peer Gynt* to exclaim "This is poetry!" you have only to turn to Herr Jaeger—whose criticism, like his namesake's underclothing, should be labelled "All Pure Natural Wool"—to find that you were mistaken and that it is really pamphleteering.

Yet Enforcing a Moral.

To be sure, in one sense *Peer Gynt* is a sermon upon a text. That is to say, it is written primarily to expound one view of man's duty, not to give a mere representation of life. The problem, not the picture, is the main thing. But then the problem, not the picture, is the main thing in *Alcestis, Hamlet, Faust.* In *Peer Gynt* the poet's own solution of the problem is presented with more insistence than in *Alcestis, Hamlet,* or *Faust*: but the problem is wider, too.

The problem is, What is self? and how shall a man be himself? And the poet's answer is, "Self is only found by being lost, gained by being given away": an answer at least as old as the gospels. The eponymous hero of the story is a man essentially half-hearted, "the incarnation of a compromising dread of self-committal to any one course," a fellow who says,

"Ay, think of it—wish it done—*will* it to boot,
But *do* it——. No, that's past my understanding!"

—who is only stung to action by pique, or by what is called the "instinct of self-preservation," an instinct which, as Ibsen shows, is the very last that will preserve self.

The Story.

This fellow, Peer Gynt, wins the love of Solveig, a woman essentially whole-hearted, who has no dread of self-committal, who surrenders self. Solveig, in short, stands in perfect antithesis to Peer. When Peer is an outlaw she deserts her father's house and follows him to his hut in the forest. The scene in which she presents herself before Peer and claims to share his lot is worthy to stand beside the ballad of the Nut-browne Mayde: indeed, as a confessed romantic I must own to thinking Solveig one of the most beautiful figures in poetry. Peer deserts her, and she lives in the hut alone and grows an old woman while her lover roams the world, seeking everywhere and through the wildest adventures the satisfaction of his Self, acting everywhere on the Troll's motto, "To thyself be enough," and finding everywhere his major premiss turned against him, to his own discomfiture, by an ironical fate. We have one glimpse of Solveig, meanwhile, in a little scene of eight lines. She is now a middle-aged woman, up in her forest hut in the far north. She sits spinning in the sunshine outside her door and sings:—

"Maybe both the winter and spring will pass by,
And the next summer too, and the whole of the year;
But thou wilt come one day....
*   *   *   *   *   *   *

God strengthen thee, whereso thou goest in the world!
God gladden thee, if at His footstool thou stand!

Here will I await thee till thou comest again;
And if thou wait up yonder, then there we'll meet, my friend!"

At last Peer, an old man, comes home. On the heath around his old hut he finds (in a passage which the translators call "fantastic," intending, I hope, approval by this word) the thoughts he has missed thinking, the watchword he has failed to utter, the tears he has missed shedding, the deed he has missed doing. The thoughts are thread-balls, the watchword withered leaves, the tears dewdrops, etc. Also he finds on that heath a Button-Moulder with an immense ladle. The Button-Moulder explains to Peer that he must go into this ladle, for his time has come. He has neither been a good man nor a sturdy sinner, but a half-and-half fellow without any real self in him. Such men are dross, badly cast buttons with no loops to them, and must go, by the Master's orders, into the melting-pot again. Is there no escape? None, unless Peer can find the loop of the button, his real Self, the Peer Gynt that God made. After vain and frantic searching across the heath, Peer reaches the door of his own old hut. Solveig stands on the threshold.

As Peer flings himself to earth before her, calling out upon her to denounce him, she sits down by his side and says—

"Thou hast made all my life as a beautiful song.
Blessed be thou that at last thou hast come!
Blessed, thrice-blessed our Whitsun-morn meeting!"

"But," says Peer, "I am lost, unless thou canst answer riddles." "Tell me them," tranquilly answers Solveig. And Peer asks, while the Button-Moulder listens behind the hut—

"Canst thou tell me where Peer Gynt has been since we parted?"

Solveig.—*Been?*

Peer.— *With his destiny's seal on his brow;*
Been, as in God's thought he first sprang forth?
Canst thou tell me? If not, I must get me home,—
Go down to the mist-shrouded regions.

Solveig (smiling).—*Oh, that riddle is easy.*

Peer.— *Then tell what thou knowest!*
Where was I, as myself, as the whole man, the true man?
Where was I, with God's sigil upon my brow?

Solveig.—*In my faith, in my hope, in my love.*

A Shirking of the Ethical Problem?

"This," says the Messrs. Archer, in effect, "may be—indeed is—magnificent: but it is not Ibsen." To quote their very words—

"The redemption of the hero through a woman's love ... we take to be a mere commonplace of romanticism, which Ibsen, though he satirised it, had by no means fully outgrown when he wrote *Peer Gynt*. Peer's return to Solveig is (in the original) a passage of the most poignant lyric beauty, but it is surely a shirking, not a solution, of the ethical problem. It would be impossible to the Ibsen of to-day, who knows (none better) that *No man can save his brother's soul, or pay his brother's debt*."

In a footnote to the italicized words Messrs. Archer add the quotation—

"No, nor woman, neither."

Oct. 22, 1892. The main Problem.

"Peer's return to Solveig is surely a shirking, not a solution of the ethical problem." Of what ethical problem? The main ethical problem of the poem is, What is self? And how shall a man be himself? As Mr. Wicksteed puts it in his "Four Lectures on Henrik Ibsen," "What is it to be one's self? God *meant something* when He made each one of us. For a man to embody that meaning of God in his words and deeds, and so become, in a degree, 'a word of God made flesh' is to be himself. But thus to be himself he must slay himself. That is to say, he must slay the craving to make himself the centre round which others revolve, and must strive to find his true orbit, and swing, self poised, round the great central light. But what if a poor devil can never puzzle out what God *did* mean when He made him? Why, then he must *feel* it. But how often your 'feeling' misses fire! Ay, there you have it. The devil has no stancher ally than *want of perception*."

And its Solution.

This is a fair statement of Ibsen's problem and his solution of it. In the poem he solves it by the aid of two characters, two diagrams we may say. Diagram I. is Peer Gynt, a man who is always striving to make himself the centre round which others revolve, who never sacrifices his Self generously for another's good, nor surrenders it to a decided course of action. Diagram II. is Solveig, a woman who has no dread of self-committal, who surrenders Self and is, in short, Peer's perfect antithesis. When Peer is an outlaw she forsakes all and follows him to his hut in the forest. Peer deserts her and roams the world, where he finds his theory of Self upset by one adventure after another and at last reduced to absurdity in the madhouse at Cairo. But though his own theory is discredited, he has not yet found the true one. To find this he must be brought face to face in the last scene with his deserted wife. There, for the first time, he asks the question and receives the answer. "Where," he asks, "has Peer Gynt's true self been since we parted:—

"Where was I, as myself, as the whole man, the true man?
Where was I with God's sigil upon my brow?"

And Solveig answers:—

"In my faith, in my hope, in my love."

In these words we have the main ethical problem solved; and Peer's *perception* of the truth (*vide* Mr. Wicksteed's remarks quoted above) is the one necessary climax of the poem. We do not care a farthing—at least, I do not care a farthing—whether Peer escape the Button-Moulder or not. It may be too late for him, or there may be yet time to live another life; but whatever the case may be, it doesn't alter what Ibsen set out to prove. The problem which Ibsen shirks (if indeed he does shirk it) is a subsidiary problem—a rider, so to speak. Can Solveig by her love redeem Peer Gynt? Can the woman save the man's soul? Will she, after all, cheat the Button-Moulder of his victim?

The poet, by giving Solveig the last word, seems to think it possible. According to Mr. Archer, the Ibsen of to-day would know it to be impossible. He knows (none better) that "No man can save his brother's soul or pay his brother's debt." "No, nor women neither," adds Mr. Archer.

Is Peer's Redemption a romantic Fallacy?

But is this so? *Peer Gynt* was published in 1867. I turn to *A Doll's House*, written twelve years later, and I find there a woman preparing to redeem a man just as Solveig prepares to redeem Peer. I find in Mr. Archer's translation of that play the following page of dialogue:—

Mrs. Linden: There's no happiness in working for oneself, Nils; give me somebody and something to work for.

Krogstad: No, no; that can never be. It's simply a woman's romantic notion of self-sacrifice.

Mrs. Linden: Have you ever found me romantic?

Krogstad: Would you really—? Tell me, do you know my past?

Mrs. Linden: Yes.

Krogstad: And do you know what people say of me?

Mrs. Linden: Didn't you say just now that with me you could have been another man?

Krogstad: I am sure of it.

Mrs. Linden: Is it too late?

Krogstad: Christina, do you know what you are doing? Yes, you do; I see it in your face. Have you the courage—?

Mrs. Linden: I need someone to tend, and your children need a mother. You need me, and I—I need you. Nils, I believe in your better self. With you I fear nothing.

Ibsen's hopes of Enfranchised Women.

Again, we are not told if Mrs. Linden's experiment is successful; but Ibsen certainly gives no hint that she is likely to fail. This was in 1879. In 1885 Ibsen paid a visit to Norway and made a speech to some workingmen at Drontheim, in which this passage occurred:—

"Democracy by itself cannot solve the social question. We must introduce an aristocratic element into our life. I am not referring, of course, to an aristocracy of birth, or of purse, or even of intellect. I mean an aristocracy of character, of will, of mind. That alone can make us free. From two classes will this aristocracy I desire come to us—*from our women and our workmen*. The social revolution, now preparing in Europe, is chiefly concerned with the future of the workers and the women. On this I set all my hopes and expectations...."

I think it would be easy to multiply instances showing that, though Ibsen may hold that no man can save his brother's soul, he does not extend this disability to women, but hopes and believes, on the contrary, that women will redeem mankind. On men he builds little hope. To speak roughly, men are all in Peer Gynt's case, or Torvald Helmer's. They are swathed in timid conventions, blindfolded with selfishness, so that they cannot perceive, and unable with their own hands to tear off these bandages. They are incapable of the highest renunciation. "No man," says Torvald Helmer, "sacrifices his honor, even for one he loves." Those who heard Miss Achurch deliver Nora's reply will not easily forget it. "Millions of women have done so." The effect in the theatre was tremendous. This sentence clinched the whole play.

Millions of women are, like Solveig, capable of renouncing all for love, of surrendering self altogether; and, as I read Ibsen, it is precisely on this power of renunciation that he builds his hope of man's redemption. So that, unless I err greatly, the scene in *Peer Gynt* which Mr. Archer calls a shirking of the ethical problem, is just the solution which Ibsen has been persistent in presenting to the world.

Let it be understood, of course, that it is only your Solveigs and Mrs. Lindens who can thus save a brother's soul: women who have made their own way in the world, thinking for themselves, working for themselves, freed from the conventions which man would impose on them. I know Mr. Archer will not retort on me with Nora, who leaves her husband and children, and claims that her first duty is to herself. Nora is just the woman who cannot redeem a man. Her Doll's House training is the very opposite of Solveig's and Mrs. Linden's. She is a silly girl brought up amid conventions, and awakened, by one blow, to the responsibilities of life. That she should at once know the right course to take would be incredible in real life, and impossible in a play the action of which has been evolved as inevitably as real life. Many critics have supposed Ibsen to commend Nora's conduct in the last act of the play. He neither sanctions nor condemns. But he does contrast her in the play with Mrs. Linden, and I do not think that contrast can be too carefully studied.

MR. SWINBURNE'S LATER MANNER

May 5, 1894. Aloofness of Mr. Swinburne's Muse.

There was a time—let us say, in the early seventies—when many young men tried to write like Mr. Swinburne. Remarkably small success waited on their efforts. Still their numbers and their youth and (for a while also) their persistency seemed to promise a new school of poesy, with Mr. Swinburne for its head and great exemplar: exemplar rather than head, for Mr. Swinburne's attitude amid all this devotion was rather that of the god than of the priest. He sang, and left the worshippers to work up their own enthusiasm. And to this attitude he has been constant. Unstinting, and occasionally unmeasured, in praise and dispraise of other men, he has allowed his own reputation the noble liberty to look after itself. Nothing, for instance, could have been finer than the careless, almost disdainful, dignity of his bearing in the months that followed Tennyson's death. The cats were out upon the tiles, then, and his was the luminous, expressive silence of a sphere. One felt, "whether he received it or no, here is the man who can wear the crown."

And Her Tendency towards Abstractions.

It was not, however, the aloofness of Mr. Swinburne's bearing that checked the formation of a Swinburnian school of poetry. The cause lay deeper, and has come more and more into the light in the course of Mr. Swinburne's poetic development—let me say, his thoroughly normal development. We can see now that from the first such a school, such a successful following, was an impossibility. The fact is that Mr. Swinburne has not only genius, but an extremely rare and individual genius. The germ of this individuality may be found, easily enough, in "Atalanta" and the Ballads; but it luxuriates in his later poems and throughout them—flower and leaf and stem. It was hardly more natural in 1870 to confess the magic of the great chorus, "Before the beginning of years," or of "Dolores," than to embark upon the vain adventure of imitating them. I cannot imagine a youth in all Great Britain so green or unknowing as to attempt an imitation of "A Nympholept," perhaps the finest poem in the volume before me.

I say "in Great Britain;" because peculiar as Mr. Swinburne's genius would be in any country, it is doubly peculiar as the endowment of an English poet. If there be one quality beloved above others by the inhabitants of this island, it is concreteness; and I suppose there never was a poet in the world who used less concreteness of speech than Mr. Swinburne. Mr. Palgrave once noted that the landscape of Keats falls short of the landscape of Shelley in its comparative lack of the larger features of sky and earth; Keats's was "foreground work" for the most part. But what shall be said of Shelley's universe after the immense vague regions inhabited by Mr. Swinburne's muse? She sings of the sea; but we never behold a sail, never a harbor: she sings of passion—among the stars. We seem never to touch earth; page after page is full of thought—for, vast as the strain may be, it is never empty—but we cannot apply it. And all this is extremely distressing to the Briton, who loves practice as his birthright. He comes on a Jacobite song. "Now, at any rate," he tells himself, "we arrive at something definite: some allusion, however small, to Bonny Prince Charlie." He reads—

"Faith speaks when hope dissembles;
Faith lives when hope lies dead:
If death as life dissembles,
And all that night assembles
Of stars at dawn lie dead,
Faint hope that smiles and trembles
May tell not well for dread:
But faith has heard it said."

"Very beautiful," says the Briton; "but why call this a 'Jacobite Song'?" Some thorough-going admirer of Mr. Swinburne will ask, no doubt, if I prefer gush about Bonny Prince Charlie. Most decidedly I do not. I am merely pointing out that the poet cares so little for the common human prejudice in favor of concreteness of speech as to give us a Jacobite song which, for all its indebtedness to the historical facts of the Jacobite Risings, might just as well have been put in the mouth of Judas Maccabæus.

Somebody—I forget for the moment who it was—compared Poetry with Antæus, who was strong when his feet touched Earth, his mother; weaker when held aloft in air. The justice of this criticism I have no space here to discuss; but the difference is patent enough between poetry such as this of Herrick—

"When as in silks my Julia goes,
Then, then, methinks, how sweetly flows
The liquefaction of her clothes."

Or this, of Burns—

"The boat rocks at the pier o' Leith,
Fu' loud the wind blaws frae the ferry,
The boat rides by the Berwick-law,
And I maun leave my bonny Mary."

Or this, of Shakespeare—

"When daisies pied, and violets blue,
And lady smocks all silver-white,

And cuckoo-buds of yellow hue
Do paint the meadows with delight."

Or this, of Milton—

"the broad circumference
Hung on his shoulders like the moon, whose orb,
Through optic glass the Tuscan artist views
At evening from the top of Fesolé,
Or in Valdarno...."

And such lines as these by Mr. Swinburne—

"The dark dumb godhead innate in the fair world's life
Imbues the rapture of dawn and of noon with dread,
Infects the peace of the star-shod night with strife,
Informs with terror the sorrow that guards the dead.
No service of bended knee or of humbled head
May soothe or subdue the God who has change to wife:
And life with death is as morning with evening wed."

Take Burns's song, "It was a' for our right-fu' King," and set it beside the Jacobite song quoted above, and it is clear at once that with Mr. Swinburne we pass from the particular and concrete to the general and abstract. And in this direction Mr. Swinburne's muse has steadily marched. In his "Erechtheus" he tells how the gods gave Pallas the lordship of Athens—

"The lordship and love of the lovely land,
The grace of the town that hath on it for crown
But a headband to wear
Of violets one-hued with her hair."

Here at least we were allowed a picture of Athens: the violet crown was something definite. But now, when Mr. Swinburne sings of England, we have to precipitate our impressions from lines fluid as these:—

"Things of night at her glance took flight: the
strengths of darkness recoiled and sank:
Sank the fires of the murderous pyres whereon wild
agony writhed and shrank:
Rose the light of the reign of right from gulfs of
years that the darkness drank."

Or—

"Change darkens and lightens around her, alternate
in hope and in fear to be:
Hope knows not if fear speak truth, nor fear whether

hope be not blind as she:
But the sun is in heaven that beholds her immortal,
and girdled with life by the sea."

I suspect, then, that a hundred years hence, when criticism speaks calm judgment upon all Mr. Swinburne's writings, she will find that his earlier and more definite poems are the edge of his blade, and such volumes as "Astrophel" the heavy metal behind it. The former penetrated the affections of his countrymen with ease: the latter followed more difficultly through the outer tissues of a people notoriously pachydermatous to abstract speech. And criticism will then know if Mr. Swinburne brought sufficient impact to drive the whole mass of metal deep.

A Voice chanting in the Void.

At present in these later volumes his must seem to us a godlike voice chanting in the void. For, fit or unfit as we may be to grasp the elusive substance of his strains, all must confess the voice of the singer to be divine. At once in the range and suppleness of his music he is not merely the first of our living poets, but incomparable. In learning he has Robert Bridges for a rival, and no other. But no amount of learning could give us 228 pages of music that from first to last has not a flaw. Rather, his marvellous ear has taken him safely through metres set by his learning as so many traps. There is one metre, for instance, that recurs again and again in this volume. Here is a specimen of it:—

"Music bright as the soul of light, for wings an eagle,
for notes a dove,
Leaps and shines from the lustrous lines wherethrough
thy soul from afar above
Shone and sang till the darkness rang with light whose
fire is the fount of love."

These lines are written of Sir Philip Sidney. Could another man have written them they had stood even better for Mr. Swinburne. But we are considering the metre, not the meaning. Now the metre may have great merits. I am disposed to say that, having fascinated Mr. Swinburne, it must have great merits. That I dislike it is, no doubt, my fault, or rather my misfortune. But undoubtedly it is a metre that no man but Mr. Swinburne could handle without producing a monotony varied only by discords.

A MORNING WITH A BOOK

April 29, 1893. Hazlitt's Stipulation.

"Food, warmth, sleep, and a book; these are all I at present ask—the *Ultima Thule* of my wandering desires. Do you not then wish for—

a friend in your retreat
Whom you may whisper, 'Solitude is sweet'?

Expected, well enough: gone, still better. Such attractions are strengthened by distance."

So Hazlitt wrote in his *Farewell to Essay Writing*. There never was such an epicure of his moods as Hazlitt. Others might add Omar's stipulation—

"—and Thou
Beside me singing in the wilderness."

But this addition would have spoiled Hazlitt's enjoyment. Let us remember that his love affairs had been unprosperous. "Such attractions," he would object, "are strengthened by distance." In any case, the book and singer go ill together, and most of us will declare for a spell of each in turn.

What are "The Best Books"?

Suppose we choose the book. What kind of book shall it be? Shall it be an old book which we have forgotten just sufficiently to taste surprise as its felicities come back to us, and remember just sufficiently to escape the attentive strain of a first reading? Or shall it be a new book by an author we love, to be glanced through with no critical purpose (this may be deferred to the second reading), but merely for the lazy pleasure of recognizing the familiar brain at work, and feeling happy, perhaps, at the success of a friend? There is no doubt which Hazlitt would have chosen; he has told us in his essay *On Reading Old Books*. But after a recent experience I am not sure that I agree with him.

That your taste should approve only the best thoughts of the best minds is a pretty counsel, but one of perfection, and is found in practice to breed prigs. It sets a man sailing round in a vicious circle. What is the best thought of the best minds? That approved by the man of highest culture. Who is the man of highest culture? He whose taste approves the best thoughts of the best minds. To escape from this foolish whirlpool, some of our stoutest bottoms run for that discredited harbor of refuge—Popular Acceptance: a harbor full of shoals, of which nobody has provided even the sketch of a chart.

Some years ago, when the *Pall Mall Gazette* sent round to all sorts and conditions of eminent men, inviting lists of "The Hundred Best Books"—the first serious attempt to introduce a decimal system into Great Britain—I remember that these eminent men's replies disclosed nothing so wonderful as their unanimity. We were prepared for Sir John Lubbock, but not, I think, for the host of celebrities who followed his hygienic example, and made a habit of taking the Rig Vedas to bed with them. Altogether their replies afforded plenty of material for a theory that to have every other body's taste in literature is the first condition of eminence in every branch of the public service. But in one of the lists—I think it was Sir Monier Williams's—the unexpected really happened. Sir Monier thought that Mr. T.E. Brown's *The Doctor* was one of the best books in the world.

Now, the poems of Mr. T.E. Brown are not known to the million. But, like Mr. Robert Bridges, Mr. Brown has always had a band of readers to whom his name is more than that of many an acknowledged classic. I fancy it is a case of liking deeply or scarce at all. Those of us who are not celebrities may be allowed to have favorites who are not the favorites of others, writers who (fortuitously, perhaps) have helped us at some crisis of our life, have spoken to us the appropriate word at the moment of need, and for that reason sit cathedrally enthroned in our affections. To explain why the author of *Betsy Lee*, *Tommy Big-Eyes* and *The Doctor* is more to me than most poets—why to open a new book of his is one of the most exciting literary events that can befall me in now my twenty-ninth year—would take some time, and the explanation might poorly satisfy the reader after all.

My Morning with a Book.

But I set out to describe a morning with a book. The book was Mr. Brown's *Old John, and other Poems*, published but a few days back by Messrs. Macmillan & Co. The morning was spent in a very small garden overlooking a harbor. Hazlitt's conditions were fulfilled. I had enjoyed enough food and sleep to last me for some little time: few people, I imagine, have complained of the cold, these last few weeks: and the book was not only new to me for the most part, but certain to please. Moreover, a small incident had already put me in the best of humors. Just as I was settling down to read, a small tug came down the harbor with a barque in tow whose nationality I recognized before she cleared a corner and showed the Norwegian colors drooping from her peak. I reached for the field-glass and read her name—*Henrik Ibsen*! I imagined Mr. William Archer applauding as I ran to my own flag-staff and dipped the British ensign to that name. The Norwegians on deck stood puzzled for a moment, but, taking the compliment to themselves, gave me a cheerful hail, while one or two ran aft and dipped the Norwegian flag in response. It was still running frantically up and down the halliards when I returned to my seat, and the lines of the bark were softening to beauty in the distance—for, to tell the truth, she had looked a crazy and not altogether seaworthy craft—as I opened my book, and, by a stroke of luck, at that fine poem, *The Schooner*.

"Just mark that schooner westward far at sea—
'Tis but an hour ago
When she was lying hoggish at the quay,
And men ran to and fro
And tugged, and stamped, and shoved, and pushed, and swore.
And ever an anon, with crapulous glee,
Grinned homage to viragoes on the shore.

"So to the jetty gradual she was hauled:
Then one the tiller took,
And chewed, and spat upon his hand, and bawled;
And one the canvas shook
Forth like a mouldy bat; and one, with nods
And smiles, lay on the bowsprit end, and called
And cursed the Harbour-master by his gods.

"And rotten from the gunwale to the keel,
Rat riddled, bilge bestank,
Slime-slobbered, horrible, I saw her reel
And drag her oozy flank,
And sprawl among the deft young waves, that laughed
And leapt, and turned in many a sportive wheel
As she thumped onward with her lumbering draught.

"And now, behold! a shadow of repose
Upon a line of gray
She sleeps, that transverse cuts the evening rose,
She sleeps and dreams away,
Soft blended in a unity of rest
All jars, and strifes obscene, and turbulent throes
'Neath the broad benediction of the West—

"Sleeps; and methinks she changes as she sleeps,
And dies, and is a spirit pure;
Lo! on her deck, an angel pilot keeps
His lonely watch secure;
And at the entrance of Heaven's dockyard waits
Till from night's leash the fine-breathed morning leaps
And that strong hand within unbars the gates."

It is very far from being the finest poem in the volume. It has not the noble humanity of *Catherine Kinrade*—and if this be not a great poem I know nothing about poetry—nor the rapture of *Jessie*, nor the awful pathos of *Mater Dolorosa*, nor the gentle pathos of *Aber Stations*, nor the fine religious feeling of *Planting* and *Disguises*. But it came so pat to the occasion, and used the occasion so deftly to take hold of one's sympathy, that these other poems were read in the very mood that, I am sure, their author would have asked for them. One has not often such luck in reading—"Never the time and the place and the author all together," if I may do this violence to Browning's line. Yet I trust that in any mood I should have had the sense to pay its meed of admiration to this volume.

Now, having carefully read the opinions of some half-a-dozen reviewers upon it, I can only wonder and leave the question to my reader, warning him by no means to miss *Mater Dalorosa* and *Catherine Kinrade*. If he remain cold to these two poems, then I shall still preserve my own opinion.

MR. JOHN DAVIDSON

April 7, 1894. His Plays.

For some weeks now I have been meaning to write about Mr. John Davidson's "Plays" (Elkin Mathews and John Lane), and always shirking the task at the last moment. The book is an exceedingly difficult one to write about, and I am not at all sure that after a few sentences I shall not stick my hands in my pockets and walk off to something easier. The recent fine weather has, however, made me desperate. The windows of the room in which I sit face S. and S.-E.; consequently a deal of sunshine comes in upon my writing-table. In ninety-nine cases out of the hundred this makes for idleness; in this, the hundredth case, it constrains to energy, because it is rapidly bleaching the puce-colored boards in which Mr. Davidson's plays are bound—and (which is worse) bleaching them unevenly. I have tried (let the miserable truth be confessed) turning the book daily, as one turns a piece of toast—But this is not criticism of Mr. Davidson's "Plays."

His Style full of Imagination and Wit.

Now it would be easy and pleasant to express my great admiration of Mr. Davidson's Muse, and justify it by a score of extracts and so make an end: and nobody (except perhaps Mr. Davidson himself) would know my dishonesty. For indeed and out of doubt he is in some respects the most richly-endowed of all our younger poets. Of wit and of imagination he has almost a plethora: they crowd this book, and all his books, from end to end. And his frequent felicity of phrase is hardly less remarkable. You may turn page after page, and with each page the truth of this will become more obvious. Let me add his quick eye for natural beauty, his penetrating instinct for the principles that lie beneath its phenomena, his sympathy with all men's more generous emotions—and still I have a store of satisfactory illustrations at hand for the mere trouble of turning the leaves. Consider, for instance, the imagery in his description of the fight by Bannockburn—

Now are they hand to hand!
How short a front! How close! *They're sewn together
with steel cross-stitches, halbert over sword,
Spear across lance and death the purfled seam!*
I never saw so fierce, so lock'd a fight.
That tireless brand that like a pliant flail
Threshes the lives from sheaves of Englishmen—
Know you who wields it? Douglas, who but he!
A noble meets him now. Clifford it is!
No bitterer foes seek out each other there.
Parried! That told! And that! Clifford, good night!

And Douglas shouts to Randolf; Edward Bruce
Cheers on the Steward; while the King's voice rings
In every Scotch ear: such a narrow strait
Confines this firth of war!

Young Friar.   "God gives me strength
Again to gaze with eyes unseared. *Jewels!*
These must be jewels peering in the grass.
Cloven from helms, or on them: dead men's eyes
Scarce shine so bright. The banners dip and mount
Like masts at sea...."

Or consider the fanciful melody of the Fairies' song in *An Unhistorical Pastoral*—

"Weave the dance and sing the song;
Subterranean depths prolong
The rainy patter of our feet;
Heights of air are rendered sweet
By our singing. Let us sing,
Breathing softly, fairily,
Swelling sweetly, airily,
Till earth and sky our echo ring.
Rustling leaves chime with our song:
Fairy bells its close prolong
Ding-dong, ding-dong."

—Or the closely-packed wit in such passages as these—

Brown: "This world,
This oyster with its valves of toil and play,
Would round his corners for its own good ease,
And make a pearl of him if he'd plunge in.
* * * * * *
Jones: And in this matter we may all be pearls.

Smith: Be worldlings, truly. I would rather be
A shred of glass that sparkles in the sun,
And keeps a lowly rainbow of its own,
Than one of these so trim and patent pearls
With hearts of sand veneered, sewed up and down
The stiff brocade society affects."

I have opened the book at random for these quotations. Its pages are stuffed with scores as good. Nor will any but the least intelligent reviewer upbraid Mr. Davidson for deriving so much of his inspiration directly from Shakespeare. Mr. Davidson is still a young man; but the first of these plays, *An Unhistorical Pastoral*, was first printed so long ago as 1877; and the last, *Scaramouch in Naxos; a Pantomime*, in 1888. They are the work therefore of a very young man, who must use models while feeling his way to a style and method of his own.

Lack of "Architectonic" Quality.

But—there is a "but"; and I am coming at length to my difficulty with Mr. Davidson's work. Oddly enough, this difficulty may be referred to the circumstance that Mr. Davidson's poetry touches Shakespeare's great circle at a second point. Wordsworth, it will be remembered, once said that Shakespeare *could* not have written an Epic (Wordsworth, by the way, was rather fond of pointing out the things that Shakespeare could not have done). "Shakespeare *could* not have written an Epic; he would have died of plethora of thought." Substitute "wit" for "thought," and you have my difficulty with Mr. Davidson. It is given to few men to have great wit: it is given to fewer to carry a great wit lightly. In Mr. Davidson's case it luxuriates over the page and seems persistently to choke his sense of form. One image suggests another, one phrase springs under the very shadow of another until the fabric of his poem is completely hidden beneath luxuriant flowers of speech. Either they hide it from the author himself; or, conscious of his lack of architectonic skill, he deliberately trails these creepers over his ill-constructed walls. I think the former is the true explanation, but am not sure.

Let me be cautious here, or some remarks I made the other day upon another poet—Mr. Hosken, author of *Phaon and Sappho*, and *Verses by the Way*—will be brought up against me. Defending Mr. Hosken against certain critics who had complained of the lack of dramatic power in his tragedies, I said, "Be it allowed that he has little dramatic power, and that (since the poem professed to be a tragedy) dramatic power was what you reasonably looked for. But an alert critic, considering the work of a beginner, will have an eye for the bye-strokes as well as the main ones: and if the author, while missing the main, prove effective with the bye—if Mr. Hosken, while failing to construct a satisfactory drama, gave evidence of strength in many fine meditative passages—then at the worst he stands convicted of a youthful error in choosing a literary form unsuited to convey his thought."

Not in the "Plays" only.

These observations I believe to be just, and having entered the *caveat* in Mr. Hosken's case, I should observe it in Mr. Davidson's also, did these five youthful plays stand alone. But Mr. Davidson has published much since these plays first appeared—works both in prose and verse—*Fleet Street Eclogues, Ninian Jamieson, A Practical Novelist, A Random Itinerary, Baptist Lake*: and because I have followed his writings (I think from his first coming to London) with the greatest interest, I may possibly be excused for speaking a word of warning. I am quite certain that Mr. Davidson will never bore me: but I wish I could be half so certain that he will in time produce something in true perspective; a fabric duly proportioned, each line of which from the beginning shall guide the reader to an end which the author has in view; something which

"*Servetur ad imum
Qualis ab incepto processerit, et sibi constet.*"

Sibi constet, be it remarked. A work of art may stand very far from Nature, provided its own parts are consistent. Heaven forbid that a critic should decry an author for being fantastic, so long as he is true to his fantasy.

But Mr. Davidson's wit is so brilliant within the circles of its temporary coruscation as to leave the outline of his work in a constant penumbra. Indeed, when he wishes to unburden his mind of an idea, he seems to have less capacity than many men of half his ability to determine the form best suited for conveying it. If anything can be certain which has not been tried, it is that his story *A Practical Novelist* should have been cast in dramatic form. His vastly clever *Perfervid*: or *the Career of Ninian Jamieson* is cast in two parts which neither unite to make a whole, nor are sufficiently independent to stand complete in themselves. I find it characteristic that his *Random Itinerary*—that fresh and agreeable narrative of suburban travel—should conclude with a crashing poem, magnificent in itself, but utterly out of key with the rest of the book. Turn to the *Compleat Angler*, and note the exquisite congruity of the songs quoted by Walton with the prose in which they are set, and the difference will be apparent at once. Fate seems to dog Mr. Davidson even into his illustrations. *A Random Itinerary* and this book of *Plays* (both published by Messrs. Mathews and Lane) have each a conspicuously clever frontispiece. But the illustrator of *A Random Itinerary* has chosen as his subject the very poem which I have mentioned as out of harmony with the book; and I must protest that the vilely sensual faces in Mr. Beardsley's frontispiece to these *Plays* are hopelessly out of keeping with the sunny paganism of *Scaramouch in Naxos*. There is nothing Greek about Mr. Beardsley's figures: their only relationship with the Olympians is derived through the goddess Aselgeia.

With all this I have to repeat that Mr. Davidson is in some respects the most richly endowed of all the younger poets. The grand manner comes more easily to him than to any other: and if he can cultivate a sense of form and use this sense as a curb upon his wit, he has all the qualities that take a poet far.

Nov. 24, 1984. "Ballads and Songs."

At last there is no mistake about it: Mr. John Davidson has come by his own. And by "his own" I do not mean popularity—though I hope that in time he will have enough of this and to spare—but mastery of his poetic method. This new volume of "Ballads and Songs" (London: John Lane) justifies our hopes and removes our chief fear. You remember Mr. T.E. Brown's fine verses on "Poets and Poets"?—

He fishes in the night of deep sea pools:
For him the nets hang long and low,
Cork-buoyed and strong; the silver-gleaming schools
Come with the ebb and flow
Of universal tides, and all the channels glow.

Or holding with his hand the weighted line
He sounds the languor of the neaps,
Or feels what current of the springing brine
The cord divergent sweeps,
The throb of what great heart bestirs the middle deeps.

Thou also weavest meshes, fine and thin,
And leaguer'st all the forest ways;
But of that sea and the great heart therein
Thou knowest nought; whole days
Thou toil'st, and hast thy end—good store of pies and jays.

Mr. Davidson has never allowed us to doubt to which of these two classes he belongs. "For him the nets hang long and low." But though it may satisfy the Pumblechook within us to recall our pleasant prophesyings, we shall find it more salutary to remember our fears. We watched Mr. Davidson struggling in the thicket of his own fancies, and saw him too often break his shins over his own wit. We asked: Will he in the end overcome the defect of his qualities? Will he remain unable to see the wood for the trees? Or will he some day be giving us poems of which the whole conception and structure shall be as beautiful as the casual fragment or the single line? For this architectonic quality is just that "invidious distinction" which the fabled undergraduate declined to draw between the major and minor prophets.

The "Ballad of a Nun."

Since its appearance, a few weeks back, all the critics have spoken of "A Ballad of a Nun," and admitted its surprising strength and beauty. They have left me in the plight of that belated fiddle in "Rejected Addresses," or of the gentleman who had to be content with saying "ditto" to Mr. Burke. For once they seem unanimous, and for once they are right. The poem is beautiful indeed in detail:

"The adventurous sun took Heaven by storm;
Clouds scattered largesses of rain;
The sounding cities, rich and warm,
Smouldered and glittered in the plain."

Dickens, reading for the first time Tennyson's "Dream of Fair Women," laid down the book, saying, "What a treat it is to come across a fellow who can *write*!" The verse that moved him to exclaim it was this—

"Squadrons and squares of men in brazen plates,
Scaffolds, still sheets of water, divers woes,
Ranges of glimmering vaults with iron grates;
And hushed seraglios."

It is not necessary to compare these two stanzas. Tennyson's depicts a confused and moving dream; Mr. Davidson's a wide earthly prospect. The point to notice in each is the superlative skill with which the poet chooses the essential points of the picture and presents them so as to convey their full meaning, appealing at once to the senses and the intelligence. Tennyson, who is handling a mental condition in which the sensations are less sharply and logically separated than in a waking vision, can enforce this second appeal—this appeal to the intelligence—by introducing the indefinite "divers woes" between the definite "sheets of water" and the definite "ranges of glimmering vaults with iron grates": just as Wordsworth, to convey the vague unanalyzed charm of singing, combines the indefinite "old unhappy far-off things" with the definite "battles long ago." Mr. Davidson, on the other hand, is describing what the eye sees, and conveying what the mind suspects, in their waking hours, and is therefore restricted in his use of the abstract and indefinite. Notice, therefore, how he qualifies that which can be seen—the sun, the clouds, the plain, the cities that "smoulder" and "glitter"—with the epithets "sounding," "rich," and "warm," each an inference rather than a direct sensation: for nobody imagines that the sound of the cities actually rang in the ear of the Nun who watched them from the mountain-side. The whole picture has the effect of one of those wide conventional landscapes which old painters delighted to spread beyond the court-yard of Nazareth, or behind the pillars of the temple at Jerusalem. My attempt to analyze it is something of a folly; to understand it is impossible:

"but *if* I could understand
What you are, root and all, and all in all,"—

I should at length comprehend the divine and inexplicable gift of song.

The "Ballad of the Making of a Poet."

But beautiful as it is in detail, this poem, and at least one other in the little volume, have the great merit which has hitherto been lacking in the best of Mr. Davidson's work. They are thoroughly considered; seen as solid wholes; seen not only in front but round at the back. In fact, they are natural growths of Mr. Davidson's philosophy of life. In his "Ballad of the Making of a Poet" Mr. Davidson lets us know his conception of the poet's proper function.

"I am a man apart:
A mouthpiece for the creeds of all the world;
A soulless life that angels may possess
Or demons haunt, wherein the foulest things
May loll at ease beside the loveliest;
A martyr for all mundane moods to tear;
The slave of every passion; and the slave
Of heat and cold, of darkness and of light;
A trembling lyre for every wind to sound.
* * * * * *
Within my heart
I'll gather all the universe, and sing
As sweetly as the spheres; and I shall be
The first of men to understand himself...."

Making, of course, full concessions to the demands of poetical treatment, we may assume pretty confidently that Mr. Davidson intended this "Ballad in Blank Verse of the Making of a Poet" for a soul's autobiography, of a kind. If so, I trust he will forgive me for doubting if he is at all likely to fulfil the poet's office as he conceives it here, or even to approach within measurable distance of his ideal—

"A trembling lyre for every wind to sound."

That it is one way in which a poet may attain, I am not just now denying. But luckily men attain in many ways: and the man who sits himself down of fixed purpose to be an Æolian harp for the winds of the world, is of all men the least likely to be merely Æolian. For the first demand of Æolian sound is that the instrument should have no theories of its own; and explicitly to proclaim yourself Æolian is implicitly to proclaim yourself didactic. As a matter of fact, both the "Ballad of the Making of a Poet" and the "Ballad of a Nun" contain sharply pointed morals very stoutly driven home. In each the poet has made up his mind; he has a theory of life, and presents that theory to us under cover of a parable. The beauty of the "Ballad of a Nun"—or so much of it as stands beyond and above mere beauty of language—consists in this, that it is informed, and consciously informed, by a spirit of tolerance so exceedingly wide that to match it I can find one poem and one only among those of recent years: I mean "Catherine Kinrade." In Mr. Brown's poem the Bishop is welcomed into Heaven by the half-wilted harlot he had once condemned to painful and public punishment. In Mr. Davidson's poem, Mary, the Mother of Heaven, herself takes the form and place of the wandering nun and fills it until the penitent returns. Take either poem: take Mr. Brown's—

"Awe-stricken, he was 'ware
How on the Emerald stair
A woman sat divinely clothed in white,
And at her knees four cherubs bright.
That laid
Their heads within their lap. Then, trembling, he essayed
To speak—'Christ's mother, pity me!'
Then answered she—
'Sir, I am Catherine Kinrade.'"

Or take Mr. Davidson's—in a way, its converse—

"The wandress raised her tenderly;
She touched her wet and fast-shut eyes;
'Look, sister; sister, look at me;
Look; can you see through my disguise?'

She looked and saw her own sad face,
And trembled, wondering, 'Who art thou?'
'God sent me down to fill your place;
I am the Virgin Mary now.'

And with the word, God's mother shone;
The wanderer whispered 'Mary, hail!'
The vision helped her to put on
Bracelet and fillet, ring and veil.

'You are sister to the mountains now,
And sister to the day and night;

Sister to God.' And on her brow
She kissed her thrice and left her sight."

The voice in each case is that of a prophet rather than that of a reed shaken by the wind, or an Æolian harp played upon by the same.

March, 1895. Second Thoughts.

I have to add that, apart from the beautiful language in which they are presented, Mr. Davidson's doctrines do not appeal to me. I cannot accept his picture of the poet's as "a soulless life ... wherein the foulest things may loll at ease beside the loveliest." It seems to me at least as obligatory on a poet as on other men to keep his garden weeded and his conscience active. Indeed, I believe some asceticism of soul to be a condition of all really great poetry. Also Mr. Davidson appears to be confusing charity with an approbation of things in the strict sense damnable when he makes the Mother of Christ abet a Nun whose wanderings have no nobler excuse than a carnal desire—*savoir enfin ce que c'est un homme*. Between forgiving a lapsed man or woman and abetting the lapse I now, in a cooler hour, see an immense, an essential, moral difference. But I confess that the foregoing paper was written while my sense of this difference was temporarily blinded under the spell of Mr. Davidson's beautiful verse.

It may still be that his Nun had some nobler motive than I am able, after two or three readings of the ballad, to discover. In that case I can only ask pardon for my obtuseness.

BJÖRNSTERNE BJÖRNSON

June 1, 1895. Björnson's First Manner.

I see that the stories promised in Mr. Heinemann's new series of translations of Björnson are *Synnöve Solbakken, Arne, A Happy Boy, The Fisher Maiden, The Bridal March, Magnhild,* and *Captain Mansana.* The first, *Synnöve Solbakken,* appeared in 1857. The others are dated thus:—*Arne* in 1858, *A Happy Boy* in 1860, *The Fisher Maiden* in 1868, *The Bridal March* in 1873, *Magnhild* in 1877, and *Captain Mansana* in 1879. There are some very significant gaps here, the most important being the eight years' gap between *A Happy Boy* and *The Fisher Maiden.* Again, after 1879 Björnson ceased to write novels for a while, returning to the charge in 1884 with *Flags are Flying in Town and Haven,* and following up with *In God's Way,* 1889. Translations of these two novels have also been published by Mr. Heinemann (the former under an altered title, *The Heritage of the Kurts*) and, to use Mr. Gosse's words, are the works, by which Björnson is best known to the present generation of Englishmen. "They possess elements which have proved excessively attractive to certain sections of our public; indeed, in the case of *In God's Way,* a novel which was by no means successful in its own country at its original publication, has enjoyed an aftermath of popularity in Scandinavia, founded on reflected warmth from its English admirers."

Taking, then, Björnson's fiction apart from his other writings (with which I confess myself unacquainted), we find that it falls into three periods, pretty sharply divided. The earliest is the idyllic period, pure and simple, and includes *Synnöve, Arne,* and *A Happy Boy.* Then with *The Fisher Maiden* we enter on a stage of transition. It is still the idyll; but it grows self-conscious, elaborate, confused by the realism that was coming into fashion all over Europe; and the trouble and confusion grow until we reach *Magnhild.* With *Flags are Flying* and *In God's Way* we reach a third stage—the stage of realism, some readers would say. I should not agree. But these tales certainly differ remarkably from their predecessors. They are much longer, to begin with; in them, too, realism at length preponderates; and they are probably as near to pure realism as Björnson will ever get.

If asked to label these three periods, I should call them the periods of (1) Simplicity, (2) Confusion, (3) Dire Confusion.

I speak, of course, as a foreigner, obliged to read Björnson in translations. But perhaps the disability is not so important as it seems at first sight. Translations cannot hide Björnson's genius; nor obscure the truth that his genius is essentially idyllic. Now if one form of literary expression suffers more than another by translation it is the idyll. Its bloom is peculiarly delicate; its freshness peculiarly quick to disappear under much handling of any kind.

But all the translations leave *Arne* a masterpiece, and *Synnövé* and *The Happy Boy*.

How many artists have been twisted from their natural bent by the long vogue of "naturalism" we shall never know. We must make the best of the great works which have been produced under its influence, and be content with that. But we may say with some confidence that Björnson's genius was unfortunate in the date of its maturity. He was born on the 8th of December, 1832, in a lonely farmhouse among the mountains, at the head of the long valley called Osterdalen; his father being priest of Kvikne parish, one of the most savage in all Norway. After six years the family removed to Naesset, in the Romsdal, "a spot as enchanting and as genial as Kvikne is the reverse." Mr. Gosse, who prefaces Mr. Heinemann's new series with a study of Björnson's writings, quotes a curious passage in which Björnson records the impression of physical beauty made upon his childish mind by the physical beauty of Naesset:—

"Here in the parsonage of Naesset—one of the loveliest places in Norway, where the land lies broadly spreading where two fjords meet, with the green braeside above it, with waterfalls and farmhouses on the opposite shore, with billowy meadows and cattle away towards the foot of the valley, and, far overhead, along the line of the fjord, mountains shooting promontory after promontory out into the lake, a big farmhouse at the extremity of each— here in the parsonage of Naesset, where I would stand at the close of the day and gaze at the sunlight playing over mountain and fjord, until I wept, as though I had done something wrong; and where I, descending on my snow-shoes into some valley, would pause as though bewitched by a loveliness, by a longing, which I had not the power to explain, but which was so great that above the highest ecstasy of joy I would feel the deepest apprehension and distress—here in the parsonage of Naesset were awakened my earliest sensations."

The passage is obviously important. And Björnson shows how much importance he attaches to the experience by introducing it, or something like it, time after time into his stories. Readers of *In God's Way*—the latest of the novels under discussion—will remember its opening chapter well.

It was good fortune indeed that a boy of such gifts should pass his early boyhood in such surroundings. Nor did the luck end here. While the young Björnson accumulated these impressions, the peasant-romance, or idyll of country life, was taking its place and growing into favor as one of the most beautiful forms of modern prose-fiction. Immermann wrote *Der Oberhof* in 1839. Weill and Auerbach took up the running in 1841 and 1843. George Sand followed, and Fritz Reuter. Björnson began to write in 1856. *Synnövé Solbakken* and *Arne* came in on the high flood of this movement. "These two stories," writes Mr. Gosse, "seem to me to be almost perfect; they have an enchanting lyrical quality, without bitterness or passion, which I look for elsewhere in vain in the prose literature of the second half of the century." To my mind, without any doubt, they and *A Happy Boy* are the best work Björnson has ever done in fiction, or is ever likely to do. For they are simple, direct, congruous; all of one piece as a flower is of a piece with its root. And never since has Björnson written a tale altogether of one piece.

His later Manner.

For here the luck ended. All over Europe there began to spread influences that may have been good for some artists, but were (we may say) peculiarly injurious to so *naïf* and, at the same time, so personal a writer as Björnson. I think another age will find much the same cause to mourn over Daudet when it compares his later novels with the promise of *Lettres de Mon Moulin* and *Le Petit Chose*. Naturalism demands nothing more severely than an impersonal treatment of its themes. Of three very personal and romantic writers, our own Stevenson escaped the pit into which both Björnson and Daudet stumbled. You may say the temptation came later to him. But the temptation to follow an European fashion does, as a rule, befall a Briton last of all men, for reasons of which we need not feel proud: and the date of Mr. Hardy's stumbling is fairly recent, after all. Björnson, at any rate, began very soon to be troubled. Between 1864 and 1874, from his thirty-second to his forty-second year, his invention seemed, to some extent, paralyzed. *The Fisher Maiden*, the one story written during that time, starts as beautifully as *Arne*; but it grows complicated and introspective: the psychological experiences of the stage-struck heroine are not in the same key as the opening chapters. Passing over nine years, we find *Magnhild* much more vague and involved—

"Here he is visibly affected by French models, and by the methods of the naturalists, but he is trying to combine them with his own simpler traditions of rustic realism.... The author felt himself greatly moved by fermenting ideas and ambitions which he had not completely mastered.... There is a kind of uncomfortable discrepancy between the scene and the style, a breath of Paris and the boulevards blowing through the pine-trees of a puritanical Norwegian village.... But the book is a most interesting link between the early peasant-stories and the great novels of his latest period."

Well, of these same "great novels"—of *Flags are Flying* and *In God's Way*—people must speak as they think. They seem to me the laborious productions of a man forcing himself still further and further from his right and natural bent. In them, says Mr. Gosse, "Björnson returns, in measure, to the poetical elements of his youth. He is now capable again, as for instance in the episode of Ragni's symbolical walk in the woodlands, *In God's Way*, of passages of pure idealism." Yes, he returns—"in measure." He is "capable of idyllic passages." In other words, his nature reasserts itself, and he remains an imperfect convert. "He has striven hard to be a realist, and at times he has seemed to acquiesce altogether in the naturalistic formula, but in truth he has never had anything essential in common with M. Zola." In other words, he has fallen between two stools. He has tried to expel nature with a pitchfork and still she runs back upon him. He has put his hand to the plough and has looked back: or (if you take my view of "the naturalistic formula") he has sinned, but has not sinned with his whole heart. For to produce a homogeneous story, either the acquired Zola or the native Björnson must have been cast out utterly.

Value of Early Impressions to a Novelist.

I have quoted an example of the impressions of Björnson's childhood. I do not think critics have ever quite realized the extent to which writers of fiction—especially those who use a personal style—depend upon the remembered impressions of childhood. Such impressions—no matter how fantastic—are an author's firsthand stock: and in using them he comes much closer to nature than when he collects any number of scientifically approved data to maintain some view of life which he has derived from books. Compare *Flags are Flying* with *Arne*, and you will see my point. The longer book is ten times as realistic in treatment, and about one-tenth as true to life.

MR. GEORGE MOORE

March 31, 1894. "Esther Waters."

It is good, after all, to come across a novel written by a man who can write a novel. We have been much in the company of the Amateur of late, and I for one am very weary of him—weary of his preposterous goings-out and comings-in, of his smart ineptitudes, of his solemn zeal in reforming the decayed art of fiction, of his repeated failures to discover beneficence in all those institutions, from the Common Law of England to the Scheme of the Universe, which have managed to leave him and his aspirations out of count. I am weary of him and of his deceased wife's sister, and of their fell determination to discover each other's soul in a bottle of hay. Above all, I am weary of his writings, because he cannot write, neither has he the humility to sit down and learn.

Mr. George Moore, on the other hand, has steadily labored to make himself a fine artist, and his training has led him through many strange places. I should guess that among living novelists few have started with so scant an equipment. As far as one can tell he had, to begin with, neither a fertile invention nor a subtle dramatic instinct, nor an accurate ear for language. A week ago I should have said this very confidently: after reading *Esther Waters* I say it less confidently, but believe it to be true, nevertheless. Mr. Moore has written novels that are full of faults. These faults have been exposed mercilessly, for Mr. Moore has made many enemies. But he has always possessed an artistic conscience and an immense courage. He answered his critics briskly enough at the time, but an onlooker of common sagacity could perceive that the really convincing answer was held in reserve—that, as they say in America, Mr. Moore "allowed" he was going to write a big novel one of these days, and meanwhile we had better hold our judgment upon Mr. Moore's capacity open to revision.

What, then, is to be said of *Esther Waters*, this volume of a modest 377 pages, upon which Mr. Moore has been at work for at least two years?

"Esther" and Mr. Hardy's "Tess."

Well, in the first place, I say, without hesitation, that *Esther Waters* is the most important novel published in England during these two years. We have been suffering from the Amateur during that period, and no doubt (though it seems hard) every nation has the Amateur it deserves. To find a book to compare with *Esther Waters* we must go back to December, 1891, and to Mr. Hardy's *Tess of the D'Urbervilles*. It happens that a certain similarity in the motives of these two stories makes comparison easy. Each starts with the seduction of a young girl; and each is mainly concerned with her subsequent adventures. From the beginning the advantage of probability is with the younger novelist. Mr. Moore's "William Latch" is a thoroughly natural figure, and remains a natural figure to the end of the book: an uneducated man and full of failings, but a man always, and therefore to be forgiven by the reader only a little less readily than Esther herself forgives him. Mr. Hardy's "Alec D'Urberville" is a grotesque and violent lay figure, a wholly incredible cad. Mr. Hardy, by killing Tess's child, takes away the one means by which his heroine could have been led to return to D'Urberville without any loss of the reader's sympathy. Mr. Moore allows Esther's child to live, and thus has at hand the material for one of the most beautiful stories of maternal love ever imagined by a writer. I dislike extravagance of speech, and would run my pen through these words could I remember, in any novel I have read, a more heroic story than this of Esther Waters, a poor maid-of-all-work, without money, friends, or character, fighting for her child against the world, and in the end dragging victory out of the struggle. In spite of the Æschylean gloom in which Mr. Hardy wraps the story of Tess, I contend that Esther's fight is, from end to end, the more heroic.

Also Esther's story seems to me informed with a saner philosophy of life. There is gloom in her story; and many of the circumstances are sordid enough; but throughout I see the recognition that man and woman can at least improve and dignify their lot in this world. Many people believe *Tess* to be the finest of its author's achievements. A devoted admirer of Mr. Hardy's genius, I decline altogether to consent. To my mind, among recent developments of the English novel nothing is more lamentable than the manner in which this distinguished writer has allowed himself of late to fancy that the riddles of life are solved by pulling mouths at Providence (or whatever men choose to call the Supreme Power) and depicting it as a savage and omnipotent bully, directing human affairs after the fashion of a practical joker fresh from a village ale-house. For to this teaching his more recent writings plainly tend; and alike in *Tess* and *Life's Little Ironies* the part played by the "President of the Immortals" is no sublimer—save in the amount of force exerted—than that of a lout who pulls a chair suddenly from under an old woman. Now, by wedding Necessity with uncouth Jocularity, Mr. Hardy may have found an hypothesis that solves for him all the difficulties of life. I am not concerned in this place to deny that it may be the true explanation. I have merely to point out that art and criticism must take some time in getting accustomed to it, and that meanwhile the traditions of both are so far agreed in allowing a certain amount of free will to direct the actions of men and women that a tale which should be all necessity and no free will would, in effect, be necessity's own contrary—a merely wanton freak.

For, in effect, it comes to this:—The story of Tess, in which attention is so urgently directed to the hand of Destiny, is not felt to be inevitable, but freakish. The story of Esther Waters, in which a poor servant-girl is allowed to grapple with her destiny and, after a fashion, to defeat it, is felt (or has been felt by one reader, at any rate) to be absolutely inevitable. To reconcile us to the black flag above Wintoncester prison as to the appointed end of Tess's career, a curse at least as deep as that of Pelops should have been laid on the D'Urberville family. Tess's curse does not lie by nature on all women; nor on all Dorset women; nor on all Dorset women who have illegitimate children; for a very few even of these are hanged. We feel that we are not concerned with a type, but with an individual case deliberately chosen by the author; and no amount of talk about the "President of the Immortals" and his "Sport" can persuade us to the contrary. With Esther Waters, on the other hand, we feel we are assisting in the combat of a human life against its natural destiny; we perceive that the woman has a chance of winning; we are happy when she wins; and we are the better for helping her with our sympathy in the struggle. That is why, using the word in the Aristotelian sense, I maintain that *Esther Waters* is a more "philosophical" work than *Tess*.

The atmosphere of the low-class gambling in which Mr. Moore's characters breathe and live is no doubt a result of his careful study of Zola. It is, as everyone knows, M. Zola's habit to take one of the many pursuits of men—from War and Religion down to Haberdashery and Veterinary Surgery—and expand it into an atmosphere for a novel. But in Mr. Moore's case it may safely be urged that gambling on racehorses actually is the atmosphere in which a million or two of Londoners pass their lives. Their hopes, their very chances of a satisfying meal, hang from day to day on the performances of horses they have never seen. I cannot profess to judge with what accuracy Mr. Moore has reproduced the niceties of handicapping, bookmaking, place-betting, and the rest, the fluctuations of the gambling market, and their causes. I gather that extraordinary care has been bestowed upon these details; but criticism here must be left to experts, I only know that, not once or twice only in the course of his narrative, Mr. Moore makes us study the odds against a horse almost as eagerly as if it carried our own money: because it does indeed carry for a while the destiny of Esther Waters—and yet for a while only. We feel that, whichever horse wins the ultimate issues are inevitable.

It will be gathered from what I have said that Mr. Moore has vastly outstripped his own public form, even as shown in *A Mummer's Wife*. But it may be as well to set down, beyond possibility of misapprehension, my belief that in *Esther Waters* we have the most artistic, the most complete, and the most inevitable work of fiction that has been written in England for at least two years. Its plainness of speech may offend many. It may not be a favorite in the circulating libraries or on the bookstalls. But I shall be surprised if it fails of the place I predict for it in the esteem of those who know the true aims of fiction and respect the conscientious practice of that great art.

MRS. MARGARET L. WOODS

Nov. 28, 1891. "Esther Vanhomrigh."

Among considerable novelists who have handled historical subjects—that is to say, who have brought into their story men and women who really lived and events which have really taken place—you will find one rule strictly observed, and no single infringement of it that has been followed by success. This rule is that the historical characters and events should be mingled with poetical characters and events, and *made subservient to them*. And it holds of books as widely dissimilar as *La Vicomte de Bragelonne* and *La Guerre et la Paix*; *The Abbot* and *John Inglesant*. In history Louis XIV. and Napoleon are the most salient men of their time: in fiction they fall back and give prominence to D'Artagnan and the Prince André. They may be admirably painted, but unless they take a subordinate place in the composition, the artist scores a failure.

A Disability of "Historical Fiction."

The reason of this is, of course, very simple. If an artist is to have full power over his characters, to know their hearts, to govern their emotions and sway them at his will, they must be his own creatures and the life in them derived from him. He must have an entirely free hand with them. But the personages of history have an independent life of their own, and with them his hand is tied. Thackeray has a freehold on the soul of Beatrix Esmond, but he takes the soul of Marlborough furnished, on a short lease, and has to render an account to the Muse of History. He is lord of one and mere occupier of the other. Nor will it do to say that an artist by sympathetic and intelligent study can master the motives of any group of historical characters sufficiently for his purpose. For, since they have anticipated him and lived their lives without his help, they leave him but a choice between two poor courses. If he narrate their lives and adventures as they really befel, he is writing history. If, on the other hand, he disregard historical accuracy, he might just as well have used another set of characters or have given his characters other names. Indeed, it would be much better. For if Alcibiades went as a matter of fact to Sparta and as a matter of fiction you make him stay at home, you merely advertise to the world that there was something in Alcibiades you don't understand. And if you are writing about an Alcibiades whom you don't quite understand, you will save your readers some risk of confusion by calling him Charicles.

Now Jonathan Swift and Esther Johnson and Esther Vanhomrigh really lived; and by living, became historical. But Mrs. Woods sets forth to translate them back into fiction, not as subordinate characters, but as protagonists. She has chosen to work within the difficult limits I have indicated. But there are others which might easily have cramped her hand even more closely.

A Tale of Passion to be told in Terms of Reason.

The story of Swift and Esther Vanhomrigh is a story of passion, and runs on the confines of madness. But it happened in the Age of Reason. Doubtless men and women felt madness and passion in that age: doubtless, too, they spoke of madness and passion, but not in their literature. And now that the lips are dust and the fiery conversations lost, Mrs. Woods has only their written prose to turn to for help. To satisfy the pedant she must tell her story of passion in terms of reason. In one respect Thackeray had a more difficult task in *Esmond*; for he aimed to make his book a reflection, in every page and line, of the days of Queen Anne. Not only had he, like Mrs. Woods, to make his characters and their talk consistent with that age; but every word of the story is supposed to be told by a gentleman of that age, whereas Mrs. Woods in her narrative prose may use the language of her own century. On the other hand, the story of *Esmond* deals with comparatively temperate emotions. There is nothing in Thackeray's masterpiece to strain the prose of the Age of Reason. It is pitched in the key of those times, and the prose of those times is sufficient and exactly sufficient for it. That it should be so is all the more to Thackeray's honor, for the artist is to be praised in the conception as duly as in the execution of his work. But, the conception being granted, I think *Esther Vanhomrigh* must have been a harder book than *Esmond* to write.

For even the prose of Swift himself is inadequate to Swift. He was a great and glaring anomaly who never fell into perspective with his age while he lived, and can hardly be pulled into perspective now with the drawing materials which are left to us. Men of like abundant genius are rarely measurable in language used by their contemporaries; and this is perhaps the reason why they disquiet their contemporaries so confoundedly. Where in the books written by tye-bewigged gentlemen, or in the letters written by Swift himself, can you find words to explain that turbulent and potent man? He bursts the capacity of Addison's phrase and Pope's couplet. He was too big for a bishop's chair, and now, if a novelist attempt to clothe him in the garments of his time, he splits them down the back.

It is in meeting this difficulty that Mrs. Woods seems to me to display the courage and intelligence of a true artist. She is bound to be praised by many for her erudition; but perhaps she will let me thank her for having trodden upon her erudition. In the first volume it threatened to overload and sink her. But no sooner does she begin to catch the wind of her subject than she tosses all this superfluous cargo overboard. From the point where passion creeps into the story this learning is carried lightly and seems to be worn unconsciously. Instead of cataloguing the age, she comprehends it.

To me the warmth and pathos she packs into her eighteenth-century conversation, without modernizing it thereby, is something amazing. For this alone the book would be notable; and it can be proved to come of divination, simply because nothing exists from which she could have copied it. More obvious, though not more wonderful, is her feminine gift of rendering a scene vivid for us by describing it, not as it is, but as it excites her own intelligence or feelings. Let me explain myself: for it is the sorry fate of a book so interesting and suggestive as *Esther Vanhomrigh* to divert the critic from praise of the writer to consider a dozen problems which the writer raises.

Women and "le don pittoresque."

Well, then, M. Jules Lemaître has said somewhere—and with considerable truth—that women when they write have not *le don pittoresque*. By this he means that they do not strive to depict a scene exactly as it strikes upon their senses, but as they perceive it after testing its effect upon their emotions and experience. Suppose now we have to describe a moonlit night in May. Mrs. Woods begins as a man might begin, thus—

"The few and twinkling lights disappeared from the roadside cottages. The full white moon was high in the cloudless deep of heaven, and the sounds of the warm summer night were all about their path; the splash of leaping fish, the sleepy chirrup of birds disturbed by some night-wandering creature; the song of the reed-warbler, the persistent churring of the night jar, and the occasional hoot of the owl, far off on some ancestral tree."

Now all this, except, perhaps, the "ancestral" tree, is a direct picture, and with it some men might stop. But no woman could stop here, and Mrs. Woods does not. She goes on—

"It was such an exquisite May night, full of the mystery and beauty of moonlight and the scent of hawthorn, as makes the earth an Eden in which none but lovers should walk—happy lovers or young poets, whose large eyes, so blind in the daylight world of men, can see God walking in the Garden." ...

You see it is sensation no longer, but reflection and emotion.

Now I am only saying that women cannot avoid this. I am not condemning it. On the contrary, it is beautiful in Mrs. Woods's hand, and sometimes luminously true. Take this, for instance, of the interior of a city church:—

"It had none of the dim impressiveness of a mediæval church, that seems reared with a view to Heaven rather than Earth, and whose arches, massive or soaring, neither gain nor lose by the accidental presence of ephemeral human creatures below them. No, the building seemed to cry out for a congregation, and the mind's eye involuntarily peopled it with its Sunday complement of substantial citizens and their families."

This is not a picturesque but a reflective description. Yet how it illuminates! If we had never thought of it before we know now, once and for all, the essential difference between a Gothic church and one of Wren's building. And further, since Mrs. Woods is writing of an age that slighted Gothic for the architecture of Wren and his followers, we get a brilliant side-flash to help our comprehension. It is a hint only, but it assures us as we read that we are in the eighteenth century, when men and women were of more account than soaring aspirations.

And the conclusion is that if Mrs. Woods could not conquer the difficulties which beset any attempt to make protagonists of two historical characters, if she was obliged to follow the facts to the detriment of composition, she has vitalized and recreated a dead age in a fashion to make us all wonder. *Esther Vanhomrigh* is a great feat, and its authoress is one of the few of whom almost anything may be expected.

Jan. 26, 1895. "The Vagabonds."

In her latest book,[A] Mrs. Woods returns to that class of life—so far as life may be classified—which she handled so memorably in *A Village Tragedy*. There are differences, though. As the titles indicate, the life in the earlier story was stationary: in the latter it is nomadic—the characters are artistes in a travelling show. This at once suggests comparison with M. Edmond de Goncourt's *Les Frères Zemganno*; or rather a contrast: for the two stories, conceived in very similar surroundings, differ in at least two vital respects.

Compared with "Les Frères Zemganno."

For what, in short, is the story of *Les Frères Zemganno*? Two brothers, Gianni and Nello, tumblers in a show that travels round the village fairs and small country towns of France, are seized with an ambition to excel in their calling. They make their way to England, where they spend some years clowning in various circuses. Then they return to make their *debut* in Paris. Gianni has invented at length a trick act, a feat that will make the brothers famous. They are performing it for the first time in public, when a circus girl, who has a spite against Nello, causes him to fall and break both his legs. He can perform no more: and henceforward, as he watches his brother performing, a strange jealousy awakes and grows in him, causing him agony whenever Gianni touches a trapèze. Gianni discovers this and renounces his art.

Now here in the first place it is to be noted that the whole story depends upon the circus profession, and the brothers' love for it and desire to excel in it. The catastrophe; Nello's jealousy; Gianni's self-sacrifice; are inseparable from the atmosphere of the book. The catastrophe is a professional catastrophe; the jealousy a professional jealousy; the sacrifice a sacrifice of a profession. And in the second place we know, even if we had not his own word for it, that M. de Goncourt—contrary to his habit—deliberately etherealized the atmosphere of the circus-ring and idealized the surroundings. He calls his tale an essay in poetic realism, "Je me suis trouvé dans une de ces heures de la vie, vieillissantes, maladives, lâches devant le travail poignant et angoisseux de mes autres livres, en un état de l'âme où la vérité trop vraie m'était antipathique à moi aussi!—et j'ai fait cette fois de l'imagination dans du rêve mêlé à du souvenir." We know from the Goncourt Journals exactly what is meant by "du souvenir." We know that M. Edmond de Goncourt is but translating into the language of the circus-ring and symbolizing in the story of Gianni and Nello the story of his own literary collaboration with his brother Jules—a collaboration of quite singular intimacy, that ceased only with Jules's death in 1870. Possibly, as M. Zola once suggested, M. Edmond de Goncourt did at first intend to depict the circus-life, after his wont, in true "naturalistic" manner, softening and extenuating nothing: but "par une délicatesse qui s'explique, il a reculé devant le milieu brutal de cirques, devant certaines laideurs et certaines monstruosités des personnages qu'il choisis-sait." The two facts remain that in *Les Frères Zemganno* M. de Goncourt (1) made professional life in a circus the very blood and tissue of his story; and (2) that he softened the details of that life, and to a certain degree idealized it.

Turning to Mrs. Woods's book and taking these two points in reverse order, we find to begin with that she idealizes nothing and softens next to nothing. Where she does soften, she softens only for literary effect—to give a word its due force, or a picture its proper values. She does not, for instance, accurately report the oaths and blasphemies:—

"The tents and booths of the show were disappearing rapidly like stage scenery. The red-faced Manager, Joe, and several others in authority, ran hither and thither shouting their orders to a crowd of workmen in jackets and fustian trousers, who were piling rolls of canvas, and heavy chests, and mountains of planks and long vibrating poles, on the great waggons. Others were harnessing the big powerful horses to the carts, horses that were mostly white, and wore large red collars. The scene was so busy, so full of movement, that it would have been exhilarating had not the fresh morning air been full of senseless blasphemies and other deformities of speech, uttered casually and constantly, without any apparent consciousness on the part of the speakers that they were using strong language. Probably the lady who dropped toads and vipers from her lips whenever she opened them came in process of time to consider them the usual accompaniments of conversation."

There are a great many reasons against copious profanity of speech. Here you have the artistic reason, and, by implication, that which forbids its use in literature—namely, its ineffectiveness. But though she selects, Mrs. Woods does not refine. She exhibits the life of the travelling show in its habitual squalor as well as in its occasional brightness. How she has managed it passes my understanding: but her book leaves the impression of confident familiarity with this kind of life, of knowledge not merely accumulated, but assimilated. Knowing as we do that Mrs. Woods was not brought up in a circus, we infer that she must have spent much labor in research: but, taken by itself, her book permits no such inference. The truth is that in the case of a genuine artist no line can be drawn between knowledge and imagination. Probably—almost certainly—Mrs. Woods has to a remarkable degree that gift which Mr. Henry James describes as "the faculty which when you give it an inch takes an ell, and which for an artist is a much greater source of strength than any accident of residence or of place in the social scale ... the power to guess the unseen from the seen, to trace the implication of things, to judge the whole piece by the pattern; the condition of feeling life in general so completely that you are well on your way to knowing a particular corner of it." Be this as it may, Mrs. Woods has written a novel which, for mastery of an unfamiliar *milieu*, is almost fit to stand beside *Esther Waters*. I say "almost": for, although Mrs. Woods's mastery is easier and less conscious than Mr. Moore's, it neither goes so deep to the springs of action nor bears so intimately on the conduct of the story. But of this later.

If one thing more than another convinces me that Mrs. Woods has thoroughly realized these queer characters of hers, it is that she makes them so much like other people. Whatever our profession may be, we are generally silent upon the instincts that led us to adopt it—unless, indeed, we happen to be writers and make a living out of self-analysis. So these strollers are silent upon the attractiveness of their calling. But they crave as openly as any of us for distinction, and they worship "respectability" as heartily and outspokenly as any of the country-folk for whose amusement they tumble and pull faces. It is no small merit in this book that it reveals how much and yet how very little divides the performers in the ring from the audience in the sixpenny seats. I wish I had space to quote a particularly fine passage—you will find it on pp. 72-74—in which Mrs. Woods describes the progress of these motley characters through Midland lanes on a fresh spring morning; the shambling white horses with their red collars, the painted vans, the cages "where bears paced uneasily and strange birds thrust uncouth heads out into the sunshine," the two elephants and the camel padding through the dust and brushing the dew off English hedges, the hermetically sealed omnibus in which the artistes bumped and dozed, while the wardrobe-woman, Mrs. Thompson, held forth undeterred on "those advantages of birth, house-rent, and furniture, which made her discomforts of real importance, whatever those of the other ladies in the show might be."

But in bringing her Vagabonds into relation with ordinary English life, Mrs. Woods loses all, or nearly all, of that esoteric professional interest which, at first sight, would seem the chief reason for choosing circus people to write about. The story of *Les Frères Zemganno* has, as I have said, this esoteric professional interest. The story of *The Vagabonds* is the story of a husband and of a young wife who does not love him, but discovers that she loves another man—a story as old as the hills and common to every rank and every calling. Mrs. Woods has made the husband a middle-aged clown, the wife a girl with strict notions about respectability, and the lover, Fritz, a handsome young German gymnast. But there was no fundamental reason for this choice of professions. The tale might be every bit as true of a grocer, and a grocer's wife, and a grocer's assistant. Once or twice, indeed, in the earlier chapters we have promise of a more peculiar story when we read of Mrs. Morris's objection to seeing her husband play the clown. "No woman," she says, "that hadn't been brought up to the business would like to see her husband look like that." And of Joe Morris we read that he took an artistic pride in his clowning. But there follows no serious struggle between love and art—no such struggle, for instance, as Zola has worked out to tragic issues in his *L'Œuvre*. Mrs. Morris's shame at her husband's ridiculous appearance merely heightens the contrast in her eyes between him and the handsome young gymnast.

But though the circus-business is not essential, Mrs. Woods makes most effective use of it. I will select one notable illustration of this. When Mrs. Morris at length makes her confession—it is in the wagon, and at night—the unhappy husband wraps her up carefully in her bed and creeps away with his grief to the barn where Chang, a ferocious elephant amenable only to him, has been stabled:—

"He opened the door; the barn was pitch dark, but as he entered he could hear the noise of the chain which had been fastened to the elephant's legs being suddenly dragged. He spoke to Chang, and the noise ceased. Then running up a short ladder which was close to the door, he threw himself down on the straw and stared up into the darkness, which to his aching eyes seemed spangled with many colours. Presently he was startled by something warm touching him on the face.

"'Who's there?' he called out.

"There was no answer, but the soft thing, something like a hand, felt him cautiously and caressingly all over.

"'Oh, it's you, Chang, my boy, is it?' said Joe. 'What! are you glad to have me, old chappie? No humbug about yer, are yer sure? No lies?'"

The circus-business is employed again in the catastrophe: but, to my mind, far less happily. In spite of very admirable writing, there remains something ridiculous in the spectacle of an injured husband, armed with a Winchester rifle and mounted on a frantic elephant, pursuing his wife's lover by moonlight across an English common and finally "treeing" him up a sign-post. Mrs. Woods, indeed, means it to be grotesque: but I think it is something more.

The problem of the story is the commonest in fiction. And when I add that the injured husband has been married before and that his first wife, honestly supposed to be dead, returns to threaten his happiness, you will see that Mrs. Woods sets forth upon a path trodden by many hundreds of thousands of incompetent feet. To start with such a situation almost suggests bravado. If it be bravado, it is entirely justified as the tale proceeds: for amid the crowd of failures Mrs. Woods's solution wears the singular distinction of truth. That the book is written in restrained and beautiful English goes without saying: but the best tribute one can pay to the writing of it is to say that its style and its truthfulness are at one. If complaint must be made, it is the vulgar complaint against truth—that it leaves one a trifle cold. A less perfect story might have aroused more emotion. Yet I for one would not barter the pages that tell of Joe Morris's final surrender of his wife—with their justness of imagination and sobriety of speech—for any amount of pity and terror.

A word on the few merely descriptive passages in the book. Mrs. Woods's scene-painting has all a Frenchman's accomplishment with the addition of that open-air feeling and intimate knowledge of the phenomena of "out-of-doors" which a Frenchman seldom or never attains to. Though not, perhaps, her strongest gift, it is the one by which she stands most conspicuously above her contemporaries. The more credit, then, that she uses it so temperately.

FOOTNOTES:

[A] *The Vagabonds.* By Margaret L. Woods. London: Smith, Elder & Co.

MR. HALL CAINE

August 11, 1894. "The Manxman."

Mr. Hall Caine's new novel *The Manxman* (London: William Heinemann) is a big piece of work altogether. But, on finishing the tale, I turned back to the beginning and read the first 125 pages over again, and then came to a stop. I wish that portion of the book could be dealt with separately. It cannot: for it but sets the problem in human passion and conduct which the remaining 300 pages have to solve. Nevertheless the temptation is too much for me.

As one who thought he knew how good Mr. Hall Caine can be at his best, I must confess to a shock of delight, or rather a growing sense of delighted amazement, while reading those 125 pages. Yet the story is a very simple one—a story of two friends and a woman. The two friends are Philip Christian and Pete Quilliam: Philip talented, accomplished, ambitious, of good family, and eager to win back the social position which his father had lost by an imprudent marriage; Pete a nameless boy—the bastard son of Philip's uncle and a gawky country-girl—ignorant, brave, simple-minded, and incurably generous. The boys have grown up together, and in love are almost more than brothers when the time comes for them to part for a while—Philip leaving home for school, while Pete goes as mill-boy to one Cæsar Cregeen, who combined the occupations of miller and landlord of "The Manx Fairy" public-house. And now enters the woman—a happy child when first we make her acquaintance—in the shape of Katherine Cregeen, the daughter of Pete's employer. With her poor simple Pete falls over head and ears in love. Philip, too, when home for his holidays, is drawn by the same dark eyes; but stands aside for his friend. Naturally, the miller will not hear of Pete, a landless, moneyless, nameless, lad, as a suitor for his daughter; and so Pete sails for Kimberley to make his fortune, confiding Kitty to Philip's care.

It seems that the task undertaken by Philip—that of watching over his friend's sweetheart—is a familiar one in the Isle of Man, and he who discharges it is known by a familiar name.

"They call him the *Dooiney Molla*—literally, the 'man-praiser'; and his primary function is that of an informal, unmercenary, purely friendly and philanthropic match-maker, introduced by the young man to persuade the parents of the young woman that he is a splendid fellow, with substantial possessions or magnificent prospects, and entirely fit to marry her. But he has a secondary function, less frequent, though scarcely less familiar; and it is that of a lover by proxy, or intended husband by deputy, with duties of moral guardianship over the girl while the man himself is off 'at the herrings,' or away 'at the mackerel,' or abroad on wider voyages."

And now, of course, begins Philip Christian's ordeal: for Kitty discovers that she loves him and not Pete, and he that he loves Kitty madly. On the other hand there is the imperative duty to keep faith with his absent friend; and more than this. His future is full of high hope; the eyes of his countrymen and of the Governor himself are beginning to fasten on him as the most promising youth in the island; it is even likely that he will be made Deemster, and so win back all the position that his father threw away. But to marry Kitty—even if he can bring himself to break faith with Pete—will be to marry beneath him, to repeat his father's disaster, and estrange the favor of all the high "society" of the island. Therefore, even when the first line of resistance is broken down by a report that Pete is dead, Philip determines to cut himself free from the temptation. But the girl, who feels that he is slipping away from her, now takes fate into her own hands. It is the day of harvest-home—the "Melliah"—on her father's farm. Philip has come to put an end to her hopes, and she knows it. The "Melliah" is cut and the usual frolic begins:

"Then the young fellows went racing over the field, vaulting the stooks, stretching a straw rope for the girls to jump over, heightening and tightening it to trip them up, and slackening it and twirling it to make them skip. And the girls were falling with a laugh, and, leaping up again and flying off like the dust, tearing their frocks and dropping their sun-bonnets as if the barley-grains they had been reaping had got into their blood.

"In the midst of this maddening frolic, while Cæsar and the others were kneeling by the barley-stack, Kate snatched Philip's hat from his head and shot like a gleam into the depths of the glen.

"Philip dragged up his coat by one of its arms and fled after her."

Here, then, in Sulby Glen, the girl stakes her last throw—the last throw of every woman—and wins. It is the woman—a truly Celtic touch—who wooes the man, and secures her love and, in the end, her shame.

"When a good woman falls from honour, is it merely that she is the victim of a momentary intoxication, of stress of passion, of the fever of instinct? No. It is mainly that she is the slave of the sweetest, tenderest, most spiritual, and pathetic of all human fallacies—the fallacy that by giving herself to the man she loves she attaches him to herself for ever. This is the real betrayer of nearly all good women that are betrayed. It lies at the root of tens of thousands of the cases that make up the merciless story of man's sin and woman's weakness. Alas! it is only the woman who clings the closer. The impulse of the man is to draw apart. He must conquer it, or she is lost. Such is the old cruel difference and inequality of man and woman as Nature made them—the old trick, the old tragedy."

And meanwhile Pete is not dead; but recovered, and coming home.

Here, on p. 125, ends the second act of the drama: and the telling has been quite masterly. The passage quoted above has hitherto been the author's solitary comment. Everything has been presented in that fine objective manner which is the triumph of story-telling. As I read, I began to say to myself, "This is good"; and in a little while, "Ah, but this is very good"; and at length, "But this is amazing. If he can only keep this up, he will have written one of the finest novels of his time." The whole story was laid out so easily; with such humor, such apparent carelessness, such an instinct for the right stroke in the right place, and no more than the right stroke; the big scenes—Pete's love-making in the dawn and Kate's victory in Sulby Glen—were so poetically conceived (I use the adverb in its strictest sense) and so beautifully written; above all, the story remained so true to the soil on which it was constructed. A sworn admirer of Mr. Brown's *Betsy Lee* and *The Doctor* has no doubt great advantage over other people in approaching *The Manxman*. Who, that has read his *Fo'c's'le Yarns* worthily, can fail to feel kindly towards the little island and its shy, home-loving folk? And—by what means I do not know—Mr. Hall Caine has managed from time to time to catch Mr. Brown's very humor and set it to shine on his page. The secret, I suppose, is their common possession as Manxmen: and, like all the best art, theirs is true to its country and its material.

Pete comes home, suspecting no harm; still childish of heart and loud of voice—a trifle too loud, by the way; his shouts begin to irritate the reader, and the reader begins to feel how sorely they must have irritated his wife: for the unhappy Kate is forced, after all, into marrying Pete. And so the tragedy begins.

I wish, with my heart, I could congratulate Mr. Hall Caine as warmly upon the remainder of the book as upon its first two parts. He is too sure an artist to miss the solution—the only adequate solution—of the problem. The purification of Philip Christian and Kitty must come, if at all, "as by fire"; and Mr. Hall Caine is not afraid to take us through the deepest fire. No suffering daunts him—neither the anguish of Kitty, writhing against her marriage with Pete, nor the desperate pathos of Pete after his wife has run away, pretending to the neighbors that she has only gone to Liverpool for her health, and actually writing letters and addressing parcels to himself and posting them from out-of-the-way towns to deceive the local postman; nor the moral ruination of Philip, with whom Kitty is living in hiding; nor his final redemption by the ordeal of a public confession before the great company assembled to see him reach the height of worldly ambition and be appointed governor of his native island.

And yet—I have a suspicion that Mr. Hall Caine, who deals by preference with the elemental emotions, would rejoice in the epithet "Æschylean" applied to his work. The epithet would not be unwarranted: but it is precisely when most consciously Æschylean that Mr. Hall Caine, in my poor judgment, comes to grief. This is but to say that he possesses the defects of his qualities. There is altogether too much of the "Go to: let me be Titanic" about the book. Æschylus has grown a trifle too well aware of his reputation, has taken to underscoring his points, and tends to prolixity in consequence. Mr. Hall Caine has not a little of Hugo's audacity, but, with it, not a little of Hugo's diffuseness. Standing, like Destiny, with scourge lifted over the naked backs of his two poor sinners, he spares them no single stroke—not so much as a little one. Every detail that can possibly heighten their suffering is brought out in its place, until we feel that Life, after all, is more careless, and tell ourselves that Fate does not measure out her revenge with an inch rule. We see the machinery of pathos at work: and we are rather made incredulous than moved when the machinery works so accurately that Philip is made to betray Pete on the very night when Pete goes out to beat a big drum in Philip's honor. Nor is this by any means the only harrowing coincidence of the kind. Worse than this—for its effect upon us as a work of art—our emotions are so flogged and out-tired by detail after detail that they cannot rise at the last big fence, and so the scene of Philip's confession in the Courthouse misses half its effect. It is a fine scene. I am no bigoted admirer of Hawthorne—a very cold one, indeed—and should be the last to say that the famous scene in *The Scarlet Letter* cannot be improved upon. Nor do I make any doubt that, as originally conceived by Mr. Hall Caine, the story had its duly effective climax here. But still less do I doubt that the climax, and therefore the whole story, would have been twice as impressive had the book, from p. 125 onwards, contained just half its present number of words. But whether this opinion be right or wrong, the book remains a big book, and its story a beautiful story.

MR. ANTHONY HOPE

Oct. 27, 1894. "The God in the Car" and "The Indiscretion of the Duchess."

As I set down the titles of these two new stories by Mr. Anthony Hope, it occurs to me that combined they would make an excellent title for a third story yet to be written. For Mr. Hope's duchess, if by any chance she found herself travelling with a god in a car, would infallibly seize the occasion for a *tour de force* in charming indiscretion. That the car would travel for some part of the distance in that position of unstable equilibrium known to skaters as the "outside edge" may, I think, be taken for granted. But far be it from me to imagine bungling developments of the situation I here suggest to Mr. Hope's singular and agreeable talents. Like Mr. Stevenson's smatterer, who was asked, "What would be the result of putting a pound of potassium in a pot of porter?" I content myself with anticipating "that there would probably be a number of interesting bye-products."

Be it understood that I suggest only a combination of the titles—not of the two stories as Mr. Hope has written them: for these move on levels altogether different. The constant reader of *The Speaker's* "Causeries" will be familiar with the two propositions—not in the least contradictory—that a novel should be true to life, and that it is quite impossible for a novel to be true to life. He will also know how they are reconciled. A story, of whatever kind, must follow life at a certain remove. It is a good and consistent story if it keep at that remove from first till last. Let us have the old tag once more:

"Servetur ad inum
Qualis ab incepto processerit, et sibi constet."

A good story and real life are such that, being produced in either direction and to any extent, they never meet. The distance between the parallels does not count: or rather, it is just a matter for the author to choose. It is here that Mr. Howells makes his mistake, who speaks contemptuously of Romance as *Puss in Boots*. *Puss in Boots* is a masterpiece in its way, and in its way just as true to life—*i.e.*, to its distance from life—as that very different masterpiece *Silas Lapham*. When Mr. Howells objects to the figure of Vautrin in *Le Père Goriot*, he criticizes well: Vautrin in that tale is out of drawing and therefore monstrous. But to bring a similar objection against Porthos in *Le Vicomte de Bragelonne* would be very bad criticism; for it would ignore all the postulates of the story. In real life Vautrin and Porthos would be equally monstrous: in the stories Vautrin is monstrous and Porthos is not.

But though the distance from real life at which an author conducts his tale is just a matter for his own choice, it usually happens to him after a while, either from taste or habit, to choose a particular distance and stick to it, or near it, henceforth in all his writings. Thus Scott has his own distance, and Jane Austen hers. Balzac, Hugo, Charlotte Brontë, Dickens, Tolstoi, Mr. Howells himself—all these have their favorite distances, and all are different and cannot be confused. But a young writer usually starts in some uncertainty on this point. He has to find his range, and will quite likely lead off with a miss or a ricochet, as Mr. Hardy led off with *Desperate Remedies* before finding the target with *Under the Greenwood Tree*. Now Mr. Hope—the application of these profound remarks is coming at last—being a young writer, hovers in choice between two ranges. He has found the target with both, and cannot make up his mind between them: and I for one hope he will keep up his practice at both: for his experiments are most interesting, and in the course of them he is giving us capital books. Of the two before me, *The God in the Car* belongs to the same class as his earliest work—his *Father Stafford*, for instance, a novel that did not win one-tenth of the notice it deserved. It is practice at short range. It moves very close to real life. Real people, of course, do not converse as briskly and wittily as do Mr. Hope's characters: but these have nothing of the impossible in them, and even in the whole business of Omofaga there is nothing more fantastic than its delightful name. The book is genuinely tragic; but the tragedy lies rather in what the reader is left to imagine than in what actually occurs upon the stage. That it never comes to a more explicit and vulgar issue stands not so much to the credit of the heroine (as I suppose we must call Mrs. Dennison) as to the force of circumstances as manipulated in the tactful grasp of Mr. Hope. Nor is it to be imputed to him for a fault that the critical chapter xvii. reminds us in half a dozen oddly indirect ways of a certain chapter in *Richard Feverel*. The place, the situation, the reader's suspense, are similar; but the actors, their emotions, their purposes are vastly different. It is a fine chapter, and the page with which it opens is the worst in the book—a solitary purple patch of "fine writing." I observe without surprise that the reviewers—whose admiring attention is seldom caught but by something out of proportion—have been fastening upon it and quoting it ecstatically.

The Indiscretion of the Duchess is the tale in Mr. Hope's second manner—the manner of *The Prisoner of Zenda*. Story for story, it falls a trifle sort of *The Prisoner of Zenda*. As a set-off, the telling is firmer, surer, more accomplished. In each an aimless, superficially cynical, but naturally amiable English gentleman finds himself casually involved in circumstances which appeal first to his sportsmanlike love of adventure, and so by degrees to his chivalry, his sense of honor, and his passions. At first amused, then perplexed, then nettled, then involved heart and soul, he is left to fight his way through with the native weapons of his order—courage, tact, honesty, wit, strength of self-sacrifice, aptitude for affairs. The *donnée* of these tales, their spirit, their postulates, are nakedly romantic. In them the author deliberately lends enchantment to his view by withdrawing to a convenient distance from real life. But, once more, the enchantment is everything and the distance nothing. If I must find fault with the later of the stories, it will not be with its general extravagance—for extravagance is part of the secret of Romance—but with the sordid and very nasty Madame Delhasse. She would be repulsive enough in any case: but as Marie's mother she is peculiarly repulsive and, let me add, improbable. Nobody looks for heredity in a tale of this sort: but even in the fairy tales it is always the heroine's *step*-mother who ends very fitly with a roll downhill in a barrel full of spikes.

But great as are the differences between *The God in the Car* and *The Indiscretion of the Duchess*—and I ought to say that the former carries (as it ought) more weight of metal—they have their points of similarity. Both illustrate conspicuously Mr. Hope's gift of advancing the action of his story by the sprightly conversation of his characters. There is a touch of Dumas in their talk, and more than a touch of Sterne—the Sterne of the *Sentimental Journey*.

"I beg your pardon, madame," said I, with a whirl of my hat.

"I beg your pardon, sir," said the lady, with an inclination of her head.

"One is so careless in entering rooms hurriedly," I observed.

"Oh, but it is stupid to stand just by the door!" insisted the lady.

To sum up, these are two most entertaining books by one of the writers for whose next book one searches eagerly in the publishers' lists. If, however, he will not resent one small word of caution, it is that he should not let us find his name there too often. As far as we can see, he cannot write too much for us. But he may very easily write too much for his own health.

"TRILBY"

Sept. 14, 1895. Hypnotic Fiction.

A number of people—and I am one—cannot "abide" hypnotism in fiction. In my own case the dislike has been merely instinctive, and I have never yet found time to examine the instinct and discover whether or not it is just and reasonable. The appearance of a one-volume edition of *Trilby*—undoubtedly the most successful tale that has ever dealt with hypnotism—and the success of the dramatic version of *Trilby* presented a few days ago by Mr. Tree, invite one to apply the test. Clearly there are large numbers of people who enjoy hypnotic fiction, or whose prejudices have been effectively subdued by Mr. du Maurier's tact and talent. Must we then confess that our instinct has been unjust and unreasonable, and give it up? Or—since we *must* like *Trilby*, and there is no help for it—shall we enjoy the tale under protest and in spite of its hypnotism?

Analysis of an Aversion.

I think my first objection to these hypnotic tales is the terror they inspire. I am not talking of ordinary human terror, which, of course, is the basis of much of the best tragedy. We are terrified by the story of Macbeth; but it is with a rational and a salutary terror. We are aware all the while that the moral laws are at work. We see a hideous calamity looming, approaching, imminent: but we can see that it is the effect of causes which have been duly exhibited to us. We can reason it out: we know where we stand: our conscience approves the punishment even while our pity calls out against it. And when the blow falls, it shakes away none of our belief in the advantages of virtuous conduct. It leaves the good old impregnable position, "Be virtuous and you will be happy," stronger than ever. But the terror of these hypnotic stories resembles that of a child in a dark room. For artistic reasons too obvious to need pointing out, the hypnotizer in these stories is always the villain of the piece. For the same or similar reasons, the "subject" is always a person worthy of our sympathy, and is usually a woman. Let us suppose it to be a good and beautiful woman—for that is the commonest case. The gives us to understand that by hypnotism this good and beautiful woman is for a while completely in the power of a man who is *ex hypothesi* a beast, and who *ex hypothesi* can make her commit any excesses that his beastliness may suggest. Obviously we are removed outside the moral order altogether; and in its place we are presented with a state of things in which innocence, honesty, love, and the rest are entirely at the disposal and under the rule of malevolent brutality; the result, as presented to us, being qualified only by such tact as the author may choose to display. That Mr. du Maurier has displayed great tact is extremely creditable to Mr. du Maurier, and might have been predicted of him. But it does not alter the fact that a form of fiction which leaves us at the mercy of an author's tact is a very dangerous form in a world which contains so few Du Mauriers. It is lamentable enough to have to exclaim—as we must over so much of human history—

"Ah! what avails the sceptred race
And what the form divine?..."

But it must be quite intolerable when a story leaves us demanding, "What avail native innocence, truthfulness, chastity, when all these can be changed into guile and uncleanliness at the mere suggestion of a dirty mesmerist?"

The answer to this, I suppose, will be, "But hypnotism is a scientific fact. People can be hypnotized, and are hypnotized. Are you one of those who would exclude the novelist from this and that field of human experience?" And then I am quite prepared to hear the old tag, "*Homo sum*," etc., once more misapplied.

Limitation of Hypnotic Fiction.

Let us distinguish. Hypnotism is a proved fact: people are hypnotized. Hypnotism is not a delimited fact: nobody yet knows precisely its conditions or its effects; or, if the discovery has been made, it has certainly not yet found its way to the novelists. For them it is as yet chiefly a field of fancy. They invent vagaries for it as they invent ghosts. And as for the "*humananum nihil a me alienum*" defence, my strongest objection to hypnotic fiction is its inhumanity. An experience is not human in the proper artistic sense (with which alone we are concerned) merely because it has befallen a man or a woman. There was an Irishman, the other day, who through mere inadvertence cut off his own head with a scythe. But the story is rather inhuman than not. Still less right have we to call everything human which can be supposed by the most liberal stretch of the imagination to have happened to a man or a woman. A story is only human in so far as it is governed by the laws which are recognized as determining human action. Now according as we regard human action, its two great determinants will be free will or necessity. But hypnotism entirely does away with free will: and for necessity, fatal or circumstantial, it substitutes the lawless and irresponsible imperative of a casual individual man, who (in fiction) usually happens to be a scoundrel.

A story may be human even though it discard one or more of the recognized conditions of human life. Thus in the confessedly supernatural story of Dr. Jekyll and Mr. Hyde, the conflict between the two Jekylls is human enough and morally significant, because it answers to a conflict which is waged day by day—though as a rule less tremendously—in the soul of every human being. But the double Trilby signifies nothing. She is naturally in love with Little Billee: she is also in love with Svengali, but quite unnaturally and irresponsibly. There is no real conflict. As Gecko says of Svengali—

"He had but to say '*Dors!*' and she suddenly became an unconscious Trilby of marble, who could produce wonderful sounds—just the sounds he wanted and nothing else—and think his thoughts and wish his wishes—and love him at his bidding with a strange, unreal, factitious love ... just his own love for himself turned inside out—à l'envers—and reflected back on him as from a mirror ... un écho, un simulacre, quoi? pas autre chose!... It was not worth having! I was not even jealous!"

This last passage, I think, suggests that Mr. du Maurier would have produced a much less charming story, indeed, but a vastly more artistic one, had he directed his readers' attention rather upon the tragedy of Svengali than upon the tragedy of Trilby. For Svengali's position as complete master of a woman's will and yet unable to call forth more than a factitious love—"just his own love for himself turned inside out and reflected back on him as from a mirror"—is a really tragic one, and a fine variation on the old Frankenstein *motif*. The tragedy of Frankenstein resides in Frankenstein himself, not in his creature.

An Incongruous Story.

In short, *Trilby* seems—as *Peter Ibbetson* seemed—to fall into two parts, the natural and supernatural, which will not join. They might possibly join if Mr. du Maurier had not made the natural so exceedingly domestic, had he been less successful with the Trilby, and Little Billee, and Taffy, and the Laird, for all of whom he has taught us so extravagant a liking. But his very success with these domestic (if oddly domestic) figures, and with the very domestic tale of Little Billee's affair of the heart, proves our greatest stumbling-block when we are invited to follow the machinations of the superlative Svengali. That the story of Svengali and of Trilby's voice is a good story only a duffer would deny. So is Gautier's *La Morte Amoureuse*; perhaps the best story of its kind ever written. But suppose Thackeray had taken *La Morte Amoureuse* and tried to write it into *Pendennis!*

MR. STOCKTON

Sept. 21, 1895. Stevenson's Testimony.

In his chapter of "Personal Memories," printed in the *Century Magazine* of July last, Mr. Gosse speaks of the peculiar esteem in which Mr. Frank R. Stockton's stories were held by Robert Louis Stevenson. "When I was going to America to lecture, he was particularly anxious that I should lay at the feet of Mr. Frank R. Stockton his homage, couched in the following lines:—

My Stockton if I failed to like,
It were a sheer depravity;
For I went down with the 'Thomas Hyke,'
And up with the 'Negative Gravity.'

He adored these tales of Mr. Stockton's, a taste which must be shared by all good men."

It is shared at any rate by some thousands of people on this side of the Atlantic. Only, one is not quite sure how far their admiration extends. As far as can be guessed—for I have never come across any British attempt at a serious appreciation of Mr. Stockton—the general disposition is to regard him as an amusing kind of "cuss" with a queer kink in his fancy, who writes puzzling little stories that make you smile. As for taking him seriously, "why he doesn't even profess to write seriously"—an absurd objection, of course; but good enough for the present-day reviewer, who sits up all night in order that the public may have his earliest possible opinion on the Reminiscences of Bishop A, or the Personal Recollections of Field-Marshal B, or a Tour taken in Ireland by the Honorable Mrs. C. For criticism just now, as a mere matter of business convenience, provides a relative importance for books before they appear; and in this classification the space allotted to fiction and labelled "important" is crowded for the moment with works dealing with religious or sexual difficulties. Everyone has read *Rudder Grange*, *The Lady or the Tiger?* and *A Borrowed Month*; but somehow few people seem to think of them as subjects for serious criticism.

"Classical" qualities.

And yet these stories are almost classics. That is to say, they have the classical qualities, and only need time to ripen them into classics: for nothing but age divides a story of the quality of *The Lady or the Tiger?* (for instance) from a story of the quality of *Rip Van Winkle*. They are full of wit; but the wit never chokes the style, which is simple and pellucid. Their fanciful postulates being granted, they are absolutely rational. And they are in a high degree original. Originality, good temper, good sense, moderation, wit—these are classical qualities: and he is a rare benefactor who employs them all for the amusement of the world.

A Comparison.

At first sight it may seem absurd to compare Mr. Stockton with Defoe. You can scarcely imagine two men with more dissimilar notions of the value of gracefulness and humor, or with more divergent aims in writing. Mr. Stockton is nothing if not fanciful, and Defoe is hardly fanciful at all. Nevertheless in reading one I am constantly reminded of the other. You must remember Mr. Stockton's habit is to confine his eccentricities of fancy to the postulates of a tale. He starts with some wildly unusual—but, as a rule, not impossible—conjuncture of circumstances. This being granted, however, he deduces his story logically and precisely, appealing never to our passions and almost constantly to our common sense. His people are as full of common-sense as Defoe's. They may have more pluck than the average man or woman, and they usually have more adaptability; but they apply to extraordinary circumstances the good unsentimental reasoning of ordinary life, and usually with the happiest results. The shipwreck of Mrs. Lecks and Mrs. Aleshine was extraordinary enough, but their subsequent conduct was rational almost to precision: and in story-telling rationality does for fancy what economy of emotional utterances does for emotion. We may apply to Mr. Stockton's tales a remark which Mr. Saintsbury let fall some years ago upon dream-literature. He was speaking particularly of Flaubert's *Tentation de Saint Antoine*:—

"The capacities of dreams and hallucinations for literary treatment are undoubted. But most writers, including even De Quincey, who have tried this style, have erred, inasmuch as they have endeavoured to throw a portion of the mystery with which the waking mind invests dreams over the dream itself. Anyone's experience is sufficient to show that this is wrong. The events of dreams as they happen are quite plain and matter-of-fact, and it is only in the intervals, and, so to speak, the scene-shifting of dreaming, that any suspicion of strangeness occurs to the dreamer."

A dream, however wild, is quite plain and matter-of-fact to the dreamer; therefore, for verisimilitude, the narrative of a dream should be quite plain and matter-of-fact. In the same way the narrator of an extremely fanciful tale should—since verisimilitude is the first aim of story-telling—attempt to exclude all suspicion of the unnatural from his reader's mind. And this is only done by persuading him that no suspicion of the unnatural occurred to the actors in the story. And this again is best managed by making his characters persons of sound every-day common sense. "If *these* are not upset by what befalls them, why"—is the unconscious inference—"why in the world should *I* be upset?"

So, in spite of the enormous difference between the two writers, there has been no one since Defoe who so carefully as Mr. Stockton regulates the actions of his characters by strict common sense. Nor do I at the moment remember any writer who comes closer to Defoe in mathematical care for detail. In the case of the True-born Englishman this carefulness was sometimes overdone—as when he makes Colonel Jack remember with exactness the lists of articles he stole as a boy, and their value. In the *Adventures of Captain Horn* the machinery which conceals and guards the Peruvian treasure is so elaborately described that one is tempted to believe Mr. Stockton must have constructed a working model of it with his own hands before he sat down to write the book. In a way, this accuracy of detail is part of the common-sense character of the narrative, and undoubtedly helps the verisimilitude enormously.

A Genuine American.

But to my mind Mr. Stockton's characters are even more original than the machinery of his stories. And in their originality they reflect not only Mr. Stockton himself, but the race from which they and their author spring. In fact, they seem to me about the most genuinely American things in American fiction. After all, when one comes to think of it, Mrs. Lecks and Captain Horn merely illustrate that ready adaptation of Anglo-Saxon pluck and businesslike common sense to savage and unusual circumstances which has been the real secret of the colonization of the North American Continent. Captain Horn's discovery and winning of the treasure may differ accidentally, but do not differ in essence, from a thousand true tales of commercial triumph in the great Central Plain or on the Pacific Slope. And in the heroine of the book we recognize those very qualities and aptitudes for which we have all learnt to admire and esteem the American girl. They are hero and heroine, and so of course we are presented with the better side of a national character; but then it has been the better side which has done the business. The bitterest critic of things American will not deny that Mr. Stockton's characters are typical Americans, and could not belong to any other nation in the world. Nor can he deny that they combine sobriety with pluck, and businesslike behavior with good feeling; that they are as full of honor as of resource, and as sportsmanlike as sagacious. That people with such characteristics should be recognizable by us as typical Americans is a sufficient answer to half the nonsense which is being talked just now *à propos* of a recent silly contest for the America Cup.

Nationality apart, if anyone wants a good stirring story, *Captain Horn* is the story for his money. It has loose ends, and the concluding chapter ties up an end that might well have been left loose; but if a better story of adventure has been written of late I wish somebody would tell me its name.

BOW-WOW

August 26, 1893. Dauntless Anthology.

It is really very difficult to know what to say to Mr. Maynard Leonard, editor of *The Dog in British Poetry* (London: David Nutt). His case is something the same as Archdeacon Farrar's. The critic who desires amendment in the Archdeacon's prose, and suggests that something might be done by a study of Butler or Hume or Cobbett or Newman, is met with the cheerful retort, "But I have studied these writers, and admire them even more than you do." The position is impregnable; and the Archdeacon is only asserting that two and two make four when he goes on to confess that, "with the best will in the world to profit by the criticisms of his books, he has never profited in the least by any of them."

Now, Mr. Leonard has at least this much in common with Archdeacon Farrar, that before him criticism must sit down with folded hands. In the lightness of his heart he accepts every fresh argument against such and such a course as an added reason for following it:—

"While this collection of poems was being made," he tells us, "a well-known author and critic took occasion to gently ridicule (*sic*) anthologies and anthologists. He suggested, as if the force of foolishness could no further go, that the next anthology would deal with dogs."

"Undismayed by this," to use his own words, Mr. Leonard proceeded to prove it. Now it is obvious that no man can set a term to literary activity if it depend on the Briton's notorious unwillingness to recognize that he is beaten. I might dare, for instance, a Scotsman to compile an anthology on "The Eel in British Poetry"; but of what avail is it to challenge an indomitable race?

I am sorry Mr. Leonard has not given the name of this critic; but have a notion it must be Mr. Andrew Lang, though I am sure he is innocent of the split infinitive quoted above. It really ought to be Mr. Lang, if only for the humor of the means by which Mr. Leonard proposes to silence him. "I am confident," says he, "that the voice of the great dog-loving public in this country would drown that of the critic in question." Mr. Leonard's metaphors, you see, like the dyer's hand, are subdued to what they work in. But is not the picture delightful? Mr. Lang, the gentle of speech; who, with his master Walton, "studies to be quiet"; who tells us in his very latest verse

"I've maistly had my fill
O' this world's din"—

—Mr. Lang set down in the midst of a really representative dog show, say at Birmingham or the Crystal Palace, and there howled down! His *blandi susurri* drowned in the combined clamor of mongrel, puppy, whelp, and hound, and "the great dog-loving public in this country"!

"*Solvitur ululando*," hopes Mr. Leonard; and we will wait for the voice of the great dog-loving public to uplift itself and settle the question. Here, at any rate, is the book, beautiful in shape, and printed by the Constables upon sumptuous paper. And the title-page bears a rubric and a reference to Tobias' dog. "It is no need," says Wyclif in one of his sermons, "to busy us what hight Tobies' hound"; but Wyclif had never to reckon with a great dog-loving public. And Mr. Leonard, having considered his work and dedicated it "To the Cynics"—which, I suppose, is Greek for "dog-loving public"—observes, "It is rather remarkable that no one has yet published such a book as this." Perhaps it is.

But if we take it for granted (1) that it was worth doing, and (2) that whatever be worth doing is worth doing well, then Mr. Leonard has reason for his complacency. "It was never my intention," he says, "to gather together a complete collection of even British poems about dogs."—When will *that* come, I wonder?—"I have sought to secure a representative rather than an exhaustive anthology." His selections from a mass of poetry ranging from Homer to Mr. Mallock are judicious. He is not concerned (he assures us) to defend the poetical merits of all this verse:—

"—O, the wise contentment
Th' anthologist doth find!"

—but he has provided it with notes—and capital notes they are—with a magnificent Table of Contents, an Index of Authors, an Index of First Lines, an Index of Dogs Mentioned by Name in the Poems, and an Index of the Species of Dogs Mentioned. So that, even if he miss transportation to an equal sky, the dog has better treatment on earth than most authors. And Mr. Nutt and the Messrs. Constable have done their best; and everyone knows how good is that best. And the wonder is, as Dr. Johnson remarked (concerning a dog, by the way), not that the thing is done so well, but that it should be done at all.

OF SEASONABLE NUMBERS:

A Baconian Essay

Dec. 26, 1891.

That was a Wittie Invective made by *Montaigny* upon the *Antipodean*, Who said they must be Thieves that pulled on their breeches when Honest Folk were scarce abed. So is it Obnoxious to them that purvey *Christmas Numbers, Annuals*, and the like, that they commonly write under *Sirius* his star as it were *Capricornus*, feigning to Scate and Carol and blow warm upon their Fingers, while yet they might be culling of Strawberries. And all to this end, that Editors may take the cake. I know One, the Father of a long Family, that will sit a whole June night without queeching in a Vessel of Refrigerated Water till he be Ingaged with hard Ice, that the *Publick* may be docked no pennyweight of the Sentiments incident to the *Nativity*. For we be like Grapes, and goe to Press in August. But methinks these rigours do postulate a *Robur Corporis* more than ordinary (whereas 'tis but one in ten if a Novelist overtop in Physique); and besides will often fail of the effect. As I *myself* have asked—the Pseudonym being but gauze—

"O! Who can hold a fire in his hand
By thinking on the frosty Caucasus?"

Yet sometimes, because some things are in kind very Casuall, which if they escape prove Excellent (as the man who by Inadvertence inherited the throne of the *Grand Turk* with all appertayning) so that the kind is inferiour, being subject to Perill, but that which is Excellent being proved superior, as the Blossom of March and the Blossom of May, whereof the French verse goeth:—

"Bourgeon de Mars, enfant de Paris;
Si un eschape, il en vaut dix."

—so, as I was saying (till the Mischief infected my Protasis), albeit the gross of writings will moulder between *St. John's* feast and *St. Stephen's*, yet, if one survive, 'tis odds he will prove Money in your Pocket. Therefore I counsel that you preoccupate and tie him, by Easter at the latest, to *Forty thousand words*, naming a Figure in excess: for Operation shrinketh all things, as was observed by Galenus, who said to his Friend, "I will cut off your Leg, and then you will be lesse by a Foot." Also you will do well to provide a *Pictura* in Chromo-Lithography. For the Glaziers like it, and no harm done if they blush not: which is easily avoided by making it out of a little Child and a Puppy-dog, or else a Mother, or some such trivial Accompaniment. But Phryne marrs all. It was even rashly done of that Editor who issued a Coloured Plate, calling it "*Phryne Behind the Areopagus*": for though nothing was Seen, the pillars and Grecian elders intervening, yet 'twas Felt a great pity. And the Fellow ran for it, saying flimsily:—

"Populus me sibilat. At mihi plaudo."

Whereas I rather praise the dictum of that other writer, who said, "In this house I had sooner be turned over on the Drawing-room Table than roll under that in the Dining-room," meaning to reflect on the wine, but the Hostess took it for a compliment.

But to speak of the Letter Press. For the Sea you will use Clark Russell; for the East, Rudyard Kipling; for *Blood*, Haggard; for neat pastorall Subjects, Thomas Hardy, so he be within Bounds. I mislike his "Noble Dames." Barrie has a prettier witt; but Besant will keep in all weathers, and serve as right *Pemmican*. As for conundrums and poetry, they are but Toys: I have seen as good in crackers; which we pull, not as meaning to read or guess, but read and guess to cover the Shame of our Employment. Yet for Conundrums, if you hold the Answers till your next issue they Raise the Wind among Fools.

He that hath *Wife and Children* hath given Hostages to *Little Folks*: he will hardly redeem but by sacrifice of a Christmas Tree. The learned Poggius, that had twelve Sons and Daughters, used to note ruefully that he might never escape but by purchase of a *dozen Annuals*, citing this to prove how greatly Tastes will diverge among the Extreamely Young, even though they come of the same geniture. So will Printed Matter multiply faster than our Parents. Yet 'tis discutable that this phrensy of *Annuals* groweth staler by Recurrence. As that Helvetian lamented, whose Cuckoo-clock failed of a ready Purchaser, and he had to live with it. "*What Again?*" said he, and "*Surely Spring is not come yet, dash it?*" Also I cannot stomach that our Authors portend a Severity of Weather unseasonable in these Muggy Latitudes. I will eat my Hat if for these twenty Christmasses I have made six Slides worthy the Mention. Yet I know an Author that had his *Hero and Heroine* consent together very prettily; but 'twas in a *Thaw*, and the Editor being stout, the match was broken off unblessedly, till a Pact was made that it should indeed be a Thaw, but sufficient only to let the Heroine drop through the Ice and be Rescewed.

Without *Ghosts*, we twiddle thumbs....

THE END.